LOST ANGELS

David J. Schow

AN ONYX BOOK

NEW AMERICAN LIBRARY

PUBLISHED BY
PENGUIN BOOKS CANADA LIMITED

This book is dedicated with love
to the memory of
SHIRLEY JOAN SCHOW
the first Lost Angel

PUBLISHER'S NOTE

This book is a work of fiction. Names, characters, places, and incidents either are the product of the author's imagination or are used fictitiously, and any resemblance to actual persons, living or dead, events, or locales is entirely coincidental.

NAL BOOKS ARE AVAILABLE AT QUANTITY DISCOUNTS WHEN USED TO PROMOTE PRODUCTS OR SERVICES. FOR INFORMATION PLEASE WRITE TO PREMIUM MARKETING DIVISION. NEW AMERICAN LIBRARY. 1633 BROADWAY. NEW YORK. NEW YORK 10019.

By the time you read this, most or all of the stories in *Los Angels* have appeared previously in magazines. Revisions, additions and (I hope) improvements have been worked in all text for this editon. This means the earlier versions are (1) crippled, compromised, incomplete *things,* as well as (2) collector's items for the purist. "Brass" and "The Falling Man" appear here for the first time in their unabridged, unserialized form. "Monster Movies" is original to this volume. "Red Light" is included as appetizer to what was originally intended as a four-novella book due to (1) length problems, and (2) irresistable thematic unity. The title *Lost Angels* is integral to the mood that links these stories, and has nothing to do with the stupid movie released under the same title in 1989, a film I'm sure you've already forgotten. Cheers.

—DJS

ONYX TRADEMARK REG. U.S. PAT. OFF. AND FOREIGN COUNTRIES
REGISTERED TRADEMARK — MARCA REGISTRADA
HECHO EN WINNIPEG, CANADA

SIGNET, SIGNET CLASSIC, MENTOR, ONYX, PLUME, MERIDIAN and NAL BOOKS are published in Canada by Penguin Books Canada Limited, 2801 John Street, Markham, Ontario, L3R 1B4

First Signet Printing, March, 1990

2 3 4 5 6 7 8 9

PRINTED IN CANADA
COVER PRINTED IN U.S.A.

CONTENTS

INTRODUCTION

David J. Schow is my friend. Has been for years.

I'll try and ignore that; be objective. Either way, I promise you, this will come out the same.

If you've read even a little of David's extraordinary work, you know what I mean when I say he's something of a be-bop clairvoyant. Indirectly predicting trends. Setting others. Often mocking both; leaving unsettled imitators far behind. Indeed, in a field aclimb with performing monkeys and dextrous copycats, David is like some finely made glockenspiel; endlessly inventive, always in perfect pitch.

All the stories collected in LOST ANGELS share a jazz immediacy; radiant, unconventional meters of sound and thought. These qualities alone would be more than enough for most writers to go far. David's work only begins there.

Observe his octaves. The countless choices available to him. When it suits his peculiar recipes, however complex, he can instantly abandon the dialects of anarchy. Then, effortlessly, he'll descend into perfect pools of formalism; a skilled defector who stuns with beautiful language. Call it lyrical, I'd agree with you. For as long as I've read him, he's always been something of a choirboy, however illicit his prose. I marvel at the impossible harmony.

Indeed, if you read David's work carefully, you'll sense the secret tenderness. It hides behind savage armament, careful to give only glimpses of itself. But the shadings will move you. Maybe a phrase. A quiet observation he seemed to coin for you alone. There is poignancy everywhere in his talent, amid the exquisite threat.

I don't know exactly where his rocket-sled talent comes from. I know something about his past. Family; emotional DNA. But it's all inadequate to explain how his gift might have occurred. It doesn't really explain a writer who over and over does more with a single short story than many do with a career. Read PAMELA'S GET or RED LIGHT. They are breathtakers and put innumerable horror novels to shame.

And always, there is that precarious, nuclear hum.

That flammable sense David gives you he's working without a fuse and if he goes too far, there's nothing there to save him. His characters share this plague. Throughout LOST ANGELS stories is a sense of real dread and danger. Aching. Madness. You can sometimes know why: how he does it. What you've responded to. But there are many times it simply isn't clear. It bends around corners too deftly, graceful beyond exact definition. But you are sure it's there, out to get you. . . . Like sensing menace and loathing in a stranger's neutral expression. You feel what isn't there. How can it be explained?

How can it be denied?

In David's frantically tiered work, as with superstitions, what is evoked is always what is most disturbing. The quiet, violent ruination his people are drawn into. The blue-digits-on-the-arm eerieness. The tragedy of the blood; it's horrific inscription on walls and floors. The tension and hypnosis of the words. The perfect wrongness of everything. . .

When David moved to novel writing, his superb shorter fiction quickly got an older brother. His first major, showroom performance was THE KILL RIFF, an outlandish, razor-ride, braiding rock 'n roll and horror in startling shades of red. The book garnered much respect and excitement among critics and readers. Other novels will certainly follow. David's interests expand as quickly as his talents and movies have been the next stop in an intriguing, rather meteoric career; moving images, ideally suited to the velocity of his visions on paper.

When David recently began in scriptwriting, an important career step which I was honored to help in bringing about, he scaled one more inky Matterhorn without looking down. And his skills prevailed once again, winning him instant advocates, much new opportunity in the eccentric rapids of Hollywood and, not incidentally, his first movie script ever written, produced. This is not ususal. But somehow for David, it was.

As a man, David stands gunslinger-straight when you talk to him, gathered hair to mid-back. He is a striking Eiffel in his black clothes and boots and looks very much like a Boschian muskateer. Without intending it, he has a way of scaring people with his daunting speed of mind. But if you remain steady long enough to allow David's eclipse of lesser talents and company to simply occur, you'll find you can warm your palms on his friendship. He's also poisonously funny, with a sense of humor he should probably carry in a holster.

If you've known him for a number of years, as I have, you begin to conclude he's not unlike one of those fascinations who can catch a whizzing bullet in their smile from fifty yards away, and hand it over like a high-calibre Tic Tac. It's just David does it with dangerous ideas, provocative approaches. Thousand-mile an-hour brain twisters.

And he just smiles.

If I didn't know him better, I'd swear he was up to something. . . . The water balloon grin. The short-sheeting, sociopathic amusement. The generally perverse twinkle. Sometimes you wonder where David ends and misdemeanors begin.

As brothers of the night, I've traveled with David, hung-out together in some strange places. Talked neck-deep into very bad hours. I've been compared to him, been one fourth of our version of the British Invasion with the Splatter Punk movement, being Gear and Fab and Virulent.

David and I will probably know each other forever; connected. Likely dissected.

And through it all, however insane it gets, two things remain clear to me:

1) as a writer, David is on fire.

2) the fire can't be contained.

So, I'm done.

Take it, pal.

Richard Christian Matheson
October 1989, Malibu, Calif.

We look
    into the eyes
Of those
    we have killed
And wonder
    why they do not thank us.

RED LIGHT

Tabloid headlines always make me laugh. You know: *I Aborted Bigfoot's Quints*, or *See Elvis' Rotting Nude Corpse*, or *Exclusive on Jack the Ripper's Grandson!* Earlier today, while passing one of those Market Street newsvendors, I saw similar hyperbolic screamers, and I laughed. I did not want to laugh; it came out as a sick coughing sound.

TASHA VODE STILL MISSING
Terrorist Kidnapping of International Cover Girl Not Ruled Out

What the hell did they know about her? Not what I knew. They were like vampires; they sucked. Ethically. Morally.

But what did that make *me?*

At the top of the dungheap was the good old *National Perspirer,* loudly thumping the tub. A four-color cover claimed all the hot, steaming poop on Tasha's disappearance, enumerating each of her three juicy, potential fates. One: She had pulled a Marilyn Monroe. Two: She had had a Dorothy Stratten pulled *on* her by some gonzo fruitbag lover. Three: She was tucked away in the Frances Farmer suite at some remote, tastefully isolated lunatic asylum.

Or maybe she was forking over richly to manufacture all this furious controversy in order to boost her asking price into the troposphere—in a word, hoax time.

It was pathetic. It made my gut throb with hurt and loss, and downtown San Francisco defused behind a hot saltwash of welling tears. I blamed the emissions of the Cal Trans buses lumbering up and down the street, knowing full well I couldn't cop such a rationalization, because the buses ran off electricity, like the mostly defunct streetcars. Once, I'd nearly been decapitated by a rooftop conductor pole when it broke free of the overhead webwork of wires and came swinging past, boom-low, alongside the moving bus, sparking viciously and banging off a potted sidewalk tree a foot above my head, zizzing and snapping. Welcome to the Bay Area.

I had no real excuse for tears now, and wiped my eyes with the heel of my hand. My left hand; my *good* hand. I was still getting used to the weight of the new cast on my other one.

One of the street denizens for which Union Square is infamous had stopped to stare at me. I stared back, head to toe, from the cloud of gnats around his matted hair to the solid-carbon crustiness of his bare, black feet. He caught me crying with his mad prophet eyes, and the grin that snaked his face lewdly open suggested that yes, I *should* howl with grief, I *should* pull out a Mauser and start plugging pedestrians. I put my legs in gear instead. I left him behind with the news kiosk, the scungy, sensationalist headlines, and all those horrifyingly flawless pictures of her. The bum and I ceased to exist for each other the moment we parted.

I know what happened to Tasha. Like a recurring dream, she showed up unannounced on my doorstep just four days ago. Like a ghost then, like a ghost now.

People read *People*. The truth they never really want to know, and for good reason.

* * *

Her real name was Claudia Katz. In 1975, nobody important knew my name, or either of hers, and I'd already shot thousands of pictures of her. When I replaced my el cheapo scoop lamps with electronically synchronized umbrella shades so new that their glitter hurt your eyes even when they *weren't* flashing, I commemmorated the event by photographing her. New Year's Eve, 1974: Five seconds before midnight, I let a whole roll rip past on autowind, catching her as she passed from one year into the next. Edited down, that sequence won me a plaque. Today, it's noteworthy only because Tasha is the subject.

"Claudia Katz is too spiky and dykey," she explained later, as she pulled off her workout shirt and aired a chest that would never need the assistance of the Maidenform Corporation, breasts that would soon have the subscribership of *Playboy* eating their fingernails. *"Claudia Katz* is somebody who does chain mail and leather doggie-collar spreads for Bitch Records. *Claudia Katz* is not somebody you'll find on the staple page in *Sports Illustrated*'s Swimsuit Issue."

I pushed back an f-stop and refocused. "Part your lips. Stop. Give me the tip of your tongue, just inside your teeth." Her mouth was invitingly moist; the starfilters would trap some nice little highlights. *Clickwhirr click-whirr.* "Tilt your head back. Not so much . . . stop." I got a magnified closeup of the muscles beneath her skin, moving through the slow, programmed dance of positions. My big fan was on, making her amber hair float. "Hands together, arms back over your head. Turn, turn, turn . . . whoa, right there, stop!" *Click-whirr*—another thousandth of a second, immobilized. *"Sports Illustrated?* Why bother aiming it at a bunch of beer-swilling beat-offs in baseball caps, anyway?"

"You don't understand the way the world works, do you?" She spoke to the camera lens, because she knew

I was in there, watching. "You've got to make people look at your picture and either want you, or want to *be* you. When they anticipate your next picture, that means they're fantasizing about you. Saying to themselves, 'Geez, I wonder what she looks like in bed, without that damned bathing suit on?' "

It was my privilege to know the answer to that one already. Grinning, I baited her: "The women say that, do they?"

"No, not the women, you dork." The warm, come-hither expression on her face was entirely contrary to her tone. She was, after all, very good at her job. *Click-whirr.* "The men. When all the men in the country, in the world, lust for you, then you can say no to the lot of them. If all the men want you, then all the women lust to *be* you. Voila."

"Excluding lesbians, Tibetian lamas and some Kalahari bushmen." Her reply begged my sarcasm. She expected it. "Not that, um, lust and envy aren't *admirable* goals . . ."

If I had not been shooting, her brow would have rearranged and a familiar crease would appear between her eyes, indicating her annoyance at my childish, defeatist, irrelevant, smartass remark. And then she'd say—

"You just don't understand." Right on cue. "But I'll be on top someday. You'll see."

"I'd like to see you on top after you finish your shower." It flew out of my mouth before I could stop it. File a lawsuit if you want. "It's your turn."

She decided not to blow up, and rolled her eyes to keep from giggling. *Click-whirr.* My heart fumbled a beat. I'd just netted a shot of an honest-to-U.S.-Grant human being, peeking out from behind a cover-girl facade of plastic. Nude from the waist up, sensual not from flaunted sexuality, but because her expression let you in on the secret that the whole sham was strictly for laughs and wages. A real woman, not a fantasy image. I wanted that photo. It reduced the rest of the roll to an exhausted, mundane repertoire of tit shots—pretty billboard face, pasted-on bedroom eyes of that inhuman chromium color, the "ideal," a dime per double dozen from one shining sea to the next, from the four-star hookers at the Beverly Hills Hotel to the smartly attired, totally paranoid corporate ladies who took their Manhattan business lunches in neat quartets.

"To hell with the shower," she had said then, lunging at me with mischief in her eyes.

I still have that photo. Not framed, not displayed. I don't make the effort to look at it anymore. I can't.

Claudia—Tasha—got precisely what she wanted. That part you know, unless you've spent the last decade eating wallaby-burgers in the Australian outback. The tiny differences in the way we perceived the world and its opportunities finally grew large enough to wedge between us. Her astronomical income had little to do with it. It was me. I made the classic mistake of trying to keep her by blurting out proclamations of love before my career, my life, was fully mobilized. When you're clawing through the riptide of your twenties, it's like a cosmic rule that you cannot be totally satisfied by your emotional life and your professional life simultaneously. We had been climbing partners, until I put everything on hold to fall in love with her. So she left, and became famous. Not many people know my name even today. They don't have to; I pull down a plush enough income. But it did come to pass that everybody wanted Tasha. Everybody still does.

I was halfway through my third mug of coffee at the Hostel Restaurant when I admitted to myself that I was consciously avoiding going home. Bad stuff waited for me out there. A Latino busboy had made off with my plate. Past the smoky front windows, Geary Street was acruise with the bun-boys that gave the Tenderloin its rep. In New York, where things are less euphemistic, they're called fudgepackers. I wondered what gays made of all the media fuss over Tasha.

Nicole was giving me the eye. She's my favorite combat-hardened coffeeshop waitress in the charted universe, an elegant willowsprout of West Indies mocha black, with a heaving bosom and a lilting, exotic way of speaking the English language. When I watch her move about her chores at the Hostel, I think she'd probably jump my bones on the spot if she thought I could *click-whirr* her into the Tasha Vode saddle—worldwide model, budding cinema star, headliner. And still missing. When I try to formulate some logical nonsense for what happened to her, I fail just like I did with the street bum. Nothing comes out. Instead, I watch Nicole as she strolls over to recharge my cup. She watches me watching her.

"How'd you know I wanted more, Nicole?"

She narrows her panther eyes and blesses me with an evil smile. "Because you white boys *always* want more, hon."

My house *cum* studio hangs off the north end of the Fieldings' Point Pier, which is owned by a white-maned, sea-salt type named Dickie Barnhardt, whom no mortal dares address as "Richard." He sold me my home and plays caretaker to his pier. I live in a fabulous, indifferently-planned spill-together of rooms, like building blocks dumped haphazardly into a corner. Spiderwebbing it together are twelve crooked little stairways, inside and out. At first I called it my Dr. Seuss House. On the very top is a lighthouse tower that still works. Dickie showed me how to operate it, and from time to time I play keeper of the maritime flame because the notion is so irresistibly romantic. In return for spiffing up the place, I got another plaque—this one from the U.S. Lighthouse Society in San Francisco. Lighthouses have long been outmoded by navigational technology, and the Society is devoted to a program of historical preservation. There's no use for my little beacon. But there are nights when I cannot bear to keep it dark.

After ten years without a postcard, Tasha knew exactly where to find me. Maybe she followed the light. I answered my downstairs door with the alkaline smell of developer clinging to my hands; the doorknob was greened from all the times I'd done it. And there she was.

Was I surprised? I knew instantly it was her, knew it from the way the ocean tilted and tried to slide off the edge of the world, knew it because all the organs in my body tried to rush together and clog up my throat.

"You look like you just swallowed a starfish," she said. She was burrowed into a minky-lush fur that hid everything but the tips of her boots. The chill sea breeze pushed wisps of her hair around. I don't have to describe what her face looked like. If you want to know, just haul your ass down to Slater's Periodicals and check out the covers of any half-dozen current glamour and pop-fashion magazines. *That's* what she looked like, brother.

Her eyes seemed backed up with tears, but maybe tears alone were insufficient to breach the Tasha forcefield, or maybe she used some brand of eyeliner so expensive that it was tear-resistant. I asked her why she was crying, invited her in, and then did not give her room to answer me. I was too busy babbling, trying to race past ten years in ten minutes and disguise my nervousness with light banter. She sensed my disorientation and rode it out, patiently, the way she used to. I fixed coffee and brandy. She sipped hers with picture-perfect lips, sitting at the breakfast overlook I'd glassed-in last summer. I needed the drink. She needed contact, and hinted at it by letting her leg brush mine beneath the booth-style table. My need for chit-chat and my awareness of the past hung around, dumbing things up like a stubborn chaperone. Beyond the booth's half-turret of windowpanes, green breakers crashed onto the rocks and foamed violently away.

Her eyes cleared, marking time between me and the ocean outside. They grew darkly stormy, registering the thunderheads that were rolling in with the dusk to lash the beach with an evening sweep of rain.

At last, I ran out of stupid questions.

She closed my hand up in both of hers. My heartbeat meddled with my breathing. She had already guessed which of my odd little Caligari staircases led to the bedroom loft.

The night sky was embossed by tines of lightning somewhere between us and Japan. Fat drops splatted against the seaward hurricane glass and skidded to the right as a strong offshore wind caught and blew them. I had opened the shutters on the shore side, and the wooden blades of the ceiling fan cast down cool air to prickle our flesh, sweat-speckled from fervent but honest lovemaking.

A lot of women had drifted through my viewfinder after Tasha had left me. Except for two or three mental time-bombs and outright snow queens, I coupled enthusiastically with all of them. I forgot how to say no. Sometimes I was artificially nice; most of the time I was making the entire sex pay because one of their number had dumped on me. The right people found out my name, yes. My studio filled up with eager young lovelies. No brag, just a living. I settled into a pattern of rejecting them about the time they tried to form any sort of lasting attachment, or tried to storm my meticulously erected walls. Some of them were annoyingly persistent, but I got good at predicting when they would turn sloppy or pleading . . . and that made snuffing their flames oddly fulfilling. I was consistent, if not happy. I took a perverse pleasure in booting cover girls out of my bed on a regular basis, and hoped that Joe Normal was envious as hell.

Lust. Envy. Admirable goals, I thought, as she lay with her hair covering my face, both of her legs hugging one of mine. We had turned out to be pretty much alike after all.

When I mumbled, she stirred from her doze. "What . . . ?"

"I said, I want a picture of you, just like you are, right this moment."

Her eyes snapped open, gleaming in the faint light. "No." She spoke into the hollow of my neck, her voice distant, the sound of it barely impressing the air. "No pictures. No more pictures. Ever."

The businessman part of my brain perked up: *What neurosis could this be?* Was Tasha Vode abandoning her career? Would it be as successful as her abandonment of me? And what was the difference? For what she earned in a month, I could buy the beach frontage below, for several miles in both directions. What difference? I'd gotten her back, against all the rules of reality, and here I was looking for the loophole. Her career had cleaved us apart, and now it was making us cleave back together. Funny how a word can have opposing definitions.

After five minutes of tossing and turning, she decided not to make me work for it. "Got anything warm?" She cracked a helpless smile. "Down in the kitchen, I mean."

"Real cocoa. Loaded with crap that's bad for you. Not from an envelope. Topped with marshmallows, also real, packed with whatever carcinogens the cocoa doesn't have."

"Sounds luscious. Bring a whole pot."

"You can help."

"No. I want to watch the storm." Water pelted the glass. Now and then lightning would suggest how turbulent the ocean had gotten, and I thought of firing up my beacon. Perhaps there was a seafarer out there who was as romantic about boats as I was about light-houses, and had gotten caught in the squall without the latest in high-tech directional doodads.

I did it. Then I dusted off an old TV tray for use as a serving platter, and brought the cocoa pot and accoutrements up the narrow stairs, clanking and rattling all the way.

My carbon-arc beam scanned the surface of the water in long, lazy turns. She was facing her diaphanous reflection in the glass, looking through her own image into the dark void beyond.

I had pulled on canvas pants to make the kitchen run, but Tasha was still perfectly naked and nakedly perfect, a siren contemplating shipwrecks. She drifted back from the window. I pitied my imaginary seafarer, stuck out in the cold, away from the warmth of her.

"You know those natives in Africa?" she said as I served. "The ones who wouldn't let missionaries take their pictures because they thought the camera would trap their souls?"

"It's a common belief. West Indians still hold to the voodoo value of snapshots. *Mucho* mojo. Even bad snapshots." I couldn't help that last remark. What a pro I am.

"You remember April McClanahan?" She spoke toward the sea. To my reflection.

"You mean Crystal Climax, right?"

She nodded. "Also of wide renown as Cherry Whipp."

All three were a lady with whom Tasha had shared a garret during her flirtation with the hardcore film industry in the early 1970s. Don't swallow the negative hype for a second—every woman who is anyone in film or modeling has made similar contacts. Tasha had never moved beyond a couple of relatively innocuous missionary-position features, respectable porn for slumming yip-yups, a one-week run at the Pussycat

Theatre, max. April, on the other hand, moved into the hardcore mainstream—*Hustler* covers, videocassette toplines, "fully erect" notices in the film ratings. And no, she didn't get strangled or blow her brains all over a motel room with a Saturday Night Special. Last I heard, she was doing TV commercials for bleach and fabric softener as "Valerie Winston," a sort of Marilyn Chambers in reverse.

"April once told me she'd figured out, with a calculator, that she was responsible for more orgasms in one year than anybody else." Tasha held the big porcelain mug in both hands, to warm her palms. "She averaged out how many moviehouses were showing her films, how many times per day, multiplied by howevermany guys she figured were getting their jollies in the audience per show. Plus whoever was doing likewise to her pictures in god knows how many stroke magazines. Or gratifying themselves to the sex advice column she did for *Leather Life*. I remember her looking at me and saying, 'Think of all the energy that must produce. All those orgasms were born because of me. Me.' "

"I'm sure there are legions of guys jollying to your photos, too," I said. "No doubt, somebody out there is yanking his crank to Christie Brinkley's smile, right now."

"It's not the same thing. April was tough. She got something back." She sat on the bed facing me, legs tucked. She reminded me of Edvard Eriksen's famous sculpture of the Little Mermaid, rendered not in bronze but coaxed from milk-white moonstone, heated by living yellow electricity called down from a black sky, and warmed by warm Arctic eyes—the warmest blue that exists in our world.

"You mean April didn't mind getting that porn star rap laid on her . . . literally?"

I could see her sadness being blotted away by acid bitterness. "The people in porn have it easier. The thuds out there in Bozo-land *know* in their tiny little hearts that porn queens fuck for jobs. Whereas cover girls or legit models who rarely do buff or full-frontal are suspect.''

''You can't deny the public their imaginary intrigues.''

''What it always boils down to is, 'Climb off it, bitch—who did you *really* blow to get that last *Vogue* cover?' They feed off you. They achieve gratification in a far dirtier way, by wanting you and resenting you at the same time. By hating your success enough to keep all the tabloids in business. It's a draining thing, all taking and no giving, like . . .''

''Psychic vampirism?'' It was so easy for someone in her position to sense that her public loved her only in the way a tumor loves its host. But a blacker part of my mind tasted a subtle tang of revenge. She'd left me to go chase what she wanted . . . and when she'd finally sunk in her teeth, she'd gotten the flavor of bile and chalk and ashes. I suppose I should have been ashamed of myself for embracing that hateful satisfaction so readily. And from the hurt neutrality on her face, she might have been reading the thoughts in my head. She watched her cocoa instead of drinking it— always a bad sign.

Just as much as I never said no, I never apologized. Not for anything.

After a cool silence, she said, ''You're saying to yourself, 'She's got it made, for christsake. What right does she have to be dissatisfied with anything?' Right?''

''Maybe a tiny bit, yeah.'' She let me take her hand regardless. She needed the contact. Our missing ten years settled between us to fog the issue. I was resentful, yes. Did I want to help her? Same answer. When I guiltily tried to pull back my hand she kept ahold of it. It made me feel forgiven; absolved, almost.

"In science class, in eighth grade, they taught us that when you smell something, your nose is actually drawing in tiny molecular bits of whatever it is you're smelling. Particles."

"Which means you clamped both hands over your mouth and nose whenever you passed a dog turd on the sidewalk after school, am I right?" My prescription for sticky emotional situations is rigid: Always—*always* joke your way out.

Her smile came and went. "The idea stuck in my head. If you smelled something long enough, it would run out of molecules and poof—it wouldn't exist anymore."

"Uh-huh, if you stood around sniffing for a couple of eons." Fortunately, I'd forgotten most of the junk with which school had tried to clog my head. About hard science I knew squat, like math. But I did know that there were billions or trillions of molecules in any given object.

"My point is that each one of us only has so much to give." She cleared her throat, almost as though it hurt her, and pressed valiantly onward. "What if you were to run out of pieces all of a sudden?"

"Happens all the time," I said airily. "That's what a nervous breakdown is. Entertainers who can't give their audiences an ounce more collapse onstage. Corporate guys get physically ill and can't go near a meeting room. People exceed their operational limits . . . and you're in one of the most high-pressure professions there is."

"No." She was shaking her head to prevent me from clouding her train of thought. "I mean run out of pieces literally. Suppose every photo of me ever taken was an infinitesimal piece? Every magazine ad, every negative, every frame of motion picture film—another tiny molecule of me, stolen away to feed an audience that is *never* satiated. And when someone is fully consumed—vampirized—they move on, still hungry, to pick their next victim by making him or her a star. That's why they're called consumers."

I looked up from the muddy lees in my cup just in time to see the passing lighthouse beam blank the ghost of her reflection from the windowpanes. Just like her smile, it came and went.

Her voice had downshifted into the husky and quavering register of confession. Now I was really uncomfortable. "I know there are celebrities who've had their picture taken two million more times than I have. But maybe they can afford it." She stretched across the bed to place her head on my thigh and hug my waist, connecting herself. "Maybe some of us don't have so many pieces . . ."

I held her while the storm rallied for a renewed assault. My modest but brave beam of lamplight chopped through it. She did not grimace, or redden, or sob; her tears just began spilling out, coursing down in perfect wet lines to darken my pantleg.

Did I want to help her?

She feared that consumers wanted so much of her that pretty soon there would be nothing left to consume. And Claudia Katz no longer existed, except in my head. I'd fallen in love with her, become addicted to her . . . and now she was clinging to me because Tasha Vode was almost used up, and after that, if there was not Claudia, there was nothing. She had not brought her exhaustion home to my stoop to prove she could still jerk my leash after ten years. She had done it because the so-called friends who had gorged themselves on her personality were now nodding and clucking about celebrity lifestyles and answering their machines and juggling in new appointments to replace her as the undertow dragged her away to oblivion.

I stroked her hair until it was all out of her face. The tears dried while the seastorm churned. She snoozed, curled up, her face at peace, and I gently disengaged. Then, with a zealot's devotion toward proving her fears were all in her imagination, I went downstairs to load up one of my Nikons.

I asked her how she felt the next morning. When she said terrific, I spilled the beans.

"You *what*—?"

"I repeat for clarity: I took pictures of you while you were asleep. Over a hundred exposures of you wound up in my dark blue sheets, sleeping through a gale. And guess what—you're still among the living this morning." I refilled her coffee cup and used tongs to pluck croissants out of the warmer.

She cut loose a capacious sigh, but put her protests on hold. "Don't do that again. Or you'll lose me."

I wasn't sure whether she meant she'd fade to nothingness on the spot, or stomp out if I defied her superstitions a second time. "You slept like a stone, love. Barely changed position all night." My ego was begging to be told that our mattress gymnastics had put her under, but when I saw the care she took to lift her coffee cup with both hands, I knew better.

"Look at this shit," she said with disgust. "I can barely hold up my head, let alone my coffee. I'm slouching. Models aren't supposed to *slouch,* for christsake." She forced her sitting posture straight and smiled weakly. Her voice was a bit hoarse this morning, almost clogged.

"Hey lady—slouch away." Worry stabbed at my insides while I tried to sound expansive and confident. "Do what thou wilt. Sleep all day if that's your pleasure. Just wait till you discover what I've learned to cook in the last ten years. Real salads. Stuff you have to sauté. Food with *wine* in it. I can artistically dish up all the squares you require. Loaf on the beach. Read my library. I have said it; it is good." I watched a glint of caution try to burn away the happiness in her eyes. She did so want to believe me. "And no more photographs. Promise. Anybody who tries has gotta shoot through yours truly.''

She brightened at that. I'd gotten the reaction I wanted from her. It was the challenge-and-reward game. And goddamned if that tiny acid-drop of doubt didn't settle into my brain, sizzling—*what if what if what if.*

What if I was playing it safe because she might be right?

"I don't want to see those pictures," she said. "Don't even develop them."

"I'll toss 'em in the woodstove right now, if that's what you'd like." I'd made my point.

She gave a theatrical shudder. "Don't burn them. That's too much like a horror story I read once. I might shuffle off the coil along with my own pictures."

The rolls of film were lined up on my miscellaneous shelf downstairs, in the darkroom, the room with the red lightbulbs. Expose the film to anything but that mellow, crimson glow and it blanked into silver nitrate nothingness. The rolls could stay down there, sealed into their little black plastic vials. Forever, if that's what she wanted.

She kept watch on the sea while we destroyed our Continental breakfast. "I thought maybe we could brave the overcast later, and drive down past Point Pitt for dinner," I said. "Steaks, salads and a bottle or two of Cabernet. If anybody asks whether you're Tasha Vode, just blink and say, '' 'Who?' ''

The life had surged back into her expression. "Maybe. Or maybe seafood. But I want you to do something for me, first."

"Your wish . . ."

"Don't you have any work to do today?"

Who were we kidding; I think we both knew I'd do almost anything she asked. "Nothing that can't wait."

"Then carry me back up to the bedroom."

My narrow little stairway was a tight shot, but we

negotiated it successfully after a mild bump or two. Our robes got in the way, so we left them crumpled on the stairs about halfway up.

Her need for contact was vital.

Outside the bedroom window it got dark. I did not notice. All I could see was her.

Her eyes were capable of a breathtaking syllabary of expressions, and I felt my own eyes become lenses, trying to record them all. I stopped being friend or lover to be a camera, to trap what it was about her that made total strangers hear those jungle drums. There were thousands, maybe millions of men out there in the darkness, who fantasized about being inside her the way I was now, who played my role and spoke my half of the dialogue whenever they passed a news-stand. Their wanting never ceased.

Her eyes told me they knew what I was up to. They did not approve.

Her calling was one of the few that made you a vet-eran before puberty was done. If you lucked out, you'd become wealthy while still legally a child; if you weren't so lucky, you'd be left a burned-out has-been before you graduated high school. The attrition rate was worse than that for professional athletes, who could at least fall back on commercials for razors and lite beer when middle age called them out. But she did not seem the sort of human being who could relish the living death of celebrity game shows. Staying beauti-ful had been an unending war; each touchup a skir-mish that stole away another irreclaimable chunk of time. Doing it for ten years, and staying the best, had been draining. Her outside was being used up. Her hipbones felt like flint arrowheads beneath soft tissue paper.

Her hand slid down and felt the cingulum cinched drawstring-tight above my balls. Comprehension dawned in her eyes, followed by that strange tolerance of hers for my various idiocies. I can't relate the exact sequence (to come was, for me, a necessary agony by now), but I was almost certain that her rapidfire contractions began the instant she slipped the knot of the cingulum. Unbound, I offloaded lavishly. Her fingers whitened with pressure on my shoulders, then relaxed, reddening with blood. I watched the pupils of those warm Arctic eyes expand hotly in the dimness as she took what was mine. Until that moment, her own orgasms had seemed insubstantial somehow. Disconnected from her. Spasms of her equipment more than sparky showers in her brain. Her breath had barely raised condensation on my skin. Now she came into focus, filled, flushed, and radiating heat.

After holding me for a lapse of time impossible to measure, she said, "Don't try to impress. You're not performing with a capital *P.*" Her eyes saw that I had been intimidated by the imagined skills of her past decade of lovers, and thus the girdle cord trick. Stupid. "Don't you see? You're the only one who ever gave anything back."

"Tasha, you don't really believe that—"

"Try Claudia." It was not a command but a gentle urging. But it, too, was vital. "You're the only one who can give me back some of myself; replace what the others have taken. Give me more." Her reverent tone bordered on love—that word I could rarely force myself to speak, even frivolously.

Who better to give her back some of herself? I was a goddamn repository of her identity. With other women I had never bothered worrying, and so had never been befuddled as I was now. I'd made love to Claudia, not the exterior self that the rest of the world was busy eating. And now she was steering.

I gave her back to herself; her eyes said so, her voice said so, and I tried to hush the voice in my head that said I was not being compensated for this drain. I tried to ignore the numberless black canisters of film that beckoned me from the room with the red light. And later, past midnight, when the storm thundered in, I carefully took twice what I had given her. No matter how much we have, as Nicole the waitress would say, we always want more.

"Skull full of sparrow shit," she said the following day, as we bumped knees and elbows trying to dress for dinner. "Gorgeous but ditzy. Vacuous. Vapid. Pampered. Transient values. A real spoiled-rotten—"

"I think I get the stereotype," I said. "You're just not stupid enough to be happy as a model anymore, right?"

"Ex-model." She watched the sea bounce back the glare of late afternoon. "You don't believe me, do you?"

"What I believe scares the crap out of me." I tried to veneer what I said with good humor, to defang my fears. "I believe, for example, that you might be a ghost. And ghosts never stay."

She waggled her eyebrows. "I could haunt your lighthouse. Or maybe I'm just your wish-fulfillment."

"Don't laugh. I've often thought that I'm not really earning a living as a photographer." Merely speaking that last word caused the slightest hesitation in the natural flow of her movements; she was *that* sensitized to it. "I'm not really sleeping with Tas . . . uh, Claudia Katz." She caught that slip, too, but forgave it. "Actually, I'm really a dirtbag litter basket picker up in the Mission. And all of this is a hallucinatory fantasy I invented while loitering near a magazine rack with Tasha Vode's picture at hand, hm?"

"Ack," she said with mock horror. "You're one of *them.* The pod-folk."

"Are we gone, or what?"

She stepped back from the mirror, inside of a bulky, deep-blue ski sweater with maroon patterning, soft boots of gray suede, and black slacks so tight they made my groin ache. Her eyes filled up with me, and they were the aquamarine color of the sunlit ocean outside. "We're gone," she said, and led the way down the stairs.

I followed, thinking that when she left me again I'd at least have those hundreds of photographs of her in my bed. Ghosts never stay.

Outside there was a son of a bitch, and an asshole.

The son of a bitch was crouched in ambush right next to my front door. His partner, the asshole, was leaning on my XLS, getting cloudy fingerprints all over the front fender. I had backed out the front door, to lock it, and heard his voice talking, before anything else.

"Miss Vode, do you have any comment on your abrupt—"

Tasha—*Claudia*—started to scream.

I turned as she recoiled and grabbed my hand. I saw the asshole. Any humanity he might have claimed was obliterated by the vision of a huge, green check for an exclusive article that lit up his eyes. A pod man. Someone had recognized us in the restaurant last night, and sent him to ambush us in the name of the public's right to know. He brandished a huge audio microphone at us as though it was a scepter of power. It had a red foam windscreen and looked like a phallic lollipop.

Her scream sliced his question neatly off. She scrambled backward, hair flying, trying to interpose me between herself and the enemy, clawing at her head, crushing her eyes shut and *screaming*. That sound filled my veins with liquid nitrogen.

The son of a bitch was behind us. From the instant we had stepped into the sunlight, he'd had us nailed in his viewfinder. The video rig into which he was harnessed ground silently away; the red bubble light over the lens hood was on.

And Tasha screamed.

Maybe she jerked her hand away, maybe I let it go, but her grip went foggy in mine as I launched myself at the cameraman, eating up the distance between us like a barracuda. Only once in my whole life had I ever hit a man in anger, and now I doubled my own personal best by delivering a roundhouse punch right into the black glass maw of his lens, filling his face up with his own camera, breaking his nose, two front teeth, and the three middle fingers of my fist. He faded to black and went down like a medieval knight trapped by the weight of his own armor. I swarmed over him and used my good hand to rip out his electronic heart, wresting away porta-cam, tape and all. Cables shredded like torn ligaments and shiny tape viscera trailed as I heaved it, spinning, over the pier rail and into a sea the same color as Tasha's eyes. The red light expired.

Her scream . . . wasn't. There was a sound of pain as translucent as rice paper, thin as a flake of mica, drowned out by the roar of water meeting beach.

By the time I cranked my head around—two dozen slow-motion shots, easy—neither of her was there anymore. I thought I saw her eyes, in Arctic-cold afterburn, winking out last.

"Did you *see*—?"

"You're trespassing!" bellowed Dickie Barnhardt, wobbling toward the asshole with his side-to-side Popeye gait, pressed flat and pissed off. The asshole's face was flashfrozen into a bloodless bas-relief of shock and disbelief. His mouth hung slack, showing off a lot of expensive fillings. His mike lay forgotten at his feet.

"Did you see . . . did . . . she just . . ."

Dickie bounced his ashwood walking stick off the asshole's forehead. He joined his fallen mike in a boneless tumble to the planks of the pier. Dickie's face was alight with a bizarre expression that said it had been too long since he'd found a good excuse to raise physical mayhem, and he was proud of his forthright defense of tenant and territory. "You okay?" he said, squinting at me and spying the fresh blood on my hand.

"Dickie . . . did you see what happened to Tasha?" My voice switched in and out. My throat constricted. My unbroken hand closed on empty space. Too late.

He grinned a seaworthy grin and nudged the unconscious idiot at his feet. "Who's Tasha, son?"

I drink my coffee left-handed, and the cast mummifying my right hand gives me something to stare at contemplatively.

I think most often of that videotape, decomposing down there among the sand sharks and the jellyfish that sometimes bob to the surface near Dickie's pier, I think that the tiny bit of footage recorded by that poor, busted-up son of a bitch cameraman would not have mattered one damn, if I hadn't shot so much film of Tasha to prove she had nothing to fear. So many pieces. I pushed her right to the edge, cannibalizing her in the name of love.

The black plastic cans of film are still on the shelf down in my darkroom, lined up like inquisitors already convinced of my guilt. The thought of dunking that film in developer makes me want to stick a gun in my ear and pull the trigger, twice if I had the time.

Then I consider another way out, and wonder how long it would take me to catch up with her; how many pieces I have.

I never cried much before. Now the tears unload at the least provocation. It's sloppy, and messy, and unprofessional, and I hate it. It makes Nicole stare at me the way the street bum did, like I've tipped over into psycholand.

When she makes her rounds to fill my cup, she watches me. The wariness in her eyes is new. She sees my notice dip from her eyes to her sumptuous chest and back, in a guilty but unalterable ritual. I force a smile for her, gamely, but it stays pasted across my face a beat too long, insisting too urgently that everything is okay. She doesn't ask. I wave my unbroken hand over my cup to indicate *no more,* and Nicole tilts her head with a queer, new expression—as though this white boy is trying to trick her. But she knows better. She always has.

BRASS

The lovemaking was just fine. Stabilizing, perfect.

The medoc jug—how trendy—was a crimson third shy of empty. The sheets had been virgin cotton up until a couple of hours ago. Floating oil wicks had replaced the customary votive candles. From their many perches on a stylized bonsai of chrome, the wicks threw back tiny, star-filtered prongs of diffused white light. The air conditioner mumbled, pushing out cool. The lovemaking . . . well, the sex had been terrific. Its afterglow was comfortably disorienting, a warm feeling the man in the bed hoped might grow more familiar with time, and thus more dimensional, and more perfect.

Green amplifier telltales winked from across the room. Grant Mantell was content to stare them down from his lazy splay across his newly inaugurated bed. The tape reel was a recording-studio-style ten-incher packed with choice tracks of symphonic soundtrack music—selections Jennifer had dared him to identify without giving him a chance at fair competition. It had run dry nearly twenty minutes ago. Grant felt no digging urge to dash over and change it, or kill the machines, or anything. Apart from the new tape, Jennifer had showed up with an orgy of snackables—summer sausage, cheeses, chips, still-warm French sourdough bread—through which they had feasted shamelessly. Within arm's reach, a crumbling plug of cheddar was nailed to a small cutting board by one of Grant's carving knives. The blade caught some of the candlelight, and Grant wondered if the frequency with which he contemplated the ease of potential murder—or suicide—was abnormal. Thoughts, blackly thrilling, never straying beyond the broom-closet area of his mind, absorbed him.

He approved of his own casual control. *Good for me.* There were psychos in rubber bedrooms the world over who had somehow failed to acknowledge the sympathetic relationship cutting utensils had with food, who wound up making the Thanksgiving cutlery part of wifey's or hubby's anatomy. *Men were not meant to stick women with knives*—that was *funny,* goddamnit; funny must still be worth something. Luckily, Jenny was asleep and therefore incapable of deriding the chauvinism of her partner's dumb postcoital philosophizing. Her right arm and leg were laced over him; her breath brushed warmly against his neck in a regularly cadenced rasp that was not quite a snore. The sheets were impossibly twined around and over and under, damp-dry patches cooling in the dark.

He raised his head, the bed gave an obliging little creak, and the snow-white Alsatian snoozing beneath the stereo shelf lifted his turretlike head attentively. The broad, thick brush of white tail batted the carpeting in three hopeful thumps. When nothing happened, he lowered head to forepaws with a dog-shrug, staring into the dark with that peculiar, patient resignation that made him such an affable companion. Jenny had brought Max along, too. Max had gotten bored snitching tidbits and so had flopped near the door to doze and listen while his masters made friction.

Carefully, conscious of Jenny's slumber, Grant stretched his arms backward to lace his fingers through the intricate metal weave of the golden headboard. The bed itself was a wonder. Thinking of the bed made him look naturally toward his other recent acquisition, the mirror. It hung on the wall close by the bed's port side, overseeing the thin corridor of carpet on which he unceremoniously dumped his boots at bedtime. It was huge—three feet on a side, demanding leaded setscrews to secure its weight to the wall beams—and gaudy enough for a whorehouse. Its wide frame was of scrolled brass, inlaid with smaller idiograms reminiscent of the hood of an Indian incense burner. Hanging it next to the bed was an obvious and uninspired choice; realistically, it was the *only* place for it. The exterior wall featured timbers every three feet. This sucker was *heavy* . . . but next to the bed it was at least stable.

Inside the slightly canted sheet of silver, Grant could see himself along with parts of Jenny in the bounce-back from the amplifier and candle lights. His hair was a riot. He adjudged himself a crowd face with an Irish nose and deep-set, glittering eyes. Black eyes; so intent that one of the first observations Jennifer had made was "Your kind of eyes make stupid people feel uncomfortable." That had been at their first lunch together, and ever since their meeting she seemed to work at helping him with his self-image. She was anything but insecure herself, and his deferral to her critical abilities was great for his ego. Thus his carriage was not *masculine* (that would have been too simple) but *authoritative*. He was not movie-idol attractive, but with his character lines, what the hell difference did it make? And so forth.

It was a matter of perspective on oneself. *There, see?* He pursed his lips in the semidark. Thanks to TV commercials, nobody was happy; everyone was self-conscious and insecure. To such a cosmetically atrophied outlook, the goal of being handsome according to media rules was to end up in bed with a woman like Jennifer, he thought. It was the logic of commerce. He was outside it, totally, and here he was in bed. None of the stupid rules, therefore, were real.

Jenny would have resented comparison to a brainless TV muffin, anyway.

He looked back at himself in the mirror a second time, scrutinizing. He squinted. He wrinkled up his brow. He bared his upper row of teeth. In the dim light, and through the cheesecloth fog of his own narrowed eyelids, he saw himself reflected back as a demon. Some kind of vampire. The light molded his imagination into a vulpine countenance, satanic and grinning, just a few feet away.

He fought to maintain the accidental illusion for a few more seconds, fascinated. He perceived the gargoyle lines of the hungry face, saw the sharp slits of nostril and the pointed chin and the eyes, like glossy chips of obsidian. It was a medieval woodcut of Lucifer rendered into glass and stone.

And it returned his gaze steadily, hungering. Someone had told the bogeyman under the bed to slither forth for feeding time.

He relaxed his facial muscles and there was silent pain. The reversed image of the digital clock told him he had lain for more than five minutes with his face frozen into that bizarre rictus; five minutes that had been like thirty seconds. Now his eyes ached and his jaw was sore. A thin headache vein began to pulse wetly away and he grimaced. The face in the mirror grimaced back. It was his own face, the one with the great character lines and the Irish nose—his wild Irish nose, he thought crazily. There was no monster stalking him from the glass, no visage sporting deathshead eyebrows arched up in black contrails and fangs dripping bubbly gobbets of saliva. It had been perspective and faint light, yes, and of course the medoc. A lot of it sat in his bladder, but the alcohol fizzed away in his bloodstream with a red tingle. It reminded him of the way people got blitzed in pubs like the Hairy O or the Piece de Maurice, always winding up in the john and convincing their mirror-selves they weren't *really* drunk, before grinning like a fool and shuffling carefully out to rejoin the world.

After a moment of such roundabout contemplation (during which Max spot-checked the proceedings and, finding only more human frippery, worked on making the floor more comfortable) Grant thought he might like to try and make the demon come back for an encore. But what if he looked back up and the demon was already there, ahead of him, waiting?

He jerked his head up suddenly. A clean lick of auburn hair drooped across his forehead, simultaneously with that of the reflected Grant. No demon.

Somehow this did nothing to reassure him; he had been struck by the fancy and concentrated on it even harder. What if, someday, you were to glance into the mirror and see a malignant, demoniac version of your own face, meeting you eye-to-eye, unflinching? Smiling hideously under the awful brightness of a bathroom light, making movements you weren't making with your own face?

Dear God, what if it said something?

He glazed his eyes, the whites above the pupils becoming visible. The oil wicks seemed to intensify without providing any real light at all.

"My turn," he growled. "Now *you* get in the mirror."

A blackly exciting tendril of fear uncoiled in his stomach. His speech scared gooseflesh up along his arms, and the fine, light hairs there snapped to attention, prickling. He stopped to admire the terrorization he had wrought. Another second might have convinced him that a palpable threat perhaps existed a few feet away, in the mirror—a total product of his imagination. An English instructor at Cal State Northridge had once told Grant that he possessed no imagination whatsoever. That was not what caused his peculiar exhilaration. His actions had the tang of supernatural defiance, like pissing in Satan's face and then daring him to do something about it. Wow.

He smiled then, broadly, idiotically, thinking that this must be what was meant by the term *enjoying yourself.* Here I am, enjoying my own self (and without masturbating, the Rodney Dangerfield imp in another quadrant of his brain was quick to add), and my reflection seems to be enjoying himself—itself—too.

Grant looked up to check. Inside its weight of brass, the glass remained implacable while his image stared back at him with an identically sheepish expression. By Cromwell, he thought with detached wonder, I must still be a tad fuzzheaded.

As if agitated by his fantasizing (or stray brain-waves, leaking out to knock her rudely up from slumber), Jenny stirred, with a grunt that hinted at her return to the domain of the living and the crazy. Her hair hung everywhichway in streaming black loops, and her eyes were slightly puffy with sleep as she rose on one elbow, mouth open, and caught sight of herself in the mirror.

Her face often pushed Grant into ruminations on the strange convergence of their lives. It always seemed surprising to him that Jenny was attractive, that he knew and *she* knew it especially, and that it was no big deal. Her face was not sculptured into the clean, perfect architectural flawlessness preferred by the purveyors of sterile fashion. Her mirror might have told another woman that her mouth was a tot too large and wide, that her chin was not well defined, that her eyes seemed too far apart. The concert of her facial components, however, certainly proved Poe's dictate that true beauty was largely a matter of *strangeness of proportion*: her face was darkly compelling, rather than blandly pretty. That was as close as Grant could pin it, and it served. Her height matched his own six feet to the inch; that leonine accumulation of jet-black hair usually served to accentuate her altitude further, and when she wore heels it became impossible. But now, curled into him in bed, she did not appear even vaguely Amazonian.

Jenny looked up into the reflection of her darkly compelling face and said, "Yuck." She covered her face with her hand and immediately parted the fingers so that a single agate-gray eye peered out for a second look. "Caught unawares again. With my pants down, to wit. So to speak." She yawned.

He glided his hand into her hair; indicated he was awake. He tried to suppress a tiny belch, but it billowed up through his innards with a rumble. Why couldn't burps or the grand old anal thunder ever rattle forth when one's love partner was dead asleep? The eyeball swiveled toward him in mock reproach. "Ah, excuse me."

"Me, too." Jennifer yawned generously again. "For falling asleep on you—literally, I mean."

"That's unconditionally okay."

"You *are* rather comfortable, you know."

"Thank you."

"What is it you're doing . . . up there?"

"Staring at the pretty lights," he said. "Making faces at myself in yonder mirror."

"Aha—unbridled excitement in my absence, I see." She grimaced, trying to read the clock in the mirror, failing, then turning. "Have you been awake all this time?"

"Yep."

"Making faces for three hours?" she said as the digital box growled over to 4:02. "Since one A.M.?" When she became inquisitive her voice rose into an exotic register of inflection that almost classified as an accent. No one Grant had witnessed had ever believed her claim that it was straight Woodstock native (whatever that classified as); they always counted on some foreign port lurking in her past to validate their conjectures of mysterious background or eclectic blood.

Grant yawned this time, nodding in response.

"Thrilling," she said, deadpan.

"Yes, it was." He was not facing her. From there the conversation did not stop; rather, it became irrelevant. They ceased talking as though by telepathic agreement.

Under the hazed light the bedframe returned a golden aura as they rearranged themselves. Its brass was a bold but gentle presence in the room, like the fire of the oil wicks, or the silver and gold of the mirror in its frame.

Grant's head was angled sideways. He watched himself in the mirror, intermittently, until his eyelids became prohibitively heavy. Nothing peculiar happened.

But past this night, the first night Jennifer had passed in his new bed, he knew he would regard the mirror uneasily. It was a morbid idea, almost a touch paranoid, but he abruptly felt like the man who discovers his pretty tropical fish have teeth and an appetite for fingers. When he projected this vague fear into the future, his heart bumped faster and he thought his prospects for deep and cozy sleep to be lost.

Sleep came with almost absurd ease. He dropped off as if anesthetized and did not consider the mirror again until the following evening.

"Assuming you can trust any doctor in town further than the distance between noses, mine and thine," Jennifer said around a mouthful of niçoise salad, "what was the verdict?"

A bow-tied waiter with ridiculously wide tortoise-shell rimmed glasses flounced past long enough to re-heat Grant's coffee. Grant's eyes stayed on the curls of steam as he spoke. "Everybody else would have added, *you don't have to talk about it if you don't want to*. They tack it onto the end of their questions, like they think I'm going to start crying or something. But in the end your feelings add up to a lot less than their need to pry.''

"Like, please pass the salt . . . you don't have to if you don't want to, but *I* want the goddamn salt—?''

"Exactly.'' He was pleased she had not misinterpreted his complaint, or taken personal offense. He speared three of the smallest homefries he could find on his plate and forked them into his mouth. "You're right, though. All the lawsuits against hospitals and doctors around LA make me wonder a little bit. Anything expedient can be scribbled in on a death certificate if they're the least bit stumped, and we humble serfs will never be the wiser. But what they've settled on, as far as my father goes, is a hematoma. A little tumor full of blood in his brain. He keeled over in his living room and Mrs. Saks from next door found him in front of the fireplace. She peeked through a crack in the curtains; all the doors were locked. She hobbled back to her place and called the medics. He'd been dead almost a whole day when they collected him. A little sac swelled up with blood and burst; he hemorrhaged like mad inside his own skull and just dropped dead. When he blacked out he knocked a candle off the mantlepiece; it burned some of the carpet before it went out. Mouin shag; that goddamned carpet was brand new the last time I was inside that house.'' He had stopped eating.

"Sounds like he might have lain there a lot longer,'' Jenny said thoughtfully, still chewing, apparently determined not to let him lapse into despondency despite their topic, which had to be dealt with.

"Yeah, well, paramedics are used to finding old folks who've been stiff and dead in their bathrooms for weeks, all bloated and gassy from—oop, sorry about that.''

Across from him, Jenny's expression was that of a woman who thinks, but is not positive, that she has just eaten a cockroach instead of a carrot slice. The dab of dressing on her lower lip looked obscene. After a second, her tongue swept it away and she swallowed hard, going for her water goblet. "Just stick to the pertinent stuff. Or else." She regarded the remainder of her food uncomfortably.

"I'm—never mind." Sickly grin. At least some of his usual humor was seeping back. "Mrs. Saks. Father once told me she was the neighborhood busybody. Used to water the lawn on the east side of her house for hours, so she could peep through his side window—she must've thought something pretty hot was going on inside. Father started keeping his curtains closed."

"Logical. Sensible."

"What's weird is that burn on the carpet. It wouldn't have made any difference if the house *had* burned to the ground. There's an empty lot down there now."

"No house?" She looked genuinely surprised.

"I met Father's legal chickenhawks two days after he died. Two locals and one appointed 'personal representative' from San Francisco. Until then nobody bothered to let me know that I was required to witness the demolition of Father's house personally in order to qualify for my inheritance. Which, by the way, is paying for this lunch, so pick a dessert."

"Why, for heaven's sake? From what you said it was quite a place—all oiled mahogany and ornamental balustrades and stained-glass windows. Haven't you ever wanted a palace?"

"First of all, I want my *own* palace, by my own hand. I can afford it now anyway. There are a lot of exquisite old houses down around Pico and La Cienega, true, but it just isn't my kind of neighborhood. Somebody connected with the corporation wants the property already, and I get the profit. Fine." He finished off his roast beef. "Next, nobody, including me and the lawyers, knows the rationale . . . except Father, who currently is not talking." He was still at-

tempting to appear breezy and unconcerned whenever
they circled back to the given of his father's death. The
masque was not totally convincing; pain came at Jennifer in surges.

"That's where you vanished to a couple of weeks
ago and wouldn't enlighten me?"

"Now it can be told." He spread his hands. "The
wreckers started half an hour before I got there. It got
boring quick. The attorneys sweltered in their C&R
suits. Then a large, hairy fellow shambled over to me
and asked me what I wanted done with all the 'fuggin
antiques.' "

"Your father's furniture was still in—"

"There was no furniture. Empty house. The executors even had the light fixtures removed. They hauled
away the fireplace, which was solid Etruscan marble
and probably cost its own gross tonnage in gold doubloons. That house was as empty when my father was
buried as my checking account was before he died."
Again the strained expression, the brief silence.
"Nevertheless, this turkey comes up with a sledgehammer in one paw and says the basement room is
full of junk. I said, 'What basement room?' He looked
at me the way a librarian does when they find out you
don't know what the Dewey Decimal System is. Was."

Jennifer pushed her plate away, scanned around and
signaled for coffee. "Everybody forgot the bomb shelter."

"No bomb shelter. It was on the executor's list after
attic compartments. No doors, no vents, no new brickwork or plaster. They pulled measurements of the exterior and only came up a foot or two short compared
to the floorplan, so they assumed the basement they
saw was all there was—until they started kicking the
walls down and found—"

"A bed," she interjected. "And a mirror . . ."

"And a couple of boxes of old *Liberty* magazines."

Jennifer spooned a few drops of milk into her coffee, barely discoloring it. "Somehow I didn't think you'd *paid* for all that stuff. Even taking recent wealth into account, you should excuse the pun."

"I spent a few hernias getting it out and a day or so polishing. For your benefit."

"God preserve me—a romantic." She grinned.

"You'll pardon my recent unsociability."

To keep them both from abstracting into another clumsy silence, she spoke immediately: "I understand: You needed some time. Why do you make it sound so unreasonable?"

He jumped in after her: "Don't apologize; that I don't need." *And now comes the part where you reach across and squeeze her hand meaningfully, or she yours, or some damn thing.* To hell with it, he thought. If she really *did* understand, it was unnecessary.

Fortunately, the waiter showed up to fuss briefly over them and provide distraction. In his wake Jennifer said, "It really is a stunning bed, Grant," with a private, evil smile. "Luxuriously oversized and heavy. It doesn't squeak and it's expensive and permanent-looking. Unusual; when you think of *brass bed* you think of those bordello things—you know, incredibly tacky. I love it."

"I've never seen one remotely like it, either. That's strange. If there's anything that ran against the grain of my father's style, it was that bed. He was strictly a Danish-modern, pure-functionalism freak; nothing ornate. He had his home maintained impeccably but never decorated in the sense you or I would understand. Just a perfect, hollow, empty cavern of house, which is now gone, too. I can't believe he wasn't aware of that stuff below him; I'm sure he probably walled it up down there himself, because if it was there already he would have found it, noticed it, ferreted it out and mentioned it. He was painfully methodical. You don't capture the executive vice-presidency of Calex Corporation if you're not methodical, period."

"You sure it wasn't just a downstairs room that got
. . . um, accidentally closed off?" Her eyes flirted with
the dessert menu again as her question trailed away.
"Boy," she said, shaking her head. "Said out loud
like that it *does* sound pretty stupid. Unlikely. *Accidentally closed off.*"

"That leaves you with *intentionally* closed off,
which strands me with a *why,* either way. But there
was no evidence of there ever being a doorway or access—just a niche of the basement, bricked up tight.
No windows." He stopped to consider whether caffeine and sugar flash were helping his logic processes,
decided against more coffee, then ordered cappucino.
With a shrug he said, "I wonder if the bed has a name?
Fortunato, or something?"

"Provided your father did not indulge his Imp to the
extent of a brass bed like that one," she said (tossing
his Poe reference back in his face, gleefully). "I doubt
that he would run on to the stage of naming his furniture." She unclipped a Benson & Hedges from a flat
silver case and fired up; she was the fastest draw with
a lighter Grant had ever seen. They both ignored the
slim box of wooden matches on the table. "Okay, try
this: The bed was there. Walled up. When your father
moved in. And he never knew about it." Thin gray
smoke trailed from her lips as she spoke, now gesturing with the cigarette. "You said everything inside was
moved out by special arrangement; if he had known it
was there, it would have been inventoried, no?"

"You shouldn't smoke those things," he said, his
attention on the glowing orange tip. "They'll kill you
dead."

Jennifer ordered fresh strawberries, to counter
Grant's request for a chocolate raspberry mousse torte
so richly laced with brandy that the fumes could water
their eyes.

"That bed seemed to suit that house." He sliced
away the tip of the layered brown wedge with his fork.

Floral designs had been swirled in liquid chocolate atop the crimson bed of raspberry sauce. Peggy's was notorious for its desserts. "It was . . . overstated. Another excuse for its burial in the basement. But when the wreckers checked the bricks, they said that although the wall wasn't new, it was about fifty years younger than the rest of the house. Which brings me back to my original conundrum."

"Tastes change," she said. "A month ago you didn't even know what a torte was." Her mouth enveloped the head of a strawberry. Crunch. Grant thought of Eve and the apple: *You talked me into it, ma'am.*

"Sure I knew." He dropped into his redneck drawl. "Hell, ah seen me some torts gettin arrested on Sunset Boo-lee-vord . . ."

"You know what I mean. You just admitted you didn't know your own dad's nature *that* well."

"He was an emotional isolationist."

"So—his taste in beds might have taken a turn toward the eccentric. Or away from it. Just as his son's tastes in food have matured from cheap garbage to expensive garbage." She endured his disapproval of her cigarette for one more luxuriant puff, then butted it in the table ashtray. It fell over, smoldering, its life ebbing.

"Hold on. I didn't actually *eat* that stuff."

The memory of their first meeting filled in gaps of reference, and Grant's mind drew on it in the same languorous way Jenny had inhaled the cigarette smoke. He might never have met her had it not been for a rare, unanticipated, masochistic gut-rumble on behalf of pure sleaze food. Traditionally, Grant forced such fare on himself about once a year, to remind himself how repugnant the consumption of fast-food sewage really was, and thus reinforce against the illusory economy buying such food represented when funds were low.

His mission had been to rendezvous with his good

buddy Scott, projectionist *cum* English major at Northridge, for the purpose of roasting current movies over lunch. Their meeting had been bumped ninety minutes ahead, and Grant, anticipating food too eagerly, found himself with nothing to do but mosey into the closest, loudest conglomeration of neon and formica and order up a clownburger with all the slop, anemic string fries, and a shamelessly flat Pepsi in a go-cup. The percentages were heavily in favor of grease and ice. Sitting on a stone bench, he watched collegiate youth loiter past, bound for dipstick classes in Aerobic Video or Art and the Media Audience. His stomach recaptured sanity and the spicy garbage in the Happy Bag cooled, ignored. He tested a fry, and washed away his error with a sip from the watery Pepsi. He never got a chance at the rest.

"*Max!*" A shrill shout, from far behind him.

He turned to see the Happy Bag kidnaped and making good escape time between the jaws of a stone-white Alsatian. The big dog was being yelled at by a tall woman wearing a jacket and boots of impeccably matched soft-brown leather and a cream-colored cowlneck sweater. Black, flowing hair; lots of it. She stood her ground as the dog homed in on her; Grant stayed neutrally on the bench to observe her pet being admonished. Then, as a pair, they approached him. He forgot about her wardrobe and turned his concentration to those first few, precious seconds of new physical attraction.

The convergence of their lives was that easy, that random.

"My dear Max has what a Victorian novelist would call an 'unfortunate predilection' for fast food. I'm afraid he's done this sort of thing before." Max pulled a parade rest, his butt plunking obediently down near her feet, eyes never straying from the bag she had returned to Grant.

"I was in a suggestible state when I bought this

stuff," he said. "I don't think I could've gone through with it." He unwrapped the burger as he talked. "Does he—?"

"Cast-titanium stomach," she said, pursing her lips pleasantly and nodding approval.

Grant lofted the charred meat patty like a little frisbee. It vanished down Max's gullet with a chomp and a swallow; the dog, still sitting, looked at Grant with an expression that said all was correct in the universe.

Max seemed to prefer his fries cold, anyway.

"And now it seems I owe you a lunch—a proper lunch, at least, and not a dilemma between gastric death and food so obscene that in this state you could pull three-to-fifteen years for just sticking it in your mouth." She saw Grant smile at her and automatically begin his courteous denial. "I'll insist before you can protest," she added, on time. "Max would've let me know if you weren't okay."

Max's eyes, such a vaguely watery blue that they were nearly colorless, seemed to affirm this. It was all a con, Grant thought, but Max wound up getting the Pepsi, too.

Jennifer was new, therefore a party to the odd intimacy careful people generally allow only for strangers. Grant found he was able to edit his conversation around the death of his father and hit few chuckholes. The subject arose before the first time they bedded down together, at Jenny's, and the conversations became impartial, healing things. They consistently surprised each other, and reveled in it. The sole secret of recent weeks had been the brass bed and mirror; these being sprung on her the night before. The coronation that ensued was pleasing for both of them. Now they sat lunching, much as they had on the day Max had caused their lives to cleave, now able to joke and rebound and distill some of Grant's befuddling sense of loss into a painless void where it could not poison him.

The desserts were used up.

"When people die, the survivors always kick themselves for spending so little time with them," said Grant. "It's like a racial imperative."

"But negate the death and nothing changes." Jenny regarded the dead cigarette. "No extra time would be spent."

"My father was always with the corporation. *Always.* Until I was seven I thought 'Calex' was some little brother I'd never met, and wondered why Cal merited so much of my father's time." He shook his head to indicate he was not lapsing into Heavy Revelations; rather, he seemed to be putting the chain of events together for the first time, consumer-testing it on Jenny for stability of logic. "The only time in my life there was a real interface was when I turned eighteen and found out a junior-executive slot on the Calex board was being held for me. That was a big thing, for my father. Bigger than I knew."

"Uh-oh. Rebellious youth."

"I told him to roll and insert it. Bingo—no allowance. Calex was the Daddy Warbucks of Vietnam."

"Sounds like you were seduced by the publicity."

"I had as little social conscience then as now. All I sensed was another surefire way to rub against his grain . . . and so began my odyssey through Real Life. Jesus, what a fucking idiot. College kids who protested the war had kids who would gladly serve up their genitals, today, right here right now, with *garnish,* if the sacrifice meant they could get a toe inside the Calex door. For me, it's all academic now."

"Jeez, you're making that sound awful." After a beat she was compelled by her nature to add: *"My* father would call it 'slicing it too thick to eat.' " Her smile stole the barb from the words.

"You're right—financial autonomy is something I can live with, probably even at the cost of my father. Though I hasten to add I don't look at it that way.

What irritates me is that just now, after eighteen years of more or less standard 'family' bullshit, plus five years of requisite alienation, I'm left with this year, which is half over, plus the year before that and the year before *that*, to know my own father. Not nearly enough; we were just beginning to become friends, and he was just starting to open up, even to me. Now he's gone, prematurely, and I'm not even sure who it is that's just stepped out of my life. That hurts. I don't even know if he had anybody else besides his Calex cronies—he never remarried, unless he kept it a huge secret, and he divorced my mother the year I was born.''

"You mean you're not the black sheep of a corporate dynasty? The son errant, thrust from your birthright by scheming siblings—two older, matching Porches, one younger with a clandestine drug habit, and an iron-fisted matriarch holding illimitable dominion over all?''

He laughed aloud. She was keeping him up here as well as she had in the big brass bed.

"Seriously,'' she said. "No brothers, no sisters you disike but would lend money to out of familial obligation? No forty-five-minute phone calls to update who's divorced and who's pregnant and who's out of jail?''

"I've never been able to understand that bonding that large families claim,'' Grant said. "Maybe it's something you can never know unless you share the group's common blood.'' He had done this disclaimer before, generally using the same words to accentuate his solo nature. "There was just me and mysterious Father, at opposite polarities. Until recently.'' He pulled out a MetroBank VISA to cover the check, which had conspicuously been delivered in mid-sentence. MetroBank was owned by Calex.

"Be generous with the tip,'' Jennifer said. "We've

run the poor dear threadbare. Twenty percent; you can afford it.''

Grant wrote CASH in block letters across the tip blank on the charge flimsy, then unwalleted currency to leave on the tray. ''Better for the waiters,'' he said. ''Less paperwork; less corporate timewasting.''

They stood and he moved to knead her shoulders from behind, grateful for the renewed contact after spending the entire meal a table apart. ''Would you like to see the property?'' He asked this abruptly, feeling that he might not have asked her a day earlier, but now it was fair to offer her some involvement, if she consented. ''I have to pop in to see Father's doctor. The lot where the house stood is on the way. Yes?''

''You *would* have to ask today,'' she said as Grant reached to tear carbons. ''I've got a shoot with Toby Wolff at three, and yes, I *did* mention this last night, before we got insensate. Today he does folio shots for me; tomorrow I do nudes, for him. Barter is always the best form of negotiation—each side of the deal thinks they made out best. Once he made the offer, I figured I could get you to tag along so I could get some professional skin shots without any excess laying on of hands by jolly old Toby. He *is* a pro, but I've heard stories. I think it's backlash against the fact that most of the other LA photographers—the *good* ones—are terminally gay, and Toby fears for his macho rep.''

''*Yes* tomorrow, if *no* today is okay. Okay?''

''Deal.''

''You sure?'' He disliked the thought of abandoning her to the greedy eyes of Toby, but Montgomery Mantell's physician was a difficult guy to get an appointment to see.

''No problem.''

''Can you meet me this evening, my apartment? Whenever you finish up?''

''I thought he'd never ask.'' She spoke toward the

sky, grinning wickedly. "But how am I supposed to
do that if I don't know what time *you'll* be done?"

He suspected she knew the answer already but
dipped into his coat pocket with a flourish regardless.
Between his fingers was a shining-bronze, newly ma-
chined key. "For you."

Her expression went just slack enough to please him;
it only lasted a second. Very seriously, she said,
"Does this mean that you and I have become an 'item,'
sir?" And took the key to his apartment, wrapping it
tightly up in her fist.

"God, that's the first time I've *ever* done anything
like that," he said in a slightly stunned voice. But
inside, he felt roughly the way good old Max must
have after wolfing down his burger.

It was impossible for Grant to miss spotting the old
woman as he swung his Pinto into the wide, curving
promenade of Avalon Circle, just south of Pico and
inside the buffer zone of Century City. She was standing in the center of the empty lot at Number 307,
where the demolition had occurred, on the brink of
the pit that had formerly delineated Montgomery Mantell's basement. Her arms were akimbo against a bil-
lowing paisley dress that went neck to ankles. Grant
slowed to stop at the curb as she turned like a cat
caught in a garbage can. She had wire spectacles, a
granny bun, broad, rounded shoulders, and massive
breasts. Grant wondered what sort of ancient foundation garment held such a boldly maternal chest in
check.

When she saw him stop, she crossed herself furtively and hustled off the lot with surprising speed for
her bulk, beelining for a cottage that had been spared
the hyperthyroidal development of most of the court's
adjoining houses. It looked to be a curt, stringently
maintained one- or two-bedroom place, in the midst
of castles with octopoid wings that nearly spilled into

Avalon Circle from their own lots—a commuter-crunch of mansions.

Bam. Only after her front door pointedly slammed did it occur to Grant that this was Mrs. Saks, the nosy widow. He stayed in the pilot bucket of the Pinto for a few moments, trying to sort his thoughts amidst the heat shimmer and the stink of mown summer grass. He was glad Jenny had not rode shotgun; to have her around all the time meant no room for judging whether the episodes of his life he had begun baring to her in blurts were credible, or prudent. They were still relatively new to each other, recently unwrapped, and had within the last hour agreed to advance their relationship to a more tricky, unstable stage.

Now his palms were finally damp.

He kicked out of the Pinto, stretching, causing his spine to crackle, and crossed onto the lot he now owned, heels sinking briefly into the humid, yielding turf. The sign was conspicuously new, and proclaimed in loud red characters ANOTHER ONE FOR SALE BY McCOY AND TANNER, with three exclamation points and three phone numbers for inquiry. Grant figured McCoy and Tanner must be pretty loud red characters themselves.

By contrast, the destruction had been scrupulously neat. It was as though a UFO had swooped down to zap the Mantell house, leaving a cleancut template of lawn whose brick sidewalks wound up to a floorplan-shaped rectangle of turned earth. No debris was scattered through the grass, which was still lush and green with the phony cinematic intensity seemingly endemic to the pampered lawns of the West Coast. McCoy and Tanner's banner was planted at the head of the lot, and looked like a lonesome sentry.

When Calex did not have his father globe-trotting, this was the place, Grant thought. The place where dear old Dad spent an abnormal percentage of his valuable executive time alone, with the curtains drawn against inquisitive neighbors. For a woman, perhaps? Several? Grant had known of no cohabitants, concubines, or compatriots—at least none who could claim any legally significant amount of time served.

Upon circumnavigation of the house-shaped plot he saw the basement and foundations were now depressions of fill dirt. In the cottage across the way he saw a pasty white face duck behind an embroidered drape.

He stopped to stand with one hand on McCoy and Tanner's sign, like a hunter posing with a kill, hoping for some sympathetic vibration from the earth. None came. He realized that after today he would probably never return to this place. Calls had already come his way regarding the disposition of the property. Calls from the hemorrhoidally polite minions of Calex middle management; calls Grant did not bother to return. The house, he did not miss. It had never been a home. The few moments he spent here alone were the true eulogy for his father. It felt correct. Montgomery Mantell would call for a moment of respectful silence . . . then get on with the business of living.

For Grant, there was literally nothing here anymore. But he idled, walking the lip of the excavation one more time. A glint of metal in the topsoil arrested his notice, near what had once been the basement's east wall. He bent and collected a strand of rosary beads in his fingers—that is, what he suspected to be a rosary, having seen one twice in his life. In movies. He blew dirt crumbs through the gaps of the worked medallion that twirled from one end. He took it to be a Star of David. Closer scrutiny proved him wrong.

Three four-pointed stars were staggered to form a kind of cog or sunburst design. Within the ring, a smaller ring composed the core. It was burnished blunt, obviously old, and appeared to have been worked from pewter. It gave gently beneath the pressure of his fingers. He examined it more closely, still blowing motes of dirt away. He saw the engraving on the flip side of the half-dollar-sized disc.

Lines and circles were hammered precisely into the thin circlet. Boxed circles; others three-quarter boxed, all outwardly random, yet purposefully intricate. They lent texture to one side while the obverse was polished and nickless. Grant thought of photo negatives: the emulsion side versus the shiny side. It all depended on which side you had up.

The designs were very much like those graven in minute detail into the brass frame of the bed and mirror he had just trucked into his apartment. He looked toward Mrs. Saks's house and saw her face dip out of sight again.

That decided him.

When it became clear that he would not vacate her porch, nor stop ringing her buzzer, Mrs. Saks cracked open the door instead of calling the law. Grant soon found out why.

"I think you dropped this out there, ma'am," he said, feeling absurd, as though he were playing Huckleberry Finn, putting on manners. He held out the rosary and medallion.

She peeped out, said nothing, allowed the door a few more cautious inches. Her glasses distorted her eyes, making them look to Grant like the view through the wrong end of a thick glass loup. She canted them back on her reddened nose to squint at him. The door opened a few more inches. He could now see one broad foot, torturing a frayed house slipper just beneath the hem of the paisley dress. Her tight bun of hair, including all the flyaways, was the iron-blue tint of a gun barrel.

"Uh—you must be Mrs. Saks," he got out, teeth locked together. The silence was suffocating.

Inside, she shifted her bulk, and Grant saw the foot in the doorway expand under the pressure, the slipper growing taut. My god, there was a good eighteen or nineteen stone inside that flimsy dress. Of that, there was at least twenty pounds of bosom. Thirty.

"You're of his blood," she said, in a voice that came from the very back of the throat and dried on the way out. Her eyes behind their half-inch density of glass checked him out again, head to shoes, and sent the input to her brain for processing. *"His* blood is yours. I can smell it." Her face was puffy, as if slightly inflated, and florid. Grant imagined her heart laboring to flush the arteries in her massive corpus with blood, to keep the crimson high in her face. "But you have my string." Fat hands with short, stubby fingers drifted up to cover her mouth in slight confusion. Her eyes seemed to swim into focus, suddenly, and her tone humanized from that of a mummified harridan to a simple but concerned matron. "You have it in your hands. How can that be, boy? Tell me."

"You dropped it on my property," he said, resisting the urge to sarcasm. "In your haste to leave."

"I was afeared. But you're not who I thought you to be; I kenned a new one, a fresh one, a renewal of the evil." She watched the words have the effect she calculated on Grant's expression and stabbed an open palm toward him before he had time to react. "Give me it," she insisted.

"No." To hesitate just now would be to stumble. "It was on *my* property. If you can explain to me what you're scared of, I might give it to you as a gift."

Her eyes narrowed, were almost swallowed by sunwrinkles. For a beat he tried to appear rational but unmovable, then he conceded to the instinct that told him threats might just as easily make the old woman clam up or, worse, become more cryptic. He had blundered onto touchy, arcane ground, and needed to know more—information he could not specify, like the unknown crossword-puzzle key that will unlock eight more hidden words. If the medallion was used as some sort of talisman against a real or imagined evil connected to his father, then in her eyes he was probably the agent for some black ruse. A concession became a good gamble.

"No," he said, extending the medallion so it revolved, shining, on the end of the unwinding rosary. "I'm no good at blackmail, Mrs. Saks. Take it—it's yours. But tell me why you think my father's house was evil. Obviously you wouldn't be so scared of losing this if it wasn't?"

She snatched it, stepping one thunderous step forward to capture it in both pawlike hands. Her gaze never left him, still suspicious, and he did not budge.

Finally she said, "Tis not a trick, then."

"I'm afraid that's a little too sophisticated for me."

She relaxed another notch, taking her eyes off him for the first time and moving across the porch to stare toward the vacated lot, hands steady on the painted wood of the porch balustrade. "Air's a mess," she observed. "Stinks. Stings the eyes and parches the gullet some."

"Smog's bad because of the heat." He half-expected her to trot out lemonade to seal their truce.

"Tis the carbons. Poisons in the very air; some you can't see." A short, disinterested silence ensued, then she turned on him like a carousel on slow revolve. "I've been rude to you with no cause. Not even thanking you for returning my string." She moved back toward the door in vast, arthritic strides, her weight creaking the porch planks.

"Wait. My father's house—"

"You're not touched by the sin, thank the Lord," she said, shaking her head in judgment. "Best for you to leave it lie. The place be taken now; it can't do no more harm neither." Confidentially, proudly, she added, "I throwed salt over the tilled ground meself, through the new dawn. Two containers of Morton's."

"The house isn't all gone," he said. "Not yet."

"Then you'd best destroy whatever's left," she said

with grandmotherly certainty. Grant felt scolded.
"Fire cleanses."

"No." *I'd need a smelter, for god's sake.* "It would
take a long time. *You* can help me today."

"I know protection. *They* wanted to touch me; oh,
how they wanted to silence me, trying temptation when
the yellow failed. But I knew protection then, and
learned more since." She cocked a plump thumb toward the threshold of the front door and the hex sign
evenly painted above. It was a larger clone of the medallion design. "That prevents entry. This"—she patted the medallion, now stowed in a flapping-sail pocket
of the dress—"prevents personal harm. I laughed in
the faces of the demons, and I walk the Earth yet.
Godliness can still triumph."

"Demons . . ." It was not a question. It was dull
repetition. His mind swam.

"They worshiped the Goat. Consorted with demons—fornicators, blasphemers. The Horned One
took them all, all but your father. He forestalled somehow, made some pact of blood, gained some engine
of protection. But he was taken all the same. Just took
longer, was all. No offense."

Mrs. Saks was as crazy as a gnat in a turbine.

"Who? What others?"

"Maybe the Spilsbury Murders was before your
time," she said, squinting at him keenly.

It was one of Hollywood's meatier scandals, back in
the days before Vietnam made television so blood-
thirsty, when such things were confined to the enquir-
ing poop tabloids Mrs. Saks no doubt took stone-cold
seriously. "I've heard of it. Movie people slaughtered
by cultists, like the Manson thing, but earlier. Late
50s, early 60s . . ."

"Nineteen and fifty-nine it was."

He stopped his smile by contorting his neck muscles. "You mean the Horned One hung fire for twenty-
three years just waiting to bump off my dad?"

"Time is nothing to the Dark Lords."

"Why *my* father? This doesn't track at all—"

"To succumb to temptation is nothing new. Look to history, boy. You'll recognize evil if you keep a clear eye."

I read that once in a fortune cookie, Grant thought. *Dark Lords, my little brown eyeball.* His impulse was to attack the old woman's derangements from all vantages at once; he opted to simply fly away. There really was nothing left here for him.

"Hang back," she ordered, anticipating his leave-taking. "You'll go now from here and scoff at the visions of a foolish old woman. Your eye is clouded already. Hang back a second." She waddled back into the cool dimness of her lair. Grant clocked off time for the slowness imposed by her own girth, impatient now to be shut of this lunacy, but obligated to finish up what he had begun by ringing the bell. Stupid.

She returned, presenting him with a lump, inside of brown shopping-bag paper fuzzy with handling. It was about the size and weight of a full soup can.

"Your father died with this in his hand."

He tore open the paper quickly, too eagerly. It was a fat candle, black, greasy to the touch. The wick was charred.

"I nicked it. The ambulance boys didn't mind none. You take it. You'll see." Magnanimously she announced, "I think your father renounced the left-handed path. He only did so too late. There are greater sins, in God's eye."

Debate would not do, so Grant merely backed off the porch with the candle, feeling foolishly like a yokel with a wet-ink deed to Brooklyn's most infamous bridge. He tossed back a cursory thanks and would not have steered around a litter-grubber on Hollywood Boulevard any less. His escape was in hand.

"I wish you well, boy. I hope what you learn doesn't lay heavy on your soul. Soon enough, you'll see. I'll do a fetish for your good luck, if my feet don't need a sitz bath tonight.'' She crossed herself again.

The old woman mumbled to herself, worrying the string, as he left. He beelined straight for the Pinto and did not glance back at her.

His opening line was ''A bottle of Mondavi says my day was weirder than yours.''

''Fool's bet.'' Jennifer was on the pillowback sofa, wound thickly up in Grant's blue terrycloth bathrobe. She dropped the subscription copy of *American Film* into a slack little tent shape on the coffee table. Meryl Streep stared up, eyes puffy, nose as red as usual, face sharp enough to chip flint. ''Bottle's already by the fridge. So, tell. You have to go first.''

''I am profoundly glad you are not a woman who paints her toenails. Don't ask; it's probably very male and illogical.'' Her bare feet, still warm and pink from the shower, were braced against the table, and from the distance the robe surrendered, he assumed her clothing was still piled in the bathroom. He brushed her neck with a kiss. She smelled fragrant and clean, and that reminded him of his own stickiness and stiff neck. He paused in passing to savor the bouquet of her hair; the masses and handfuls of glossy black exuded their own intoxicating aroma.

In the kitchenette he uncorked the dry, musky red and swished out two bowl-shaped goblets under scalding water. Through their first glass, he told her most of the saga of Mrs. Saks.

''Sounds like venerable ancient curse on ye olde bed and mirror.'' She waggled her eyebrows. ''Case closed.'' Pause. ''That old lady had been spying on your father for . . . what? Twenty-five years? Thirty? Jesus.''

''She was unbalanced, sure. But what conviction. And she had a definite interest in salvaging my soul from the big bad demons, or ghosts, or whatever.''

"She push any tracts at you?" She hesitated then, the frivolous tone of her banter vanishing, as though she was deciding whether to pass on bad news. "Grant? I'm not trying to match you weirdness for weirdness . . . but you tell me whether this is stupid or not."

"I'm not laughing." He was still smiling, though.

"Okay." She squared her shoulders, inhaled deeply. "I was, how you say, disrobing awhile ago, in the bedroom. You know how shooting lights make you sweat; I was pretty gummed-up and cranky. Well, when you're near that mirror in the bedroom, you can't help but watch yourself in it. I mean, you really cannot *stop* yourself—as though something might change if you don't keep an eye on it. And I started freaking out, right there, totally by myself, because I got the idea that it was actually the other way round: I wasn't watching the mirror, the mirror was watching me—I mean *personally,* as if it was a one-way peep glass with a couple of horny Feds on the flip side. Breathing evenly. Watching me strip. Now, I was taking it off for the Wolf earlier, and I don't get nervous when his eyeballs try to gobble me up at ten thousand RPMs. That kind of self-consciousness you lose when you pose. But I didn't want to stay in the bedroom. Not alone. Not even with Max there. I started shivering, can you believe that? The next step, I'm sure, would have been seeing things in the mirror."

"Boogey-persons," Grant said.

"God knows the *bathroom* mirrors weren't freaking me out." She shook her head in semi-exasperation, a sanity-asserting gesture. "I rolled out of there, toweling off, consciously averting my eyes from the mirror. Crazy, huh?"

"I can't laugh," he said distantly, "because it gives me the creeps too—just as vaguely. Last night . . . I can't really articulate the feeling. But it unnerved me."

"Hmm. *Caveat emptor.*" She motioned for a re-charge.

"I didn't *buy* anything," he sulked. "I propose you and I confront this dumb phenomenon together and see if our Haunted Mirror has the balls to freak out more than one person at a time. Where's Battling Maxo?"

"Around. I'm surprised he didn't come out when—"

She stopped then, because they could both hear the dog growling.

"He was camping out by my clothes," she said. "Near the foot of the bed."

They moved together.

Max's ghost-white form was easily visible in the dim bedroom. His coffin-shaped head was fixed low, de-fensively, his black lips skinned back, his tail motion-less. He stood aggressively between them and the mirror on the wall. He growled at the mirror, making a steady and thoroughly ominous basso noise of warn-ing. His hindquarters rippled to spring and defend—or attack. In an unsettlingly targeted way, Max's reflected image was growling at *them*. Directly at both of them.

When he began barking angrily at the glass it nearly launched them both up to cling from the ceiling light fixtures.

"Max!" Grant shouted. "Max, goddamnit, what is it?"

It broke the spell. Max turned to them with an al-most apologetic little whine, then jogged over for congratulations.

"Good puppy," Grant said, rolling his eyes at ca-nine dumbness for Jennifer's benefit. In the mirror, he watched his own reflection scratch Max's radar ears. "You show 'em what a badass you are."

"Big jerk," muttered Jenny. "You scared the crap out of me." She forced a brutal little smile, said *"good* dog" with suffocating sarcasm, and then sighed.

"Tell you what: You sit on the john and drink while I grab a shower. If Max wants to play guard dog, fine."

"You mean you're not going to admit how *weird* that was?" Frank incredulity, now.

"Not as weird as Mrs. Saks," he said, trying to move through his bathroom routine nonchalantly. "And not as weird as the rather awesome Dr. Axel Byrd." He yanked a huge bath towel down from the cabinet; all others strung about the bathroom were still damp. His smile toward Jenny and Max was an honest one, but he was aware of consciously forced reassurance: "It's too bloody easy to overinterpret this stuff. You wind up like Mrs. Saks, with her talismans and stacks of old scandal sheets."

Max padded off to case the kitchen, tail drifting lazily with his stride. Jenny glared after him, then at the large mirror. "He always agrees with you. . . ."

The mirror did nothing but hang on the wall and reflect their lovemaking. This time the paradox struck him.

In bed, they should have been preoccupied. The mirror was hanging right there, reminding them, refusing to be ignored, daring their eyes to come back. He had been emptied by a crushing day cruising the smogscape to parley with oddballs like Mrs. Saks and Dr. Axel Byrd; Jenny had done Toby Wolff's. The one such photo session Grant had attended was exhausting simply to watch. Yet the act of boarding the monster bed seemed to flush them both with urgent adrenaline; he could *feel* it hit Jennifer. Her eyes irised to the dark gray of thunderheads. Perspiration, light, clean, dappled them before they even touched. Grant caught the aromas of musky need, of feral hunger. She not only wanted him—she lusted for him, and his heart rate jumped up from double, and he plundered her, and she drained him. The streamlined chat that so endeared them was discarded in the living room, supplanted by a dangerously new exchange: a sexual echo effect, power given and power received and power amplified; dangerous because it seemed to obliterate the humor and caring that normally accompanied them to bed. She pulled him into her as though she was starving. His body sprang alive to the nerve roots, and in that starting-gun instant he cared about nothing but taking her.

The mirror watched as they slept, woke, made love again, slept, talked as before. It watched.

The wine was gone and Max was snoozing before the topic of Dr. Axel Byrd was actually addressed.

"A big guy, gruff, stout, barrel chested. I expected a sterile Aryan type for my father's doctor. What I got was a bearded Viking in a doctor suit. It was a little surreal." He shifted uncomfortably. Jennifer was entrenched on the mirror side of the bed tonight, and that stood disturbingly at the edge of his thoughts, as though they were aboard a life-raft and a random toss of the boat would flip her, still half-awake, into a sea turbulent with sharks. He watched his own feet in the mirror, abstracted.

"I suppose he wasn't apologetic?" She yawned, turned her back to the mirror, snaked an arm around him.

"Terse at first." Actually, Dr. Byrd had somehow divined that Grant's questions about his father's health were standard and perfunctory. He had waited, patiently, for the gist, his replies crisp and dull as he outlined the senior Mantell's assorted minor distresses, shrugging them all equally—a little justifiable high blood pressure, a false-alarm ulcer, a brief problem sleeping.

It had all seemed a burden of trivia to Dr. Byrd. No big deal. "Your father phoned me once, bursting with questions about narcolepsy. About coma." *So get on with it.*

Abruptly Grant's throat felt as if it was trying to swallow a golf ball. "Coma I know about, but . . ."

"Ah, you've seen that dreadful film, I suppose." The huge shoulders rolled, the encompassing hands dangled between his knees in the overburdened desk chair.

"But narcolepsy—isn't that sleeping sickness?"

"More properly summed up by the term 'sleep attacks,' " said Dr. Byrd. "As in angina attacks, or attacks of intestinal gas. They can occur anytime, anywhere. A person with a case of bonafide narcolepsy is capable of dropping into a very deep sleep state with no warning whatsoever, and during any activity—driving, sex, playing basketball." He swept a clearing between beard and mustache to insert a gray stick of spearmint gum.

"My father?"

"Claimed he had been oversleeping. Many questions on what a 'normal' amount of sleeptime was. For him I estimated six to eight hours; that didn't satisfy him. Even at six you're spending nearly a third of your life in bed, semiconscious or unconscious. For a corporate eagle like your father, the idea of too much sleep would've been very frustrating. Less time for work, you see. He would become agitated at the idea, tax himself even harder—more wear and tear on his metabolism."

"Was he actually sick?"

"Apart from the development of the tumor, nothing. I'd say it was very easy for him to focus his work stress on his sleeping habits. But psychology isn't my field."

It's probably nothing, Grant thought. Yeah, that's what they say in the movies, *it's probably nothing,* right before they get eaten by a giant cockroach.

Up, down, around, the gentle curve of Jennifer's waist in the mirror, a fold of sheet cutting just below the two indentations in the small of her back, like a toga in a posed picture. Beyond it, his reflection.

"So then?" she said.

"So then he booked me for a physical examination next week. I didn't protest; I'm overdue, I guess." He ran his palm along the smooth warmth of her hip. "He seemed privately pleased that he managed to trade one Mantell for another, as though I'd just go into the file in my father's folder or something." He continued to stroke her reflexively. She mumbled and snuggled in tighter.

"Hey?" he said, realizing she had slipped away. No reaction. He kept caressing her while his treacherous eyes instantly sought the mirror. Its panorama was nominal.

First there was his father's death and the hints of narcolepsy or some other sleep affliction. Then the mirror: brass encircling a lens, backed by silver . . . oh, yes, vaguely malignant somehow. Mrs. Saks, plus her hex signs. Blasphemers. Fornicators. Those were the strings; where in hell was the common knot?

His morning coffee mug was still on the nightstand, the one closest the mirror. He craned to see and saw the coagulated brown dregs, like a crust of blood. He had to do the dishes more often than once weekly; chances were tomorrow he'd dump fresh-brewed on top of the scum and dust without even rinsing the cup.

Something moved inside the mirror.

He fought not to see it from the visual periphery, tried to keep contemplating his stupid coffee mug, stubbornly, until he realized that it was merely Max, bopping back into the bedroom with the arrogant, hipshot stride of a *pachuco* casing Van Nuys Boulevard.

And abruptly, comfortingly, he felt that Max would warn them if the mirror was plotting anything weird. Animals knew.

Sleep came easier, though he kept thinking of sleep

as a symptom. No, he was simply bashed from the day.

Or maybe he was not exhausted. Not technically, not for real.

He fell asleep and reaped a few hours of peace. Then the grandaddy of all nightmares smashed into his mind, head-on, a freight train vaporizing a prairie dog transfixed by the high-beams. There was no defense, nothing he could do.

He had nobody's recommendation to use as a quality filter, and did not consult the yellow pages. He merely cut out of traffic, slewing into a curbspace bordering the first shop he saw. Paint peeled in sharp strips from the billboard overhead. It was lit at night by two senile floods hanging from top on ugly pipe armatures wired into place against the weather, orange with rust.

To Grant, the rust was an indication the place had been in business for awhile, stable in one locale.

DARKMOON OCCULT SUPPLIES
Tools ☆ Literature ☆ Incunabula

The logo was subdued, as far as Grant's nonknowledge of such things went: It was surrounded by a fresco of stars and planetoids in half-eclipse, with elliptical Saturnian ringwork, fretted with lines (beams? rays?) radiating (force? light? Bosco?) outward.

Beams of force. Grant felt suddenly idiotic again, and he almost gunned the Pinto away from the witchcraft shoppe in embarrassment. On cue, the memory of the dream stopped him, causing his backbone to horripilate coldly even in the thick heat of urban summer. His teeth were tightly set; his jaw muscles nudged a baby migraine toward maturity. The Pinto idled. He smelled or imagined petrofumes bonking away at his headache, worsening it. Almost as an omen of inevitability, the motor stalled out—committing him.

He grabbed the fat candle in its paper wrapping from the passenger bucket, along with the graphite-smeared pages of pencil rubbings, and did it.

He jolted awake, or dreamed he did, staring into the mirror again. The past played back. "Monty" Mantell, sweating, furtive, rushed up to his Etruscan marble fireplace, mouthing words Grant could not understand beyond identifying their pattern of repetition. He shot them out anxiously, below his breath, in the desperate cadence of the slightly mad, fumbling for a butane cigarette lighter, grabbing the black candle on the mantle. The fat wick touched the fire and sputtered as though wet, at last catching. Sweatdrops of relief broke freely and Grant's father almost smiled, still muttering the incomprehensible litany. His free hand ditched the lighter and went for his coat pocket, digging, still furtively, for something small within. He appeared more normal, more in control now, the image of resourcefulness Grant usually ascribed to his father.

The black candle slipped from his grasp and bounced onto the carpet. He grabbed wildly to intercept and missed; the wick was still improbably alight. He forgot whatever was in his pocket and tried to retrieve the candle. He bent, then fell as the hematoma in his brain burst.

Perhaps he could still see, Grant thought with a shudder. *Perhaps his father's wide, unfocused eyes noted, as they fogged over in death, the candle, crisping a brown oval into the new shag carpeting, five inches too far from his outstretched hand. His final breath eased out, in no hurry. The wick extinguished itself. A web of gray smoke uncoiled toward the ceiling.*

The inside of Darkmoon Occult Supplies' front door was festooned with tiny brass bells. Grant's eyes quickly dealt with the chaotic junkyard of merchandise

and decoration and zeroed in on the store's only occupant.

"Hey man," said the apparent proprietor, a man
with a long ponytail of black hair topped by a French
beret. Black leather vest over a neon-red T-shirt overwhelmed by a black image of a bare-chested, love-
beaded Jim Morrison, with the Doors logo in blocky
letters. Black mustache, waxed at the tips. Black
goatee. He cupped his hand over the phone receiver
crooked into his shoulder and said, "Welcome to
Darkmoon. Browse away; I'll catch up with you in a
second."

Grant nodded as a tirade from the phone drew the
man back. "No, no, no," he interposed. "You're not
listening. Cardamom for love spells you can buy at
Lucky's. The supermarket. It's the same as—no, just
buy Spice Islands; it's the same stuff. Look, Mrs. Fetters—"

Grant drifted, tuning out the chatter. Darkmoon's
ceiling was a good thirty feet from the floor; stout
beams of oily wood were hung with stuffed birds and
odd mobiles that revolved sluggishly in the eddies of
heat. The entire west wall was absorbed by floor-to-
ceiling bookshelves of stained pine: *Numerology, Astrology, Tarot, Wicca, Satanism, Voodoo*, more. Grant
saw one presstape label that read *Blank Books of Art*.
The library balanced the old of crusted leather bind-
ings with the new of glossy trade paperbacks. The goa-
teed clerk's voice continued to drone, patiently; he had
switched topics from cardamom to arrowroot.

A gray anatomy skeleton guarded the corner of the
first display case. Within were hundreds of orderly
ranks and files of philtres and potions—spellcasting
ingredients in cork-stoppered vials of blown glass, like
tiny test tubes; larger, hermetically sealed jars of dull-
colored powders. A plastic bag of "dream bones."
Joss sticks of consecration incense and bottles of
brown oil. The shelves to Grant's right were laden with

lanterns, candles, silver knives, small braziers, tools whose purpose was a mystery. Tarot decks carefully wrapped in silk. Beyond the shelves, a rack of tabards—black, white, brown, some silk—and cowled monk's robes with braid. A card near his nose read *Chalice—Thurible—Athamé / Set (Ready to Use):* $65.95. There was a ''chic shelf'' of pop power objects: ankhs, pyramid necklaces, icons so commercial they were the most familiar items to Grant. A hand-calligraphed index card thumbtacked to the shelf informed him that jewelry could be inscribed with his Witchcraft Name free of charge, with a $25 purchase.

Nearer the counter was a thick wooden shelf bearing tarantulas and scorpions encased in lucite, and a dead snake in a rubber-lipped bell jar of formaldehyde. Other floating dead things inspected him from their glass coffins. There was a small fireplace hewn from a block of weathered gray stone. Below its mantle, etched as though by centuries of rain, was the word INRUS. From a strategic roost above, a ratty stuffed goat's head glared with golden eyes. Grant saw it was a ram. Its cornucopian horns had been gilded, its dead teeth looked plastic; beyond them, a tongue that resembled a stale, petrified piece of luncheon meat.

Across the counter, powerful corporate mojo for Visa, Mastercard, and American Express asserted themselves. Everything surrounding him was priced with those nasty disintegrating pricetags he hated—even the ram's head had one, curling away from the patch of hair it had obviously occupied for years. The cooling fan of the register hummed; the blue digital display glowed. Grant thought abruptly of how the ultrasimplified logos of the Fortune 500, the top corporations in the country, were really modernized mutations of the hex sign Mrs. Saks had sworn by. IBM, Exxon, Randcorp, all used as mastheads a letter or a geometric line design that had undergone decades of refinement and simplification, like a distilling process. Using charge plates in a witchcraft shoppe exemplified the head-on crash of ancient superstition into modern technology. He considered the combination of sorcery and computers and guessed the slant must have been tried a thousand times by now.

The logo for Calex Corporation was a *C* inside a *C*, two letters linked by orthographic projection; two looking like one. Very snazzy industrial fashion. Design of and decision on the logo had encompassed an expenditure (carefully itemized and, of course, wholly deductible) in the neighborhood of $25,000. How valuable might protection and image be if they boiled away to the same thing?

His imagination jumped ahead to an image of the governing board of Calex chanting the Lord's Prayer backwards; all those constipated execs prancing around in the buff and impaling a stray cat on a spike for sacrifice . . . it was beautifully obscene.

". . . but that was Mrs. Fetters making her daily call."

"I'm sorry?" Grant had not noticed the counterman hanging up. *You did it again, stupid*—he had blanked out, had gone away and not noticed.

"Mrs. Fetters, jeez." The man in the black vest spread his hands across the fingerprinty glass of the counter. "She has a standing account here. Calls in with her daily order. Has these spellbooks specifying really hard-to-get items, you know? Like clove oil, paprika, A-1 Sauce . . . And every day I tell the old broad that in *this* century we have supermarkets. I'm broadcasting; she's not receiving." He shrugged. A button pinned to the lapel of his vest read *So Mote It Be, goddammit*.

Grant dropped a tiny Indian tetraskelion on a leather thong back into a display box between them. "But you oblige her."

"She spends a coupla thou a year here, my friend.

A veritable patron, in the old, renowned sense of the word.''

The thought occurred; burst out: "You don't have a customer named Mrs. Saks, do you?"

His eyes narrowed. "You a PI? Hey, I got all the entrapment flubs I need this year, ace." The humor drained from his face, leaving it swarthy.

"No, no," Grant said, trying to restore order. "Just a vagrant thought. I knew—"

"Never heard of her," he said, relaxing.

"Oh." His attention returned to the package, the papers he had brought. "I was wondering if you could tell me about these."

The clerk took the candle first, hefting it in his hand, not opening it. "Yeah, I said to myself when you came in, 'this guy ain't no practitioner,' you know what I mean? Now, I don't care one way or the other—I mean, we exist but to serve." He stepped back for gesturing room. "But it's been my experience, limited though it may be in this game, that, ahh—guys like you who wander into places like this, your newspaper reporters, your snoops and PIs, your tourists—usually wander out shaking their heads, like *I'm* the one who's crazy. Without purchasing anything. This ain't a library, John Henry. You planning on wasting my time, or you got a legit interest?" He placed the wrapped candle back onto the counter, pointedly, and waited with folded arms.

"Legit enough to even allow for a consultation fee," Grant said, without grinning.

"You've just entered the realm of the occult," the clerk said, smiling wide and toothy, looking like Rasputin in a beret. "I am Jade Wing, your humble guide." A stage bow.

And the meter is now running, Grant thought, amused.

"And this thing," he said, unfurling the candle like a toilet-paper streamer fron the windings of sack, "this guy is . . . ahhuummm . . . tallow candle. Made out of sheep fat. What'd you do, leave it sitting on your dashboard in the heat? Dumb.'' He flipped it in the air; caught it. It glistened with beads of oil prompted by the temperature.

Grant remembered now: He had not shown Jennifer the candle. He'd left it in the car. Gradually the sweltering heat had molded one side of it to the juncture of seat and backrest; now the thick, greasy cylinder had a crude corner.

"You're gonna ask me what's it for,'' Jade Wing said from behind a pointed finger. "Basic spellcasting ordnance. Like I said, sheep fat. You can't buy it at the Mayfair Supermarket with the chip dips and bargain liquor.''

"Or cardamom,'' Grant said.

"Yeah, right! I mean, you may have noticed, but they don't *make* that many black candles. Gotta get 'em at an occult dimestore like this, or maybe mold 'em yourself.'' He stroked his goatee. "Presuming you have a fat sheep.'' He joggled his eyebrows and winked. "The M-16 of witchcraft. Use it for almost anything.''

"You're beginning to sound less like a 'practitioner' yourself.''

"Oh, hey—this is a pickup, I mean, don't kid yourself, I'm a knowledgeable employee. I did the groundwork. But this place *isn't* mine. I can tell you've never met Annabella. Miz Darkmoon. A very strange lady. Wears her hair in a huge Victorian bun; long dresses, like Morticia on *The Addams Family*. Too much eye makeup by half. Long fingernails. I *mean*''—he set his fluid, expressive face into neutral, as though posing for a sculptor—"do I look to you like some kinda *warlock?*''

He shook his head at the density of the uninitiated. "Man, I look like Joe Suburban next to the regulars.''

"How about these?'' Grant produced the three pages

of white typing bond on which he had done pencil
rubbings of the designs on the headboard of the brass
bed. "Can you tell me what these symbols mean?"

Jade stared, squinted, stared again, his eyebrows
arching into a little peak of intrigue. "Hey wow," he
said. "What a mess." He fanned the three pages
across the counter, and with a nod of permission from
Grant, began to sketch the rubbings into bold, black
lines with an indelible marker, making small sounds
of recognition, *yeah, yeah, and this goes like. . . .*

"Bells ringing?"

"Tiny ones, my man. I know some of these, but
some I don't. Have to check the shelf; get some ref-
erences. Just a sec, okay?" He was already moving.

"Sure." Grant was perversely pleased to see that
whatever books Jade needed were obscure enough to
be slotted into the very topmost shelves. He dashed
up the ladder like a lithe, rakishly dressed lizard.

The bad part of the nightmare had followed the mirror replay of Montgomery Mantell's death.

As if the moment his father's life had winked out
was a cue, Grant's eyes snapped open to meet themselves, in the mirror. It was not like surfacing from
sleep; he awoke feeling more like he had just wrestled
out from beneath a massive weight that had immobilized him and blotted out his consciousness by force,
some dark fugue he now feared Dr. Byrd had pin-
pointed with hideous ease. He saw the reflection of his
face—not the vampire demon, but his own normal
face. He saw the reflection of the shining brass bed in
which he lay. And he saw something else.

*The image of his father shaded to transparency; the
candlesmoke fogged the room. In the mirror, the bed
was alive with writhing, naked bodies. Diaphanous
hands fisted the bedpost knobs, sweat-sheens dulling
the brass. Ghostflesh jerked together soundlessly, cou-
pling in an abstract that rendered numbers and sexes
indiscernible, a thrusting frenzy of bestial rut.*

Grant lost his breath. He was not in the reflection. And Jennifer was not in bed beside him.

They've got her was his only panicked thought.

His hands grabbed uselessly through the twisted rills of sheet. She was gone.

He damned his brain for making his eyes accuse the mirror so readily. But she was not among the orgiasts. Was the triphammer pounding of his heart against his ribcage evidence that he was awake? Was this still the dream, the nightmare?

Mockingly, the faces of the madly fucking troupe seemed familiar. If Grant's presence was real, they did not acknowledge it. The melding bodies boiled together, wrenched apart. The wisps of dead candle-smoke began to dissolve them.

Grant focused his eyes painfully. They watered, as if from the stench of a putrefacting corpse. They saw.

Beyond the bed, in the darkest corner of the room, the reflected blackness of his *real* room, behind him, he saw a blocky shape overseeing the tableau. Its ursine skull cut just short of the canted reflection of the ceiling. It watched with faceted diamond eyes, eyes that glinted hard blue-silver with the lust to turn the coital ritual into a carnage of feeding.

It was black, unfathomable, definitely *there*.

It shifted its attention from the group to the observer, the nonparticipant, the silent watcher beyond.

The sound Grant made was primal, scoured clean of civilized distraction. His left hand swept the heavy coffee mug free of the nightstand and hooked it into the face of the mirror. Both disintegrated. A down-shower of steely glass splinters exploded toward him with an ear-grating, metallic din. The shattering noise swept him beneath an avalanche of sound; needlelike shrapnel sought him, and he shielded his eyes with a forearm and screamed, a long braying sound that chafed his throat and failed to exceed that of the deadly hailstorm of breaking glass.

He uncovered his eyes at last.

He saw himself, peeking out from behind his hands, panting hard now, still alone in bed. Jennifer was not reflected because she was not there at all.

Naked, he scrambled from the bed, stealing yesterday's clothes from the bathroom, hurrying out and slamming the bedroom door. Max wasn't around, either. Quickly, too nervously, he grabbed cash, keys, and the pencil rubbings he had done of the brass headboard days previously, during the polishing stage. He fumbled them and they fanned. When he gathered them, he dropped his keyring. His movements began to betray his panic. He fled with a hard slam of the front door.

He could not force himself to recheck the bedroom. He knew that if he had, he could have verified that the coffee mug was gone from the nightstand and nowhere to be found. And that the mirror might be intact, unbroken, still waiting.

The beige business card on Darkmoon's bulletin board resolved into readability: *MISS MIRIAM— Profundo conocedor de las Ciencias Ocultas y Consejero Espiritual de Fama Internationale.*

He was back again, confused.

Spanish, stupid; it's a foreign language, remember?

Fortunately, Jade Wing had not noted him. He was still mountaineering among the dust of Darkmoon's bookshelves.

Safely locked into his Pinto, Grant had finally discovered Jenny's note—laid blatantly atop the pencil rubbings, totally overlooked in his, er, altered state of consciousness. Signed *love*. A surge of 100-proof idiocy wormed his cheesy grin to a rictus of embarrassment. She had probably kissed him goodbye for the day and he had probably grunted and rolled over.

Her answering machine would do him no good; he'd turned up a Hamburger Hamlet and begun to drink coffee—to help his mind get linear again, and then until he could no longer sit still, unacting. *Beds That Eat People;* hadn't he caught that at a grindhouse somewhere a year or two back? Awake, in the real world, it was no longer the supernatural histrionics of sleazy horror films that unnerved him but the reasoned likelihood that he might face-first into his banana-creme pie, with no twinge or mental klaxon of warning—and then he would be alone, with the dream-state.

The eyes had been like mean little chromium ball bearings, he thought—rather the way Max's eyes had glinted in the mirror, earlier. And he had definitely *heard* the sharp crack of the heavy porcelain mug introducing itself to the fragile glass.

Looking at the note signed *love* made him feel more a renewed occupant of the real world. It was like a notarized letter of transit for hazardous terrain, folded now into quarters and stowed safely in his shirt pocket. He had reread it a hundred times. Jenny almost never left written evidence of her passage or feelings. It would take longer to discover whether she was a letter writer or not.

"Still with us, ace?" Jade Wing was leaning toward him, elbows on the glass, head propped in hands.

Again, Grant refolded the note and pocketed it. "I have some other questions—more general, I think, than—"

Jade held up a hand. Stop sign. "If it's about the notice board, that stuff is Annabella's fault. I can't endorse individual covens. The competition knows automatically, and they toss revenge magic at you for favoritism." He balanced forward on the counter to peek at the Black Forest cuckoo clock mounted near the ram's head. "Hey, noon-and-a-half. Lunchtime!" He squatted, dropping out of sight, and Grant heard him rustling a paper sack around.

"Do you have to leave?"

"No sir," came Jade's voice. "Annabella's out sick with the shingles. Ran right around her waistline; made her walk funny, so she's home trying to magick it away. I'm marooned here till nine tonight. A lot of the regulars don't come in till dusk anyway. I mean, at this moment I got nothing better to do than help you, if you'll be patient. Undivided professional attention is rare to chance across, y'know.'' He surfaced with a fistful of fudge cookies, building a little column with them on the countertop next to the books he'd selected, popping them into his mouth whole and dusting the crumbs on his chinos as he riffled through one text, marked a place, consulted another, munched. Grant wound up bringing him a Diet Pepsi from the 7-11 on the north side of Beverly Boulevard.

"What are your other questions?" Jade shouted hollowly as Grant re-entered. "Maybe I can put all this into some kind of perspective if I can get a bigger picture."

"You're supposed to be the expert," Grant said as Jade cracked his cold can and drank. "Tell me what all that has to do with, uh, fornicators."

Jade tapped the rubbings. "The reason this looks so confusing is that it's a bunch of different symbols run together, as far as I can tell." He drew a pencil circle around one, to isolate it. "See? There you have a variation on the Greek cross, that thing you were looking at awhile ago." He pointed to the display box. "A swastika. A pagan fertility symbol, a solar emblem signifying the female principle in Nature." He circled another. "This little squiggle is a rune for the succubus—female sexual demon—and *this* one is for the incubus."

"Male version of same?"

"And this thing is called the *satyrica signa*—the sign of the satyr. A little penis shape. And here's a set of 'Lilith bars,' a kind of perverted cross. Know your Bible?"

"No."

"Lilith was supposedly Adam's first wife. Supposedly a succubus. But this thing over here is the Zracine Vile—signifying spirits that tease you when they're benign. When they get pissed off, they kill you. The hexagram enclosing the symbol is protective. And most of these symbols are in octets, groups of eight, enclosed by octagons. Eight is the number of regeneration and again, fertility. But over here are some perfectly mundane astrological signs—the barbed *M* for Scorpio; the 69 for Cancer. In astrology, the eighth house is the house of death.'' Jade shook his head, appearing honestly perplexed. ''Are these from a gravestone, or a wailing wall somewhere I don't know about?''

''They're from the headboard of a bed. The symbols are all along the frame, on all sides, and the footboard.''

''Jesus. Carved out of wood?''

''Solid brass.''

''Are you *serious?*'' He skipped it. ''Bright yellow brass or dull gold brass?'' He waggled his head. ''You *are* serious.''

''It's bright yellow.''

''Then it's brass with a low copper content. Called 'high brass.' Know anything about brass, ace?''

''It's a bitch to polish.''

''Okay.'' Jade was clearly eager to explain. ''Brass is an alloy of copper and zinc. High brass is about seventy percent copper or less. The more zinc, the tougher—that's called 'cartridge' brass; they make bullets out of it. Into that you put a very small percentage of lead, to improve machinability—high-wear clock parts are made of leaded brass—plus tin and nickel to increase resistance to corrosion and wear. Enough nickel lightens the color more. Are you with me so far?''

''Copper, zinc, lead, tin, nickel,'' said Grant.

''And iron: Mix 'em all together and you get brass.

Each metal has protective significance in one form of sorcery or another. Is it a big bed? All one piece?''

"Super kingsize. And completely covered with symbols like those.'' He felt on the brink again, ready to slam the brakes.

"Looks like what you got is the biggest goddamn protective amulet in history.'' Jade wiped his lips. "If I was a righteous fornicator, like Aleister Crowley, I'd kill for that bed.''

"I'm thinking about selling it,'' Grant said, to bait him. "Maybe Crowley would be interested?''

"If he was alive. He died in 1947. He was what is lightly referred to as a voluptuary He sort of stirred the occult together with Rosecrucianism, Eastern religions, a lot of coke, heroin, and sexual gluttony. *He* was an alloy. Believed that orgiasm allowed mystic communication with the forces of magic; that each orgasm he had took him closer to becoming one with the power, understanding and mastering it. He started his own church, even established an abbey in Sicily. His gospel was 'Do what thou wilt shall be the whole of the law.' ''

"He'd put the bed on the altar?'' Grant was almost lost.

"The bed would *be* the altar for somebody like that,'' said Jade, flustered. "Don't you get it? With a bed like that, you could whistle up sexual demons, imps, incubi, succubi that could do things to you they've never even *dreamed* of down at the Leather Castle. And you wouldn't have to worry about them gobbling you up afterward. Or during. The protected circle inside the bed is like a pentagram. See, succubi, for example, are designed to seduce mortals, and usually wind up frightening them to death. Inside the arms of the bed you've got nothing to worry about; you can fornicate your little heart out, and the forces of darkness can't lay a glove on you.''

"What about sex with a normal person?''

"Who can say? It'd make good sex into great sex, great sex into transcendant sex—do what thou wilt, literally."

"Could it cause nightmares, sleeping sickness?" The morning's overdose of coffee was starting to pump acidic bile up his throat.

"Not the bed. But if I was a bully, and couldn't punch you out because you were inside a fence, I'd still try to lob rocks at you over the fence, you get what I mean?"

"Wear me down . . ." Grant said, with no inflection.

"If something—some entity or force—was pissed off at you but only capable of pestering you long-distance because you had protection . . . ?" He raised open hands; *quien sabe?* Half of Jade Wing's statements curled up at the end, sounding like questions even if they were not. Grant had known this peculiar pattern of speech since grade school.

"So if I had protection, so?"

"The bad guy might sock you with dizziness, fainting spells, or bad dreams. Sudden feelings of personal danger. Vertigo. Hair loss. Everything from fear to pimples. The Navajo Indians call it the ghost sickness. It feeds on the ego." He smoothed his stiff, gleaming mustaches between his fingertips.

"I don't know any demons." *But I might have inherited one or two.*

"You don't have to. They might know you, though. Easy." He pulled a thin volume from the bottom of the stack he'd brought and let it fall open to a page marked by a mauve ribbon—"here. You light the candle—it doesn't matter that it's been lit already—and recite this, over and over." He indicated a short paragraph. "Might help if you did it on the bed. Keep saying it for, I don't know, five minutes or so. It's simple. Fewer words than the Equal Rights Amendment. Just make sure the candle doesn't go out, or you have to start over.''

Grant felt like fainting. Evil spirits had nothing to do with the feeling that surged up inside of him as Jade rambled.

"Mind you," he said. "Unless you get specific, a lot of this is conjecture. But you seem to be going pale at key moments; I'd wager that you've felt the pull of the old strings, supernaturally speaking, and recently, too. Stop me when I get outrageous." He restacked the books, the rubbings, and stuck his pencil and marker back into a cup shaped like a skull. "But of course, you don't *really* believe in any of this shit, do you?" Eyebrows up.

"Certainly not," he said, returning Jade's corner-of-the-mouth smile. "I'll take the book just as a curio."

"Born pitchman, am I not?" he said as he punched it into the humming register. It peeped and clicked and burped out a skinny receipt designed to read *Blessed Be* just shy of the sawtoothed perforation.

Grant unclipped a fifty and folded it double in his hand, making ready. "Tell me one more thing."

"Business is so brisk I don't have a second to breathe," Jade said, opening his arms to indicate the empty store.

"What do you know about the Spilsbury Murders—cult killing, happened in 1959? Could that have had something to do with witchcraft or some kind of cult or coven?"

"Never heard of it."

He slid the fifty across. "Keep the change. For consultation rendered."

Jade and Ulysses S. Grant stared each other down for an instant. "Where ya off to now, ace?" he said, tucking the bill away.

"To talk to a little old lady who *can* tell me about

the Spilsbury Murders." He nodded. "Thanks for your time."

"It's your time," he said. "You bought it. No sweat—as soon as you walk out, somebody else'll roll in. That's the way things work around this place."

Before he left, he used Darkmoon's phone to try and warn—no, no, *ask* Jenny not to go back to his apartment alone, to let them meet at her place. He left the message on her machine. Then he made the drive back to Avalon Circle.

Mrs. Saks was already dead.

He later thought that perhaps he had pounded on Jenny's door a bit too hard, rattling it in its secure frame, very possibly stirring a neighbor. Stupidly, he at least startled her into taking her time answering the door, lest the knocker be 61-year-old Mr. Jensen from down the hall, horny and drunk again. He watched darkness swirl around the dot of light in the bull's eye of the door peephole.

The raven hair fell to mingle with her deep-burgundy robe. She waved him in without the expected admonishments, sighing heavily, and that made him feel sufficiently dumb. The jump he had just given her was not entirely gone from her eyes yet. She watched him attempt to recover from his fumble by fading around it.

"Where the hell have you been?" Instantly, he regretted the line. *Pro forma* soap opera shorthand for emotional scenes.

She would let it pass—it was in her nature, he thought—but not without retort. "You look like hell yourself." She let him shut the door himself, and preceded him into her airy and clinically ordered kitchen. Everything in Jennifer's apartment appeared to have been recently uncrated by designers, lovingly reconstructing a diorama: Quarters of Modern Professional Woman. Magazines arranged oh so artfully on the table; agate ashtrays spotless; espresso machine gleaming; kitchen tiles as radiant as those in a floor-wax commercial. At first, the entire display had made Grant feel uncomfortable and shabby. He soon decided he liked it. Other people, he supposed, would complain that it was too reminiscent of their *parents'* house. He knew, certifiably, this was nothing like *his* parents' house. He knew from experience that Jennifer *did* sit on her sofa, despite the even, directional scape of the fabric nap. From experience, he knew Jennifer had done much more acrobatic things on that sofa.

The sofa did not betray the things it had witnessed.

She had given up the idea of touching him in greeting for now. It would be awkward, inappropriate. Atonement was due. But she despised the inexorability of the ritual, so said, "Sit, you. We shall back up and start again, since I don't want either of us to be mad. It's not worth it, not at this time of night. Not for us." Water was aboil and coffee was premeasured. Of course she had expected him. Maybe. "And I won't apologize for being out of touch. I did get your message on the machine. I had to run out. A chore I couldn't avoid." She favored him by looking back for a reply. "You staying?"

"Huh?" He stumbled mentally. "Yeah. Of course."

"I don't want to bother being domestic unless you're staying. You're very late. And I haven't been able to get in touch with you, either."

He blundered about for a place to begin. With his dream, with the hideous logic chain forged at Darkmoon Occult Supplies?

With the contrite, elderly woman he had found doing sentry duty on Mrs. Saks' front porch?

"Just a pity, young sir, a shame. One of those awful vans, with the whirling lights, took her away this afternoon. If you met her, of course, then you knew she was carrying around too much, you know. Like a side of pork. Poor, dear woman. My heart couldn't stand

*a job like that, and neither could yours, for long. It
would just burst. I bet the doctor says her heart just*
POPPED *from the overload, like a circuit breaker. The
least teeny bit of tension or stress. Or excitement . . ."*

Or how about a hulking, creepy, bearish manifes-
tation, come a-calling to stamp her out before she
could tell one Grant Mantell damning facts about the
Spilsbury Murders? It might not be capable of crossing Mrs. Saks's hex sign . . . but as Jade Wing had
advised, it *could* lob a few rocks.

Grant considered the coffee, almost made. He was
not sure he needed any more stimulation this night.

Max's nails clicked on the kitchen floor. A warm,
damp, pink-black nose pressed into Grant's free hand.
The dog sat his head heavily upon Grant's knee and
proceeded to dust his jeans with white hair.

"No barking at the door allowed," said Jennifer.
"He has better-developed manners than you."

The incident with the mirror that morning seemed
years distant. He released a tired exhalation. "Remember what they told you about acne in high school?
The self-renewing cycle: Don't worry about getting
pimples, they said, because worrying *causes* them.
Talk about a fixed game." He pinched the bridge of
his nose, hard, then ruffled the dog's head without
looking. "Now I'm thinking about crap I don't want
to. But I can't help it. I can't stop it. Now, I can't."

She was pulling things down from shelves, keeping
her back to him, he thought, because he had sinned
earlier. Now he could tell she was making extra work
for herself, averting her eyes. All he heard her say was
"You're scared you've got it. That disease you think
your father had—"

Suddenly the word *narcolepsy* swelled up to ridiculous zeppelin size in his head, becoming unmanage-
able for the narrow limits inside which he wanted to
confine his explanation. Everything fizzled. "I'm terrified I've got it," he said in a small voice. "I'm scared

I've got it, and it's driving me bonkers in some weird chemical way, making me see phantoms, giving me nightmares to feed the superstitions. Another goddamn cycle, like a hungry little cancer, chomping away. Auto-cannibalism of the sanity, to the point where a missing coffee cup sends me into an untethered panic.''

"Hang onto this one." She handed over a steaming mug, eyes still direct and dry.

He preferred not to exchange meaningful silences. "It just figures, you know. Now that I've come into all the cash I'll ever need, it so happens I've also got"—he flubbed the word; had to force it out—"a disease. *And* inherited insanity. I can afford the best hospitals. Custom-tailored strait-jackets, when the hallucinations get *really* pro.''

"Stop." She sat within reach, knees poking from the division of robe.

"Stop thinking about it? That's what they'd say in high school—*don't think about getting zits all over your face or you'll get 'em*—and thinking this thing to death is what will shove me off the proverbial edge. Did I mention the nightmares I'm having about the mirror are progressive? More information each time; definitely freaky enough to certify me for a private closet. Classic pattern of decay. Did I mention that I've gone in for occult consultation?'' A wild laugh squirmed free and sounded unhealthy. "Did I mention I'm about this far away from actually believing a corpulent little old lady was somehow killed by the forces of darkness this morning? Jesus H. goddamn *Christ.''* He let the mug warm his hands. Max, bored with this trifling, checked his dish to see if anything edible had appeared in his absence.

"So wallow if you want," she countered sharply. "But if you're going on that kind of drunk, get your terminology right. Try corybantiasm, I quote, 'a sleepless delirium accompanied by wild and frightening hallucinations.' Not *narcolepsy*. Try getting a definite prognosis if you really think you're sick. Get a different doctor. Stay away from your father's camp. And why not just *dump* the fucking mirror—no antique is worth this kind of anguish." *Clunk*—her mug came down like a gavel on the breakfast bar.

"You really have been listening," he said, as though at last recognizing her through a fogbank of vertigo. He raised the cup and tasted chocolate, cinnamon, coffee, cream, all spiked with something that imparted a nice, subtle bite.

She made a futile gesture, as if trying to encompass the improbability of it all. "Suppose your mirror isn't haunted, Grant?"

"Then I guess we're back to the stuff that bothers me a bit deeper."

"No, I mean, what if it's the bed that's evil and not the mirror?"

"Now who's being superstitious?"

She lept to correct: "Assuming, just assuming for a moment that there's any profit to be had from that line of logic." For the record, she qualified: "And *not* that I believe it, anyway." She killed a bit more thinking time by drinking from her own mug, then picking up the slim silver cigarette case from the counter. Its mechanistic Deco engraving caught light. Trapped it. "By the way—is this yours?"

Disorientation crept up his skeleton. "No. They're *yours.*"

Her expression told him she was being unfairly toyed with. "These are lady cigarettes, doll, but they're not mine. I wouldn't smoke these things. They'd kill me dead." She smiled, shrugged, put the case aside.

A sophisticated little jest, Grant thought; that's it. He tried to hold down his unease. Grow up, spud, learn some adult humor, get some subtlety into your wit. Keep up with her. Forsake the puns and fart jokes, huh?

Do nothing. Pretend you get it. And let her play with the wolves awhile.

"Okay," she said. "So—think about this for a moment, Goodman Mantell. Your problems are all sleep-related, from the nightmares to the real-or-imagined illness. Think of what a holding tank for fear a bed could be—*your* new bed could be. Think of all the fears beds are party to. When you were a little kid, how many things about your bed scared you?"

"I had at least two boogeymen in residence underneath," he said, warming to the idea. "There must've been some kid somewhere without one. I wouldn't let my feet hang over the edge; I still don't. But it was a place of security, too—where else can you hide under the covers, except in bed?"

"But that security was a result of the fear, the thing you were hiding *from*. I used to think there were monster hermit crabs who wanted to clip my bare toes off with their pincers. And think—when you get older, schedules start to victimize you. You fear being up too late, fear your parents will whack you for reading under the blanket with a flashlight. Then you fear oversleeping—you'll be late for school. Late for work. Then you fear not sleeping enough—*what am I doing to my body?*"

"And then there's my father," Grant said, hating the way the progression formed a neat, ordered chain. "He resents sleeping at all because it detracts from work-time with Calex. His body starts compensating and he immediately thinks he's sick, and starts worrying over how such a sickness could ball up his high-gear corporate life." He suddenly felt his stomach roll. "Pimples."

"Thinks of the attendant fear standing in line, ready, when sex becomes an issue in life," she said, pleased now with the wealth of examples. "Fear of the first time. Very powerful; very scary. Some people worry about loss of virginity; more people worry about how they'll perform. Fear of missing an orgasm, or messing one up, or not feeling what you think you're supposed to. A million fears regarding the person who has consented to get into such a ridiculous position with you." After a beat, she added, "Fear of impotence."

"God, do I hate the *sound* of that word," he said. "Another one that feeds on itself. You either best it, or just have to find somebody who doesn't scare you so much. . . ."

"And how many people die in bed?"

Now *that*, he thought, was terrific PR for what inane waterbed ads called "sleep systems." A lot of people died flatbacking it in their own, comfy, familiar beds, without any special supernatural assistance. Death and beds. Deathbeds. Could a long enough association between the two lead to some kind of causal relationship? A coffin, to be sure, was just a narrow bed with silk cushions and a lid.

"No bedsores and senility, not for me, not at this rate," he said. Jenny's brewed concoction was beveling the sharp corners in his head.

"I can think of better ways to go," she said, inclining her head downward, her eyes darkening, having much the same effect as the drink. "Enough for one more?" She indicated the glass pot, the tiny silver pitchers, the condiments on the counter.

"Sure, I—" He stopped cold. Something, a thought, had just fallen out of his head like a chunk of rotten insulation. *It's happening again!* He clenched his fists. No, surely it was the mad whipsaw of tension-stress; having made it intact to Jenny's, he relaxed (*let his guard down?*) and had momentarily forgotten what he was going to—

He gave his coffee mug a secret-agent glance of doubt. No, *that* suspicion was even dumber.

He looked up; saw her watching him with a most peculiar expression. The mug made him remember.

"The mirror," he said, giving over the cup. "Jenny, I've got to go back to the apartment and see if the mirror is unbroken, if the mug is still gone. See if I fantasized this whole thing. I need you to come with me. Remember what you said about being alone with the damned thing? If this was all a hallucination, then I've got my mental stability to fret about. But if it wasn't—then I've got palpable proof.

"Of what?" she said, appearing derailed, annoyed. "Either a busted mirror or a coffee cup that's MIA. Truly substantial evidence, my love."

"To *me* it is, yeah!" He nearly shouted. "I *know* the goddamn thing was shining back at me when I left. I pitched the cup at it, and broke it, and *didn't* break it! I know—"

"I'll go, I'll go, cease fire." She took the cup from his hands and returned it, steaming, full. "But in the morning, Grant, okay? I'm shagged." She braced him, placing her hands on his shoulders and pushing her own shoulders back. Her vertebrae pop-pop-popped. She sighed in relief. The belt of the burgundy robe gave up a few inches. "Seriously."

His reserves of iron were crapping out. "No, Jenny. Now. Don't you get it? I can know one way or the other, now, tonight, and I need you . . . well, to notarize what I find out."

She tapped away his iron with her touch, seemingly absorbing it through her fingertips. "No, yourself. If it's such cosmic proof, it can wait till sunrise, because I need *you* right now." She guided his hands into the slack of the robe. "Pause a moment to let it sink in, boy."

The solid rise of her chest, between her breasts, seemed to be raging with warmth. He squashed the nutty urge to ask if she was running a fever. An imp stationed near his ear counseled him not to blow it twice in one night, and capitulation began.

Her hand pushed his to the knotting of belt. "I don't

have a stitch on under this thing,'' she said, her breath carrying her voice to him in soft little clouds. ''You might have guessed.''

He croaked out a syllable of agreement. The thin belt surrendered faster than an Italian infantryman and she arched into his grasp.

''I don't want you to go right now,'' she said. *''I* don't want to go. It's night out there, Grant, and now you've got *me* scared of it. Love me instead?''

The attitude of her face was a picture Grant had imagined on a thousand nights he had spent alone, and he shut up protesting, for his own good. He stifled himself despite the renegade interior voice, the imp, warning him that manipulation of this brazen sort was a diversion one of the bad guys might pull. One of the enemy; one of *them.* He tried to see clues in the familiar agate-gray eyes of his lover. The newly poured coffee began to cool.

Bed was an utter disaster.

He sat in the cold concrete night of the parking garage below his apartment. He chuckled. It was a small, fatal sound; a noise of self-destruction.

''I'm going. Over there. Right now.'' Still groggy *with new sleep, she had said,* ''No. Not yet.'' *He said* okay; *she had rolled over. Then he sneaked his clothing out of her bedroom on tiptoe. Edging out the door, he heard a final syllable:* ''Don't.''

He did not attempt to join the ends of the circle by leaving her a note, signed *love.*

Don't.

Perversely, the center of his attention had become Jenny's digital clock. He had watched it tote up elapsed time as he kissed her once more, caressed her again, and nothing else happened. More lost time. Panic. He felt displaced, goading his own erection as though he was inside a different, uncooperative skin. Coaching had never been needed before. He came up mechani-

cally hard and lost it before he could even move, before his brain could pester him about the trouble he
was experiencing. The second time was worse, pyra-
miding his frustration.

Jennifer's calm disclaimers only angered him inside.
*You're exhausted distracted frightened tired. It's all
right. It's not necessary. You're just—*

Impotent. The reflex cliché locked smoothly on, extracted blood and detached. Getting old, ditto.

He thought disgustedly that excuses like age were
still decades away. Not only that, but through it all his
apartment, his bedroom, was still waiting with open
arms and maybe jaws, perhaps getting itchy for action.

He thought of boffing Max on the snout to keep him
from thundering through the living room, wagging and
rowfing, but instead mutely motioned him out the
door. He'd gotten it into his pinpoint doggie brain that
there was *A RIDE* to be had, and he would wake up
the entire building should Grant refuse him a chance
to stick his head out the car window into the mesmer-
izing slipstream of moving air. He piled himself into
the suicide seat of the Pinto and panted. His breath
was awful this morning.

Grant thought of the clock, counting time, and
booted his door open. "Okay, dogface, let's go do it."

On the way up, it occurred to him that the culpabil-
ity for last night's performance might not be entirely
his—what if the brass bed was some kind of sexual
exciter, as Jade Wing had claimed, the way the mirror
seemed to be a paranormal videotape deck, rerunning
the past?

Past tense operative, he thought. Was, not is. He
had broken the mirror yesterday morning. Maybe.

His rioting metabolism was in hard contrast to the
mundane view inside his door. He was overcranked,
attack-ready, flushed full of fresh adrenaline, and everything looked damnably regular. The rickrack he'd
spilled off the desk was still in the same position he'd

abandoned it on the floor. Yet something else, a calm resonant mental tone, quietly contradicted the apartment's masque of normalcy.

Perhaps it was the set of air in the room that told him the apartment *had* been entered and changes unobtrusively worked.

There was no need to cautiously ease the bedroom door open with an extended foot (the sound of its slam the day before rolled back to him now, full volume). He had begun to twist the knob when Max nosed blithely through ahead of him.

In just a few days of ownership, he had become accustomed to the way the big mirror beamed light around the bedroom, formerly the dimmest box in the place. That light was gone now. The scrolled brass frame hung dark, like the pit of an empty eyesocket, or a television with a kicked-in tube. Tiny motes of brass-yellow glinted feebly. The mirror glass was salted all over the bed, the carpet, the nightstand, in glittering splinters, shiny and slim and pointed like the fangs from a burnished mechanical rattlesnake. They broadcast a galaxy of light points across the ceiling, sharp white. It was broken, all right, shattered into a million million polished smithereens. He waded into the densest spill of broken glass, his shoes imbedding needled fragments into the carpet. He bent and retrieved a cup handle snapped open to porous tooth-white on each end, a curve like a skeleton's knuckle joint. Chunkier, triangular wedges of the dead coffee mug were plainly mingled with the obliterated mirror's metallic remains.

"Don't walk on the glass, Max," he said, lacking anything else.

His decision was already made. If he was crazy enough to hallucinate the mirror whole, the cup vanished, then one more spurt of lunacy could not curse him any more before calling the medics—or finding himself a razor blade.

"Come on, Max, we gotta visit the car again." The tallow candle and the spellbook from Darkmoon were still in the Pinto. He had left them behind, thinking that to tote them up to the apartment before *seeing* might jinx what he was to discover. He felt sure that deep inside he did not *want* to believe, no. Now it made no difference to go through the motions, complete the dance as a matter of style, neutrally, since sillier things had already been done.

On his way out it occurred to him to case the kitchen.

He knew what he had. Between the dust of the cabinets and the grease of the sink, he owned three large dinner plates, two salad plates, two mismatched short-stem wine goblets, a few plastic baseball trading cups from 7-11, a Pyrex bowl for all purposes, some Melmac plates he never used, and four coffee cups—one bowl-shaped Shafford cup with no saucer and three identical dark brown mugs. The unbroken pair would be in the kitchen.

He looked and found one mug, dirty. He looked twice. He began to search. After inventing unlikely hiding places—in the refrigerator, under the sofa cushions—he stopped and still had exactly one mug accounted for.

Yes, there was a chance Jenny might have busted it and slipped it into the trash and forgotten it. There also seemed to be a chance that she had broken it on purpose, more recently, in the bedroom. She had a key to his apartment; he'd been gone all day yesterday.

Jenny. Jennifer. Preternaturally beautiful and obviously well off. Why would she have anything to do with him unless—

Mrs. Saks had told him *you'd best destroy whatever's left.*

The tallow candle was yielding now to the dashboard and windshield, no longer even remotely a cylinder so much as an amorphous mass inside the paper.

It smelled like stale bacon. Max chased Grant happily down the service stairs. Avoiding the elevator forced him to fry off loose blood sugar. As he shut his door, his phone began ringing. He ignored it.

Let her come on her own.

Her presence could render him vertiginous, almost always had. She wobbled him. Could make him just a touch weak in the knees. A barely noticeable form of control . . . or mere proof of the intensity with which he realized he wanted her?

Sure.

"What about you, old pal?" he said to Max. "How real are you?"

Max sneezed explosively, as if to vindicate his actuality. Certainly nothing metaphysical could sneeze or fart with Max's style.

Maybe the dog merely served the purpose of helping to snare him in the first place. Let's be thorough now, not reluctant, he thought; let's run this little extrapolation to earth. Dogs were a soft spot of his. The current apartment (like all the others) was too small to keep one, and his list of second-string wants perpetually included a canine buddy. But if Jenny was something other than . . . if she was *different* in some way, wouldn't Max sense it, and react as he had to the authentically bad vibes of the mirror? Didn't animals *know?*

Grant camped out on the brass bed with his souvenirs until Jennifer's form filled up the bedroom doorway. He heard his door close and imagined the number of paces across the living room, and there she was, having obviously rolled out of bed and into jeans and a loose, billowy workshirt. Her hair was free, mussed from the rush.

"I'm conducting an experiment in pop craziness, the kind we generally ascribe to the Boulevard loons," he said to her silhouette. "And if nothing comes of it, I'm entitled to feel supremely stupid.

Should that happen, you may not want to be everything for me anymore. But if something does happen . . . god, then I've got a whole additional set of problems, don't I?''

Now she did not talk of doctors, or urge calm, or coo reassurance, or protect her innocence with a flood of examples. She had helped him with the chain of conjecture that led here. Motives could be dealt with after the fact. She said what she had said earlier, and now the word chilled him.

"Don't."

Her breath was labored, he noticed. What would've happened if he'd answered the phone instead?

"I can't stop you, can I?" she said.

"I'm afraid not, Jenny. I mean *afraid*. Not knowing scares me witless. I don't know that I've ever loved anything, either—maybe I never spent enough time contemplating it—but I'd apply that word, love, for whatever value it's worth with you. But my brain can't just disengage or ignore things. And that means if not today, I'd do this next week, assuming my days weren't numbered.'' The words came out shakily.

"I understand," she said. "I mean, I know. It's the way you are.''

"What the hell else can I do?"

Max, put off by their sloth, sought his place beneath the stereo shelf. Grant abruptly felt like a general abandoned in a trench during a banzai charge, his heart racing because Jenny had not budged from the doorway. She would not come near the bed now. *He gained some engine of protection*, Mrs. Saks's reedy voice said inside his head. *But he was taken anyway.*

"You can let me tell you a story," she said finally, the hurt plainly clogging her speech.

"I'm listening." No concessions. You're committed, boy.

"Once upon a time there were some no-talent Hollywood leeches.'' There was no sarcasm in her tone.

"They got off by claiming to be attendants of Cybele; whether they actually believed in such a nature goddess doesn't matter. It was just a thin license for fucking their brains out at ritual orgies. They managed to attract the attention of some jaded business mavens, ledger hacks who wanted to cop a feel on the Hollywood action they'd always coveted, and become part of the big, glittery Movie Machine. They got to bare their butts and indulge their wet dreams in exchange for bankrolling this erstwhile Bad Actor's Club. Eventually, the financial grease permitted a few of these no-talents to slide through into the filmaking mainstream. The Business Administration dropouts formed a big, bad corporation. And their olypmian sexual repetoire began to get eccentric."

Grant wondered if Aleister Crowley had fancied himself a corybant. Or if Jennifer knew how sharp her teeth could look to someone else, in the dark.

"Blood got spilled," she said. "Then imbibed. Some of these worthies got 'accidentally' killed. The group began to study, delving into ways to make their orgies more radical, once they'd passed beyond mere torture and murder. Cybele had nothing to do with the kind of special assistance they eventually fomented. Their custom-made patron. It whistled up all manner of brand new sexual diversions. But it was a newly-born thing, hungry, and not a little bit insane. It was like a nuclear pile. The group discovered that in order to keep going, they would require protection against the benefactor they'd created . . . or it would consume *them* when it tired of sacrifices. In due course they contrived a way to keep from getting gobbled up. Everything stayed copacetic: The smarmy occult rumors helped the film careers along. Jase Spilsbury became a minor star; his was the orgy mansion, the demon spa. Colette Nichols, Bryan Thorne, Davis T.J. Stone, Julia Cushing-Jones—all prospered. And the new corporation that spawned them broke ground in plastics

and petroleum at the right time and became a mega-
monolith. That part I think you already know about.''

She had not moved. Grant could not even make out
her lips in the bad light, telling the tale.

Blasphemers. Fornicators.

''The club, however, would not countenance split-
ters, and when one man wanted to pay accounts and
leave, they voted no. Easy. He was a resourceful man,
with a facile mind that had elevated him greatly inside
the Corporation. He arranged to quite audaciously steal
away their hallowed protection, at night, practically
from under their muzzles, and without it they were
lost. Their pet monster scooped them up on the night
of May first, 1959. Walpurgisnacht, coincidentally—a
night when witches and demons and so forth are supposed to swarm forth to revel amidst unwary humans.
That's pop occult stuff, though, too fairytale. *They* sure
didn't believe in it. It was clearly a cult murder; one
of Hollywood's first.

''The beast they'd created, however, did not evap-
orate at *their* passing. There was still the rogue member of the Club.''

''Say it,'' Grant said dully. ''My father.''

''He shut away the protection where it could shield
him and occasionally availed himself of the pleasures
the Beast could offer. After a decade, forgetting became easy—he never truly *liked* his ex-cohorts. And
soon he got around to the homework they had all ne-
glected. The existence of the Beast was threatened,
and subtle combat was engaged. As he looked for ways
to vanquish the nuisance he'd helped to call up, the
Beast tried beguiling him into giving up his protection.''

''He was baited with a beautiful woman,'' said
Grant. ''One he kept to himself. Outsiders shrugged
her off as some mystery bimbo; no big deal.'' He did
not have to ask why his mother had divorced his fa-

ther; why the money had flowed in but the contact had been sparse all these years.

"An alternate avenue of attack, a gradual blood clot growing quietly in the brain, finally had the desired effect. Stupid Beast. With the death of the last believer, it dwindled away to nothing. The bait it had abandoned survived it by flowing naturally toward the only outlet possible—the son."

"The son." *You're of his blood. I can smell it.*

"I'm perfect for you, Grant. I can't help but be— emotionally, sexually. There's nothing malign involved with actually becoming corporeal, being *real* unexpectedly. Accidentally. And there you were, with your simple emotional stresses, the answers to which were so easy for me. There you were. Your existence helped make me a fact. I'm *real*. And you looked so helpless when we met, I . . ." A trace of her customary humor seeped into her recollection. "The more real I became, the more I fell in love with you. I couldn't help that, either. And I never wanted to leave you. Don't ask me, but . . . the mirror somehow stockpiled everything it witnessed. And the bed was the charmed circle. Surely you've noticed how sex on it is. But now you're dabbling in things that could erase me. I wasn't lying when I said I was scared."

Her voice quavered now. It was too convincing, Grant thought, hating it. "I saw the Beast in the mirror; it still exists."

"No. That's the past; it was only showing you the past."

"Then why did you sneak back here and break it?"

He heard a sigh come out in the dark. "You seemed so convinced you were seeing things I thought I could solidify your problems into reality. Without the glass the visions would stop, and you'd eventually believe the disappearance of your coffee cup into it was a hallucination. An overwrought mental state I could nurse you out of; magic mirrors, no. For the same reason I tried to get to Mrs. Saks' house ahead of you.''

"You killed her?''

"No.'' He thought he could feel her sheer frustration. "I went to her house. That's why all you got on the phone was my machine. I knew about her but never suspected she was tangled up in the occultism and had gotten the Beast after her ass, as well. She was obviously inside when I knocked. When I wouldn't leave, she started screeching things about *smelling* what I was in God's eye, and how she had been tempted with the figure of her dead husband. Just *screaming*—totally out of it. So I left. I could only hope you wouldn't take her too seriously if she told you some embellished riff about the Spilsbury Murders.''

"Sounds like she might've wailed loud and hard enough to make her heart explode,'' Grant ventured. "It also sounds, therefore, like the Beast is still with us. A hematoma, a coronary, my nightmares, hallucinations and—''

"Don't you *grasp?!*'' She was angered but perfectly in character as Grant knew her and exasperated by what seemed his congenital male thickheadedness. "It's not me you have to be afraid of, it's that Dr. Byrd, it's your father's Calex buddies—*they're* the ones interested in starting the whole stinking cycle up again! That's why they're so anxious to buy that property out from under you—you haven't heard from them, but you will. Why Byrd wants to poke and prod you. They're holding off now because of death protocol, a grace period between you and your father. If there's one thing they respect, it's protocol. And they'll be the death of you, when they find they can't groom you!''

"What about you?'' Again, it sounded too logical to Grant. Diversions, successful ones, always sounded good, were well planned, like battle strategy.

"I don't know. And I don't care about any of them.

You have the savvy to steer around the greedy ones, the incompetent ones, the ladder-climbers that started all the bad things. I just want to *leave*. I need to know if you have enough faith in me to throw the junk away, get it clear of *them*. No hocus-pocus, no candles, no visions. Melt the goddamned bed down and sell it as lamp chains. But let's leave it behind.''

"Toss away my supposed protection, Jenny? Sounds like something the old Beast would cotton to real fast.''

"Oh, god, I know how I must sound!'' Her voice cracked with tears, hopelessness.

His thumb was marking the page Jade Wing had recommended in the book. "Let's try an alternate scenario,'' he said, "just for argument's sake. Devil's advocate time, right? Let's propose that the bed, being a huge protective amulet (bless you, Jade Wing, for the jargon, at least), is the only roadblock in the Beast's way. Its power is already diminished, and the bed retards it from getting more serious, more real. So Mister Beast, while it can't get physical, can still harass me with visions, nightmares. Grant suspects a relationship between the bed and the Beast he sees in the mirror. Bad news. The Beast needs to eighty-six the bed before Grant can investigate and maybe find a way to rub it out. Little Jenny trots along and smashes the mirror, strictly to help Grant with his head problem, but coincidentally helping the Beast—since Grant will now not see any more disturbing revelations. Little Jenny beats Grant back to Mrs. Saks, again strictly to help Grant. And Mrs. Saks' heart bursts before I can grill her about my father. And then little Jenny finally gets around to spinning this tale for Grant—when were you planning to let me in on all this? And her closing remark is 'Gee, Grant, get rid of the bed, huh?' '' He let the book drop open to the place Jade Wing had marked. "Little Jenny begins to look like the Beast's hole card against oblivion. I think that going through with the candle trick, all the way, since my father never got a chance at the finale, might make everyone here honest, for good. Or not so good."

"And it might destroy me. If your father had managed to complete the recitation, I wouldn't be here."

"But according to your own story, you might have ended up as a participant in my father's demise. Bait for Mister Beast. No? Then how about this, Jenny: If you've been absolutely straight with me, this little spellbreaker might not do a damned thing to you."

"You're gambling." She did not approve.

"I don't really think so. Your presence, just standing there, constitutes a fair argument for you're being a good guy. Max—whom I am convinced is a real dog—likes you. And if you're not lying, then *you* gambled, by breaking the mirror without knowing the consequences in advance. You gambled on saving me the most painless way and my nosiness botched the plan. You weren't *sure* what would happen. Some thing, like the Beast, would be sure, I think. And—also if you're not lying—you went to Mrs. Saks and stood right underneath a protective hex sign. If you were a bad guy and could do that, Mrs. Saks would've died a long time ago. Yeah, I'm gambling now: I'm betting that you've become real enough, strong enough for the bed or the words in here not to matter."

"Assuming you just haven't lost your mind," she said, her tone acknowledging the small hope he'd made implicit.

"If I *am* crazy, you've got a lot of explaining to do for that story about Spilsbury and the Beast," he said, almost smiling. "Let's get this over with."

"Wait," she said, hands coming up. "No. I guess not." She shook her head wonderingly, sniffed. "You have to do it, don't you? If I'm lying, I'm a threat, and the only way you'll really know if I'm lying is to . . ." Her extended hands dropped to her sides. "I can't even kiss you, before, just in case." She wiped away tears. "I can't even cry, because it might be a con."

A surge inside him insisted *this* was real. She was real, and her love for him was chewing up her insides. *I can't* not *do this*. His fingers snapped the butane lighter to life, and the wick of the lumpy tallow stump sputtered and caught.

"A moment," she said. Strength tried to slither away and was recaptured. "I'm going down to your car to wait. If I know you at all, you ran off and left it open. Let's pretend I went to check to see if it was locked. You come down looking for me. If you see me sitting there wiping my eyes, then all is well, and we can fight later. And I won't say I love you, because by now you either know it or you don't. I don't want to just loiter here, with you watching, in case anything *does* happen. That's strange, isn't it? I should know whether something should happen. Or shouldn't. But I don't." Her voice stayed low and level, like a worker, newly fired. "Goodbye, then. Lover."

"Not goodbye," he said as she turned to leave, and he reckoned he saw her eyes glint toward him, briefly chromium in the dim light. "Not ever."

Jennifer was gone. She closed the front door behind her, but only after Max, anticipating another jaunt in the car, perked up and followed her out hopefully. *Damned pointy-eared turncoat.* The gentle way Jenny closed the door was more horrible than a million doors slammed hard against nightmares.

Grant never saw her again.

Once again he was here in the brass bed, by candle-light. This time he was utterly alone, and his nose told him the sheets needed changing. The odor of the candle made itself thickly evident; he could hear the wick sizzling in the absolute quiet. There was no way the candle could tip over, or roll away, as it had in his father's hands. Summer heat plus the Pinto's dashboard had conspired to reform the tallow cylinder into an Impressionist mini-pyramid. Grant read aloud.

After the flat, parched echo of his own voice died,

he sat there like the village idiot. He had expected the air in the room to roil, to hear a distant, unearthly howl as the teardrop of fire flickered while he recited the words. He made it to the end of the passage. His hands were shaking. Nothing provocative happened. The sun did not break the clouds.

Max sat in the cockpit of the Pinto, licking his toes. His tail started wagging, in hopes of A RIDE. There was nothing so dramatic as a note using the word *love* and ending in midsentence. There was no residue, no evidence. Jennifer could just as easily have hailed a cab for parts unknown. Max's tail ceased moving as Grant sat down hard on the oil and soot-stained concrete, his back pressed to a hubcap, and wept the first honest tears he had known in twenty-eight years. The dog cocked his head, sympathetically.

Before he cleared out of Los Angeles for good he made a lot of phone calls. He told Toby Wolff, the photographer, that Jennifer had pulled stakes for the gauntlet of modeling agencies in Manhattan, and indeed, this was an impression Grant's own gut feelings clung to—that she had merely walked out of the garage and out of his life. It was the way many people dealt with death. The lost one was assigned a status of permanent incommunicado, making them unreachable instead of obliterated. He felt certain that some blinking mental telltale-lamp would have gone dark if she really was dead . . . provided that she was ever really alive. She had been alive enough to photograph. And Toby Wolff had chalked up a lot of photographs. They all hurt to look at, even the bad ones.

With the help of a rented van and some able bodies from Starving Students, Grant engineered the transport of the bed, mirror frame, the candle and book, plus every shard of broken glass up the Pacific Coast Highway, to a secluded lookout called Point Pitt. In the middle of the night, the load went into the ocean and the movers pocketed big tips. Grant felt good when he saw how fast the baroque brasswork sank into the boiling whitecaps of seawater. Up at Point Pitt, the water ran deep close to shore. The admonition of the late Mrs. Saks still nagged, however: *Fire cleanses.* Not water. That sort of detail was important to the folks who kept Darkmoon Occult Supplies in business. But the act made him feel relieved in a bitter, minor way, and upon his return to the city he left an extra hundred bucks in an envelope for Jade Wing, slipping it through the door slot at an hour when even Darkmoon's lamps were out. Go and try to bribe the forces of darkness, sure. But it, too, felt correct.

The inheritance funds were tapped and new lawyers and accountants were engaged. The proper city officials got their palms crossed with *baksheesh*. Grant's representatives secured Mrs. Saks' property, tore down her house, and dedicated the resultant residential park to his father, via a bronze plaque. Calex never got ahold of the property, and the plaque stands there to this day.

Max happily rose shotgun as LA shrank in the car's rearview. Grant wondered if the dog sensed, or knew. He wished he could know if Max had sat thumping his tail while Jennifer walked quickly out of the parking garage . . . or phased into thin air like a lap-dissolve in a TV commercial. He wondered about the dog, but not too much, because that was the road back to paranoia and lunacy.

Instead, he drove north to begin waiting.

He forced himself not to notice when Max's brilliant, clear blue eyes began to darken into a unique shade of agate-gray.

PAMELA'S GET

"This is a scam, young lady. Or some sort of unpolished joke I lack the crust to understand."

That *young lady* had been aimed and fired like a bullet: *Me Caesar—you bimbo.* Jaime's lip tried to curl, but when pow-wowing with Pavel Drake it was always a more prudent strategy to maintain a corporate attitude, an unfeeling stonewall posture. Beneath the black slate circle of the cocktail table her fist locked tight, an evil flower, slowly feeding. She was going to have to tread very cautiously to get what she wanted from this man—this cruel and condescending being whom she had kept distant from any part of her life he might corrupt. Until tonight. Now she had a painful lot to do, and maybe not much time left to do it in.

That Obscure Object of Desire was a membership-only Beverly Hills venue waitressed by foldout-class women two steps down from the game show and soap opera stratum of failure. Some still managed a local television commercial or two; all were leftovers, staling, what a Hollywood Hopeful looks like on the wane. The cheap thrill was to witness these budding stars as they shanghaied themselves into topless duty after hawking carpets and spas on the tube, still desperately pretty, willing to risk nearly anything for one more shot at popcorn fame. Every customer was therefore a potential backer for a career breakthrough, so each got a generous smile . . . and the only thing tainting the biological purity of such mutual parasitism was the bitterness calcifying each smile. Those smiles told you stories of how hope could sabotage lives.

Industry people—that is, movie, TV, and music video rollers, high and low—pointedly shunned the Object; some kinds of failures might prove disastrously communicable. The mainstay clientele consisted of businessmen who could appreciate such failure, in the way a conqueror might savor the captured vintages of a newly ransacked village. The Object offered the opportunity to taste the blood of one killed right beside you, and enjoy that taste because it meant you were still alive. Fat billfolds were entreated and a Hellfire Club mentality encouraged.

It was not a place a man would invite a woman for whom he held the slightest degree of good regard. It was a useful arena for tacit humiliation, or the nastier subtleties of revenge.

Jaime watched Pamela Drake's father reread the single typed page she had given him. "Maybe you should order a drink," he said, releasing a huge sigh, his eyes still relentlessly scanning. Seeking faults, footholds for assault.

A thinly misted glass of ice water stood untouched before her on its cocktail napkin. Drake's purely professional scotch and soda was half dead. At his beckoning a splay-breasted cooch hostess jiggled over to swap empties for fulls. Jaime did not want anything from the Object getting inside of her, but her throat was arid and she knew the way Drake's brain worked. A libation might signal some rough truce. Just this once. That was all she needed.

"White wine," she said. "Dry." Stay generic. One glass. Give a little that you might gain everything. If she had been out boozing with Pamela, outrageous new drinks in funny colors would have been the ground rule.

Fifty-six, without a thread of gray, was Pavel Drake

of Drake Polyvinyl Products Inc. *He dyes his hair,* she thought, suddenly shocked. Any vanity implied a crumb of human feeling somewhere in the convolutions of this man's mean, small mind. In this place of hopelessness, where women were literally Objectified, it was a spark of hope.

Jaime needed hope. Because if the man sitting across from her did not affix his signature to that piece of paper, she was going to die.

Tears had rinsed the mascara down Jaime's face hours before. There was no denying that the person in the box had been her best friend—the kind you are permitted one per lifetime, with luck; the kind you win if the timing is just so and the clockwork of the universe smiles on you in its random way. Jaime had watched the box slide into the ground at half past ten in the morning, signing off the eight years of that friendship, leaving her to hold nothing but death and thoughts of death.

She refused to believe the way she had just *stood* there, dumbly, Wayfarer shades hiding the ravaged state of her eyes, her black stiletto heels sinking slowly into the cemetery turf as Pamela was subjected to ritual and clumsy eulogizing. She had died intestate so there had been no cremation; whatever she had insisted upon in private did not count here. Case closed. The box's showroom finish was kissed by grave dirt, and the strangers in attendance (relatives lacking better diversions this weekend) would soon depart to make merry on Pavel Drake's tab, their pocket obligation dispatched. If there was a casting house where one rented extras for funerals—natty folks with gerbil eyes and tight, insurance-broker smiles—then Drake had scribbled them a hefty check. It was all very businesslike. Jaime's eyes kept looking for the camera crews.

Thank God for Jason.

He ignored the cattle and stepped across the line to wrap Jaime up in a genuine hug. She linked arms with him and hung on. They were the only two attendees on the far side of the grave, away from the tent and folding chairs.

People expect their parents to die some dim date in the future. No one is surprised when Grandpa stops drooling long enough to bite the big one. Jaime knew she herself would experience what the medics called an "event" if she drank or tooted or drove too fast, or kept getting horizontal with those faceless and monied Brentwood body-builders. They had great asses, charm and cash to burn, and hard chromium eyes that flattened and rejected her once the contour of flesh beneath clothing was no longer sufficient mystery to hold them. When you saw yourself crying in the mirrors, when your own eyes reflected back the pain inside, then you expected bad news, if only subconsciously. But buddies just did not keel over from unannounced pulmonary embolisms, not after a 20/20 checkup. Especially not buddies like Pamela, who seemed put on the earth to babysit you through one crisis after another. They were not supposed to die at twenty-eight, sitting on a sofa, eyes open, holding cold coffee in a mug that read MY OTHER COFFEE CUP IS A MERCEDES. No.

The tears just would not stanch, and Jaime hated her own loss of control. There could never be enough tears for Pamela. Mickey was nowhere in sight; he hadn't bothered to show up. This angered Jaime, and she saw that Jason was flat pissed. His eyes glinted as they scanned the group and came back to her, minus Mickey. Then they settled into a dull expression of hurt and loss.

Jaime knew then just what had been lost, to all of them.

She could call up a picture-post-card-perfect image of the foursome right now: Pamela, cross-legged on a leather hassock in her living room, sipping white Bordeaux and waving her hands. Jason would be on the floor, unconsciously assuming a Sears catalogue model pose so perfect it was funny. He'd refill glasses and sit with one forearm hooked around Pamela's thigh in a comfy way that looked possessive yet not restrictive. He hated being what he called the "whore of fashion" and so was shaggier than *GQ* might dictate. He was sexier than an incubus anyway. While Pamela animatedly held forth, he'd roll his eyes in that here-we-go-again expression that made him look like a befuddled cocker spaniel.

And then came Mickey, less polished, not as brash, but still a contender. His position would be directly across from Pamela's, and he would lean into her commentary as though inviting charades. Unerringly, he would call from the air the very words her gesticulations begged, causing her to take a big gulp of wine and nod yes, *yes!*

Last, watching all, submerged in the cushions of Pamela's thronelike Prince recliner, eyes bemused and just visible above the silvery rim of the wine goblet, would be her. Jaime. Thinking.

A perverse, I-told-you-so feeling welled up within her. More than once, she had dutifully dunned Pamela about neatening her affairs on paper. Both had acknowledged that day in the misty future when one would precede the other into death, leaving the other to clean up and carry on. Neither of them had counted on their coffee conversation lopping over into nerve-numbing reality so bloody soon.

Now it was just one more thing to prompt the tears.

"I want to be cremated when I buy it," Pamela had said. "I hate the idea of people standing around, sniffling, going *oh woe!* while I do nothing but suck formaldehyde, you know what I mean? Yuck." Her eyes, deep green, lambent as the glass of a champagne bot-

tle, scanned Jaime's neat rooms. Her lips busied themselves, worrying, as she contemplated just what she
did want at her funeral, instead.

Pamela was a slender woman, given to jeans and
Reeboks and the first tee or sweat off a chairback or
doorknob that could pass the Pamela Drake patented
Nasal Cleanliness Test. She'd settled down on the floor,
nursing one of Jaime's new Napas mugs, heavy porcelain and full of hot cinnamon coffee. Her fingertips,
nails bitten rigorously to the quick, traced patterns in
the burgundy carpeting.

Jaime had gone to the bedroom to shuck her working duds. Pamela raised her voice. "Don't you ever
get the feeling those uniforms are gonna smother
you?" She rose and wandered into the hallway. The
bedroom door was demurely half-shut.

"Nope," came Jaime's voice from beyond. "Did it
ever occur to you that if you had been born ten years
earlier, you would have been sucked into the hippie
mythos and would now be a screaming, headband-
wearing anachronism?"

"Ho, ho, ho."

"I'm serious, girl. Put together *1984* and designer
denim and you get uniforms that would do Orwell
proud."

Pamela booted the door open, grinning like a grem-
lin. Jaime, naked to the waist, yelped and jumped for
cover, then gave it up as hopeless.

"Hey, whoa, it's only me!" Pamela's hands were
up. "I come to learn, not to grope. I want to glimpse
corporate America with its uniform off."

"Do you *mind?*" Pamela was always jumping frantically ahead, and Jaime resented straining to keep
pace. When the decorum had been passed out, Jaime
had gotten both her own and Pamela's shares.

Pamela blew out breath in a huff. "Geez, okay, already!" She lifted her arms and stripped off her Ducks
Deluxe t-shirt, tossing it to the floor and seizing

Jaime's bare arm to drag her to the dressing mirror.
She posed them side-by-side, adopting an exaggerated
buddy stance with one hip cocked. "There. Check this
out. The gene pool doesn't have a prayer."

Jaime covered her eyes and laughed, helpless now.

She admired the casual street-poet disdain with
which Pamela wore clothes, or discarded them. She
liked Pamela's body as well. It was lower slung, larger
breasted, not padded. She had scrappy, healthy honey-
blond hair in contrast to Jaime's overstyled brunette,
which got trimmed shorter every year in an endless
process of distillation. Where Pamela had none, Jaime
had fingernails—sculpted, medium length, glossy, perfect. Pamela had wide tiger-paw feet that Jaime at first
thought were snubbed and odd looking, then came to
love for their musculature and power. Pamela squinted,
going on tiptoe to hold her right breast level with
Jaime's left. "I think your tits are more proportionate
than mine," she said with an absolutely straight face.
"I'm gonna be in trouble when I turn fifty."

The contact was unexpectedly electric; a thrill
zipped through Jaime's skin and her nipple condensed
to a nub.

She had never wanted to have sex with Pamela. *Call
me Victorian.* Many times she had wanted to hold
Pamela while she slept, to warm her when the emotionally calloused men she attracted called "time" and
began sniffing elsewhere. But she was pretty sure this
did not mean she wanted to jump Pamela's bones.

Well. Maybe once.

Women had invented the thing the magazines now
called "male bonding," she thought. Her love and
friendship with Pamela expressed itself in a million
tiny gestures and touches—tactile reassurance for the
constitutionally handicapped. A superstitious shield-
ing against urban hostilities, built like a flawless pearl,
layer upon layer accumulating day by day. Pamela was
her Hyde half, different, damned near opposite, but

essential. At times she could be infuriating. Jaime had
recorded so much about her—things that were annoy-
ing, even insignificant, but which resonated later and
now made her want to weep to mourn their permanent
loss. The queer tic Pamela developed, for example,
when something pierced her armor and punctured her
feelings—a rapid-fire batting of one eyelid plus a startled, quick sniffing noise, as though she was recoiling
from an actual blow. Her maddening use of nonwords.
Excape. Idear. Irregardlessly. Her approach to laun-
dry, which up until recently had been to dump in half
a box of detergent and set the machine on HOT.

HOT could deal with anything. Other traits were less
quaint.

"You didn't ask me how my folio went down at
Avatar Publishing," Pamela would say. "I took it in
two days ago."

"Oh, I was wondering about that," Jaime would
begin, dreading what came next. "How'd it go?"

"You're so tied up in what *you're* doing, you don't
care."

"Don't give me that, of course I care." Jaime was
confrontational and often not as gentle as she might
be in such engagements. She had to stay in character.
"So, how'd—"

"You're just asking me *now* because I brought it
up!" Pamela would get petulant and stick out her lip
(*See, you* don't *really care.*)

"No. Seriously. How'd it go (*Goddamnit!*)?"

"I don't want to talk about it." Which meant, of
course, *I win.* And just when Jaime would be ready to
scream and tear hair, Pamela would humanize. "I
guess I'm really a bitch, huh?"

(Go on, tell me I'm a bitch, that's what you want.)
Ready to shriek . . .

At times like that, Jaime hated her best friend,
knowing all along she still loved her twice as strongly.
It was a problem now and then, as it is any time you

get to know another human being intimately. But she did need Pamela to know she would always be there for her . . . even if Pamela pissed her off beyond rational endurance.

The carpeting, the Napas mugs, the wardrobe were all courtesy of Jaime's rise in retail from assistant buyer to buyer for Sanger Harris. Now, instead of lording over the paperwork for Glassware, Linens, and Bath Shoppe, she got to make the purchasing trips to New York and points past. Such work necessitated a wardrobe that Pamela would have considered an insurmountable feat of program planning, and a methodical approach to documents totally at odds with her pile-file habit.

"1984 has come and gone," Pamela said, jumping ahead to pour Jaime coffee while her friend made a pit stop in the bathroom. "In 1980, I figured we'd all be dead by then anyhow. Now I guess it's 1990."

Jaime emerged in slacks and an oversized, shapeless epaulette shirt from Banana Republic. On anyone else it would have been all wrinkles. "You'd better *not* just die on me! Without telling me, warning me first."

"I won't. I promise. But did you hear what I said about cremation? What do you think?"

"I want to sell my body to science—if I don't die old and doorspit, that is. Let 'em recycle me. Why trash corneas like these? I mean, have you ever *seen* corneas this classy?"

Pamela giggled. "Not a bad idea." She pondered it, but only for an instant. Then she was off and running toward whatever came next. She never wasted too much time on a single topic; it was another lineament of her character that her anal-retentive corporate daddy hated most. Finally, she said, "Have you got a will, Jaime?"

Her response was too offhand. "Sure." She had never mentioned it to anyone. More forgotten paper.

Pamela seemed to go far away fast. "I didn't know."

"Hey . . . I left everything to you, kiddo." It was the only response Jaime could think of to lighten the tone.

Pamela's voice remained tiny. "Oh. Good."

That, for Jaime, summed up Pamela's lifelong hate affair with documents. It had been inspired, doubtless, by her father's obsession with same. No insurance. No will. No messages. Nothing.

Nobody dies this young.

When Jason caught Pavel Drake staring at them over the flower-bedecked casket, he put a protective arm around Jaime. His nearness was comforting, even if the day was too muggy and her glove-tight formal get-up too close.

"He's probably checking out my legs," she said.

"It's sweltering out here," Jason said, breaking eye contact with the far side of the fresh grave. "But I'll be goddamned if I'm going to stand around with those mouth breathers under her dad's little circus tent."

"I was thinking the same thing. Have I ever told you what dear Daddy did at Pamela's birthday party?"

"You'll have to . . . some other time." They leaned into each other. It would be so easy to simply split the funeral and go home with Jason. If they no longer had Pamela . . . well, who did they have?

It was Maurois, as Jaime recollected, who wrote "In literature, as in love, we are astonished at what is chosen by others." Approval of your best friend's lovemates (or books) was nice but usually inappropriate, if not embarrassing. In the case of Jason Parrish, the test was irrelevant. He was the sort of guy whose food looked better than yours because *he* had ordered it.

Pamela and Jason had met in Chicago at a horror film titled *Piece by Piece*. Charming. The screening had been downtown at Facett's Multimedia, and Jason had come to review it for the *Trib*. They were the only two who lasted through to the end credits. They wound up warming a booth at some sleepy suburban coffee shop while predawn snow drifted down to bury the city.

Career-wise, Pamela had lit off on another of her flank attacks, and half a year had passed. Jaime knew she would soon be magnetized back to her home ground. The care packages and correspondence were voluminous enough to fill a Knudsen dairy crate. When Pamela returned, live and in person, Jaime had filed the crateful of memories in the rear of her clothes closet.

Near the end of the Chicago phase had come one postcard Jaime never forgot. In it, Pamela had specified the qualities she preferred in her closest friends, and its implication was that the arrival of Jason on the scene had completed her personal equation for happiness. During one of their thousands of long-distance calls (the bills for which overrode the gross national product of Paraguay), Jaime had gotten the lowdown on Jason in salacious detail.

Pamela had gone on at length about how considerate he was in the sack, and Jaime thought ruefully of little acorns and mighty oaks.

Jason got fired from the *Tribune,* but he had savings, and Pamela gladly filled the gaps. Then the film magazine she was designing collapsed, and she flew back to Jaime. Two months later, her connections in graphics yielded up a post at the *Herald Examiner,* and Jason was booked west on United.

Jaime's attraction to Jason was crude, at first, and entirely the fault of Pamela's giddy enthusiasm. She had seeded in Jaime the sort of interest that could not really be helped. Or stopped. It had taken a few months, but the inevitable finally happened.

Jaime felt the sparks jump across her nerve endings.

Pamela had gotten roped into an all-night session of paste-up, purely à la carte, at good pay. Jason had been loafing around her apartment; it was his day off. And Jaime had dropped by with a bottle of Gray Reisling. No excuse was needed.

It was not merely the unspoken commonality between them. In the end, Jaime had moved first, casually touching him when their automatic dialogue ran thin. Their embrace quickly waxed to critical mass. They were blameless. They finished folded together on Pamela's fake Persian rug, naked, purring, and spent.

To Jaime's certain knowledge, Pamela had never guessed. Today, only the vibrations of unease lingered. She found it difficult, even with him right beside her, to recall the specifics of how they furiously plundered each other in a pile of still-warm clothing, except that she had passed into light unconsciousness following her third orgasm. Pamela had been right about his magic tongue.

"I'm sorry," she said to the casket. "I wish you were here so I could tell you I'm sorry, so you could get mad, so we could make up. It only happened that once. I guess I messed up. But you promised you wouldn't die on me. Does this make us even?"

It was too damned easy to forget how much you could love someone, until they died and it became impossible.

The unconcerned mourners filed away and Pavel Drake beckoned the cemetery attendant, who released the catches on the aluminum rack supporting the casket. Canvas straps slowly unreeled, clicking metronomically, and the box containing Pamela settled into the dark hole.

It was almost as if Jason's infidelity was unthinkable to Pamela. Or just not relevant. With Mickey, she'd tried to matchmake.

"You want to fuck Mickey, *doncha?*" Pamela had opined at lunch one day. It was during the hiatus before Jason had come to Los Angeles and he and Pamela had spent a whole weekend in bed before emerging into the daylight to say hello. She could get spiteful or sharp when she wasn't getting laid regularly.

"Say what?" Jaime returned with a pained expression.

"Oh, Mickey's attracted, you bet. I saw him gobbling you up with his eyeballs."

"Jump his bones, maybe, but sleep with him, never. I'd get athlete's sheet." They both laughed. Tension defused.

Mickey was the one who never forgot Pamela. He picked the most appropriate oddball Christmas gifts for her and beat everyone to the punchline by phoning her at midnight sharp on each of her birthdays. Mickey Banks and Pamela were a pair that quickly discovered they were better friends than lovers. The thing that endeared Mickey was his knack for bestowing just the right words to vocalize feelings, on those rare days Pamela found herself inarticulate over some transient grief. He never overlooked dates important to her. He was constitutionally incapable of it. Maybe that was why he had ducked the burial. There was no more Pamela to remember . . . except for the one inside their heads.

Mickey had saved Jaime from Pavel Drake at Pamela's twenty-fifth birthday party.

After four flutes of Perrier Jouet, Pamela had begun to pout and sink into her "quarter of a century" badrap. Her smile had turned tipsy, brittle, and forced. The whole awkward bash had come at the insistence of Pamela's father, who Jaime had heard was a big plastics baron. She had retreated to the wet bar to grab a sparkling mineral water, and somewhere behind her Jason proposed a jokey toast to lighten the mood. Ah, the things we suffer for our friends . . .

"We've achieved eye contact several times, dear, but I don't believe we've been formally inflicted on each other." Jaime turned around and shook a hand. "Pavel Drake. I'm Pamela's father. The one who's getting stuck with the bill for this rodeo.''

They traded chat; Jaime thought of empty calories. She had only heard penny dreadfuls about Pamela's father, from Pamela. By the time she got a peek at his engraved business card and had mentioned her own job in retail, she saw the wattage in his eyes bump up and realized that the brown stuff eroding the ice in his glass was not tea.

He nodded too much as he talked, working his lips, probably because they were getting numb. ''Good advancement in retail,'' he said. ''Upward mobility. I admire that. It's always been Pamela's big problem— no ambition. She daydreams, you see. Twenty-five and nowhere, and she wonders why she's not happy, and with her great imagination she can't figure out why.'' He sniffed imperiously and glanced at Jaime's bosom before meeting her eyes again. ''Oh, my daughter has a terrific imagination, Miss Ralston. But it's unproductive; she can't turn a penny profit with it. Twenty-five now. And I'm beginning to fear she's never going to amount to anything.''

Already Jaime's body was begging to flee, but for Pamela's sake she made a game try: ''I wouldn't say that, Mr. Drake. She's knocking out a nice little berth for herself with the graphics and designs and layouts. She's always seemed most interested in the mechanics of publishing, and she's fascinated by *processes,* not—''

He cut her off with an impatient *ahhh* noise of discontent and a wave of his hand. She counted three gold rings. ''That magazine horseshit,'' he spat. ''I offered her a fucking vice-presidency and apprenticeship when she turned twenty-one. None of this entry-level asscrap. Fifty large per annum to start, with perks and deductions out the wazoo. And here she is . . . farting around with this pissant magazine diddly. Jesus Christ in a Handi-Van . . .''

He drifted, then refocused. His hand lit upon her

shoulder, to perch. "Now, I think *you* understand how the business world works, don't you, dear? What'd you think if I offered *you* a position, hmm? I don't know where you came from, but you look like you'd be pretty good."

Jaime could not believe she was staring into his sharktooth leer, wincing at his one-hundred-proof breath, suffering a snapshot nightmare of the sort of position Pamela's father had in mind. It almost took her balance away.

Someone tapped her shoulder, causing Drake to snatch his hand back. "Care to dance, m'lady?"

It was Mickey Banks, in his black shirt and jeans and corduroy jacket and cowboy boots, and Jaime wanted to embrace him madly. She turned while Pavel Drake was still on hold. "There's no music," she said.

"I'll hum," he said, and did, pulling her free. Jaime knew Mickey's combat smile. The grin on his face was almost it. "Excuse us, please, Mr. Drake."

"Yeah, right." Drake gestured loose-jointedly with his glass. As Mickey led Jaime away, she thought she heard Drake mutter *fucking cooze* . . .

"Anything you want is yours, Banks," she said once they were across the room and safe. "God, my brain just blanked, Pamela's *dad* . . ." She bit her knuckle and made a face.

"Yep. Pretty repulsive, huh?" He took a neat gulp of vodka and orange juice. "Whenever he starts cranking up his blood alcohol, I get this knotted fist right in my sternum. It won't unclench till I get out of range. I see his sheer charm rubbed you the same way."

A sympathetic phantom pain blossomed near her heart, in the hard knot of cartilage where her ribs met. "I feel sorry for Pamela, most of all."

"Me too. Imagine having that guy bounce you on his knee. Daddy Dearest. He drove Pamela's mom straight into the most expensive lunatic asylum in town. She died there.'' He saluted something imaginary with his glass.

Jaime paled. ''I had no idea.'' Pamela had made a few shrugging allusions to an unpleasant childhood but had never burdened anyone with specifics. Except Mickey. It figured.

''It is but one single chapter in a whole rancid serial,'' he said knowingly, squeezing her hand.

She nodded. ''I guess I didn't realize what she was up against. But she's got you and me, right? And Jason. Jason's good for her.''

''She's nuts about him.''

Several couples away, Pamela was threatening to douse Jason with bubbly if he did not cease with the dumb toasts. A cork went *bang* and somebody got drenched. Everybody laughed.

''Thanks, Mickey.'' She tilted forward to kiss him. Just as she made lip contact, he averted his head so that she got his cheek.

''Be good.'' He smiled, putting two fingers to her lips. ''I'm not made of iron, you know.''

Jaime knew. Athlete's sheet, indeed.

This was no joke. The casket lid was not going to pop back; Pamela was not going to sit up and yell *gotcha*. That would have blown Pavel Drake's tubes, all right. On the other side of the hole, Pamela's father shook hands and kept a stiff upper. He might have been blowing smoke at some fund raiser. Jaime imagined his eyes, behind their tinted glass, stripping and ravishing her.

The burden of remembrance is a weighty thing, she knew now, intimidating enough to bow the shoulders of the spiritually weak. Responsibility to the dead often starts time bombs ticking within the survivors when they discover that death is not TV, not Disney, never easy or graceful or clean. Or temporary. Maybe Mickey was manufacturing his own brand of anguish right this moment. Jaime could not shove the Kipling poem "The Thousandth Man" from her mind, where it skip-repeated like a scratched record.

> *Nine hundred and ninety-nine depend*
> *On what the world sees in you,*
> *But the Thousandth Man will stand your friend*
> *With the whole round world agin you.*

And that goes double for girls, she thought. There were nine hundred and ninety-nine usurious fuckers, and more, afoot and breathing while Pamela was not. How could you be expected to stand against the world's indifferences and banal evils when the good guys kept dropping? No fair. And Pamela was becoming a larger part of her life every moment Jaime herself breathed. That dull void in her heart, the Pamela-sized hole that had been ripped in her, was the worst thing she could ever feel.

The hole filled by Pamela's casket was beginning to look more and more like a mass grave for all the good things they had shared. Four people had gone under today, not one. Jaime stepped backward, away from the loamy darkness of that pit, as though there was a risk of slipping in.

"I want to find Mickey," she said, "Now."

Jason shook his head. He was despondent now and had withdrawn to the point where he had not even noticed Jaime talking to herself—to Pamela—at graveside. "I have to go home," he said after a deep breath. "I have something to do."

It's hitting him, she thought. He was going to burst into tears if she didn't stop hanging onto him, if she did not leave him alone right now. And the more she thought about Mickey's truancy, the madder she got. She could do this by herself. "Well . . . fine. We'll link up later, yes?"

"Yeah. We'll all get together later."

He escorted her to her car and kissed her. It was like cold, damp fog on her lips. Like nothing.

Terrific—some moron was trying to pummel the front door right out of its rickety frame.

Mick's brain thumped right along. A caber had crash-landed on his skull. He shot to wakefulness muggy with sweat, his throat arid, his mouth clogged with a thick, dog-turd tang that had reached up and nailed his sinuses shut. He had come up from sleep too fast; his eyes had the bends. This was definitely the most cacklingly awful biorhythmic phase of his entire life. He *arrghed* to the corners of his studio apartment. The mambo beat between his head and the door just kept right on rocking.

The doorknob began rattling. Foot-shadows interrupted the clean crack of daylight separating the bottom of the door from its threshold.

"Coming!" he croaked, at his faceless tormentor. He rubbed his face, and his palm came away glistening with perspiration and oil. Falling asleep fully dressed had made him look like his own unmade bed. His hair was . . . awful. His stereo stylus, long since finished with side one of *Goodbye Yellow Brick Road,* skritched out a soft cadence. Mick had once bragged—to somebody or other—about his totally manual, belt-driven, smooth-as-lucite turntable with its twelve-pound professional deejay platter. Now a forty-dollar needle was grinding itself to diamond dust because he had passed out, and not even in the middle of a decent album. Whatever had inspired him to unsleeve the Elton John oldie was forgotten now, irrelevant.

Pound, thump, pound, skritch-skritch. It was not a sterling afternoon.

He yawned cavernously, smoothed back his hair, and struggled to look intelligent as he unbolted and opened up.

"*Christ*, Mickey, I've been beating on this goddamned thing for five minutes! Why aren't you answering your phone?''

The adrenaline jolt helped wake him up. The woman on his stoop was simply lovely. His brain raced to catalogue her assets and did not resist the list as it rolled up. Though cogent, he was still woozy and fantasy-inclined.

The gray suit-dress was strictly conservative chic. Short, peppy dark brown hair. Large-lensed glasses in spidery frames, more young-exec stuff. The eyes, the color of amber and brandied chocolate. She was sinfully tall, cut with confidence and regal bearing. Strong chin, small mouth, laugh lines. His eyes gave her the once-over. Twice. A . . .

''What the hell is *wrong* with you? Do I have a tarantula on my head?'' She rolled her eyes and began to push past him. ''Let me in—it's broiling out here.''

. . . a charming stranger indeed, Mick's romanticist brain concluded. But his body instinctively shifted to block intrusion into his home by a stranger, charming or less, and when they collided she dropped her shoulder bag.

''I'm sorry?'' he said, bending to retrieve. They nearly bonked heads. ''I mean, I beg your pardon? You're not a Jehovah's Witness or something . . . I hope?''

She yanked the bag free of him without thanks and gaped as though he had just asked her to suck his toes.

He shrugged. ''So what is it? Census bureau? Meter reader? Avon lady? What can I do for you, um . . . ?'' His eyebrows went up, urging her to reveal her identity. It was a good place to begin.

She stopped dead for only an instant, then shook her head with the fatefulness of a woman who must endure a thick-headed little brother. ''You picked a hell of a day to screw around with stupid jokes, love. It hasn't even been six hours. You going to tell me you forgot to set your alarm?'' Her anger was growing. Past the frank glare in her eyes, Mick could see the redness of some recent hurt.

He coughed out a commiserative laugh, which she did not share. "Uh . . . what are you talking about, Miss?"

"*Mickey!* What's the secret word today? Too much blow on our Fruit Loops this morning? Why are you being such an asshole?"

She tried to enter; he rebuffed her again.

"I'd really rather not let anyone in," he said. "My place is kind of a mess."

She looked upset, disoriented. "Your place is always a hog wallow, Mickey."

That was another thing, Mick thought, his pique kicking up from preheat to simmer. Where did this (admittedly gorgeous) nonentity get off calling him that? *Mick* was clipped, sharp, rock and roll, he liked it. *Mickey* preceded *mouse,* and he could live without either.

He overrode her, firming up. "Lady, I do *not* know what you're talking about. Honest. I do *not* know who you are. And I don't know if I'm as eager to talk to you as I was fifteen seconds ago."

He saw the change wash over her expression, and its speed caught him unprepared. He could sense the gooseflesh scaring up on her back, the snap chill of a suppressed shudder, so out of place in the midday heat. Her mouth unhinged, drifting open. She seemed to dwindle horribly, like a person trying to shrink against an unyielding wall.

"Oh . . . no," she whispered. Not to him.

He fought to lighten up, be boyish on short notice, to bring her back to where she had been seconds before, because her irritation was better to experience than her abrupt fear. He could hate himself later. "Hey, no, I—"

At the sound of his voice she began to edge back

along the narrow breezeway, as though she could see him transmogrifying into a drooling werewolf.

He shook his head and got pain. The woman on his stoop was crazy; next case. His concern was easily overwhelmed by the idea that this was more than a joke . . . it was an assault entrapment, or apartment filmflam, or other setup. Los Angeles was packed to the spires with predators that could look like this woman.

"Fine," he said, shutting the door. The bolt sprang to automatically.

He heard a muffled *no,* almost a cry of pain, and the futile thump of a small fist against the door. He ignored it, making for the bathroom and many aspirins. He was in no mood; he just wanted to lie down and go away for a while. His bones and muscles ached, empty of vitality. He felt like a train wreck.

After a while the woman, whoever she was, however she had gotten his name, gave up and went away for good.

Jaime tried to swallow hot tears and her throat knotted shut. Strangers gawked at her wet face from their own cars.

It was Mickey, Mickey Banks, he of the corduroy jacket and cowboy boots and athlete's sheet, who had just slammed his door in her face. His rejection, his wariness, his utter nonrecognition of her was frightening. It made her stomach cramp helplessly. His eyes held the same lost expression as Jason's had, at Pamela's gravesite. Jaime's hand tried to quiver; she gripped the wheel tighter.

Jason's machine had answered five times when Jaime ran out of payphone change. When she pulled up at his address, she saw exactly what she would see again on that evening's metro news.

The manner in which Jason Parrish had killed himself after Pamela Drake's funeral was reeled off in a hydrophobic torrent of babble by a TV newshound broadcasting from inside a fluttering yellow LAPD cordon. Jaime watched the slow zoom up to the wide-open main door and the equally predictable closeup of a body-bagged shape on a stretcher en route to the ambulance. It lolled.

Tomorrow the *Herald Examiner* would bid adieu to one of its own, with an even bigger wallow in the grisly Known Facts.

Jason Arthur Parrish, 31, was found dangling from his dining-room archway, his neck pulled long, face a deep indigo from cyanosis, eyes bloated and dry. His tongue had swollen to the size of a black hockey puck. The nylon cord that had strangled him had stretched as his corpse sagged, but the give did not matter. His feet still cleared the floor by ten inches.

There was a note, displayed prominently on an antique writing desk Pamela had helped him pick out at Poor Ruth's. The nylon cord had come from a camping trip to the Sierra Nevada range that life in retail had prevented Jaime from joining.

Mercifully, the only photo to be included in the paper would be a staff glossy three years old. The note would not be reproduced. Jaime already knew it was about nothing but Pamela.

Jason was gone. Mickey was gone. While Jaime had endured a nasal recitation of the Twenty-third Psalm by a hired minister with a game leg, Pavel Drake's hired movers had lain siege to Pamela's apartment. They received time-and-a-half for Sunday work, plus a fat tip for speed. By the time Pamela had filled the boxlike hole she would never leave, another box—a U-Haul storage locker much like a tomb itself—had been efficiently loaded with her possessions. The slickness of the arrangement would have offended Pamela, who would resent being so easily erased.

There was only one piece of Pamela left, and Jaime fled to it.

The anarchic untidiness of Jaime's clothes closet was a source of queer pride. With her promotion had come total whirlpool chaos in this one niche of her otherwise ordered living space; here was a guilty pleasure she could hold in common with Pamela. In the back of the closet (perhaps sucked back there as food by the forgotten and now-sentient blobs of polyester waiting in the darkness) was the Knudsen crate. In it were the letters, the snapshots, the physical residue of Pamela's passage through her life. It was more than enough to get drunk on.

The crate was the only piece of Pamela that Pavel Drake had not absorbed. There had to be a reason Jaime was permitted this one piece, and she found it, forgotten, buried in the back of the crate, Jaime thought of a Chinese box puzzle.

It was a fireproof Smythe document box, a steel rectangle in outdated industrial maroon, with a lock. Pamela had provided no key. Dimly, Jaime remembered being handed the box and being asked in a casual way to stash it.

Pamela's irresponsibility with minutiae was legendary. Jaime maintained a rolodex; Pamela had been known to write phone numbers in ink on the back of her hand. She only threw out the receipts she would later need. Jaime balanced her checkbook; Pamela's utilities usually avoided termination by scant hours. Clearly, more complex items like insurance—or wills, say—were scheduled for the turn of the century, because twenty-eight-year-olds should not have to worry about dying until later.

The incidents with Mickey, with Jason, had flooded Jaime with a sense of lost control, urgently accelerating. If her best friend Pamela had anything to say to her after her death, now was the time to hear it.

Breaking the Smythe box's lock with the blade of a

butcher knife was distasteful, akin to violation. A rape. Jaime wondered whether Pavel Drake's movers had broken into Jaime's apartment, similarly, to plunder.

The lid squeaked when she bent it back. Even if she had recalled the box earlier, she never would have considered peeking. Pamela had banked successfully on her trust. Jaime felt a pang of resentment at being so predictable.

Boxes within boxes. Suddenly this did not look so random, so unplanned, so Pamela.

The tear tracks were dry on her face. She lifted out long pages, legal sized, stapled to sky-blue stock backings, folded into oblongs and tucked into a vinyl folder. Her heart thudded and her breath pulled short. From Pamela of all people, could this be something for the record in black on white?

A handwritten note had been placed on top but had fallen to one side and gotten creased thanks to the box's rough ride. Jaime immediately recognized the distinctive paraph of her best friend's script:

Dear Jaime,
　　Please trust me when I say what your going to see here is real. I'm sorry you have to find out this way, but if your reading this than I'm probabbly dead. You know how I work, your my best friend. So maybe youll understand without bad explanations. Your the puzzle solver. I love you.
　　　　　　　　　　　　　　　　　Pamela.

It was Pamela, sure as hell. The horrific spelling and grammar were ironclad verification. New tears made a bid for escape but Jaime swallowed them down. The note had been rendered with a soft-tipped art pen, in purple, Pamela's favorite color. She favored such pens for all kinds of jotting and had thrown a fit when the manufacturer terminated them a couple of years back. The violet ink had already begun to fade.

You could not buy these pens anymore at any price. Like Pamela, they were part of the past now.

Jaime unsnapped the folder and counted three separate documents, each headed with the legend AGREEMENT in Gothic. The text nosedove straight away into legalese so dense that Jaime's eye rejected such unpalatably large glops. These were contracts. Her recognition of them scared her a bit—it was like Pamela sneaking into the paperwork she hustled daily at Sanger Harris.

The top one was drawn between PAMELA LYNN DRAKE and JAIME ANYA RALSTON. On the last page she saw Pamela's signature, again in florid purple ink.

In the adjacent blank, written with the same pen, Jaime found her own signature.

The contracts seemed to jump from her lap, to fan themselves across the floor. Her throat dried up and began to pulse achingly. She had never seen these papers before.

Nervously, she gathered them, checking the other two, fearing what she would see.

The second bore the name JASON ARTHUR PARRISH. Jason had been at the funeral, holding Jaime because there was no longer a Pamela to hold. The third contract was in the name of MICHAEL MARQUIS BANKS.

Known to his intimates as Mickey.

Her eyes hurt from scrutinizing the contracts. She squeezed them shut; tried to force more tears to come . . . and got nothing.

She sat rereading Pamela's postcard, the specific one from Chicago she had remembered earlier. It had waited for her in the crate. Her eyes drifted over it dryly. Here was Pamela's description of their cozy little foursome in the days before madness and funerals.

From the bedamned contracts to the postcard and back again she went . . . and her heart began to thud hard and fast. The love had been drained out, but there was still enough muscle remaining to give her whole body a sound jump at a sudden shock of inspiration.

The trendy pressure to have babies before thirty-five was nothing compared to the deadline with which she was now squared off. She raced back to her closet. An old Smith-Corona manual typewriter had been lost in there for at least as long as the Knudsen crate, and now she needed it as badly as air to breathe.

When she found it, she phoned Pavel Drake.

The silence on the line was adjudicatory, punctuated by the measured respiration of a self-important man, weighing trifles. Drake had delivered a terse reminder that any imposition less than twenty-four hours after his only child's funeral deserved nothing from him past an angry hang-up. Jaime had known he would not disconnect for two reasons.

Once she had rejected him. By making contact now, she was offering him another shot, an opportunity to salve his bruised ego. His was the type of mercenary business mind that would never forget any slight, no matter how trivial. Now he might make her crawl, or wait, or beg his help. Now he might do something so small as make her run the telephonic gauntlet to be granted the privilege of speaking with him.

More important, she mentioned the Smythe box—the single item that had eluded the neat dragnet of Pamela's life arranged by Drake's legal chickenhawks.

Beats of silence on the telephone can be exquisitely cruel. Drake wanted this acid quiet to slowly tear Jaime's heart out. He could not know that an hour ago she had run out of tears, and now her heart functioned only as a pump.

He instructed Jaime to ask for his table at That Obscure Object of Desire in half an hour. He called her *Miz Ralston* and made sure that he sounded properly put upon.

Before she flew out the door, she tried one last time

to call Mickey. Or Mick. His line was already out of service.

Charlene the waitress faded, butt switching saucily to let Pavel Drake know she was still on call. Jaime took a tentative sip of her white wine, watching as the frost of condensation filled in her lip prints and restored uniformity to the surface of the glass. Drake had just made his snide remark about scams and polish and *crust* . . . whatever the hell that meant.

"You want me to sign this," he said. His voice was low, disbelieving, calculatedly ugly.

"You have Pamela's power of attorney," Jaime said. "She can't sign it."

He caught her off guard by evidencing interest in her explanation. It was a trick of executive strategy—the lull before the kicker—but Jaime knew it. She had seen the momentary glint in his eyes. "Now . . . you're trying to say that Pamela . . . made up her friends? Imaginary friends, like little kids have?"

"She *conceptualized* her ideal friends. Then she created pacts, promises of duties including every trait from loyalty to good housekeeping, and inscribed them with pseudonyms. See? They're even notarized. I don't have to remind you how imaginative she was."

No, that was the thing Drake had disliked most about his daughter. It had prevented her from becoming like him and following his corporate footprint trail. That would have been an alternative version of Pamela . . . and what had become of that possibility, Jaime now realized with abrupt horror. It was spelled out in one of the clauses on the contract headed JAIME ANYA RALSTON, because there is a fragment of every daughter that wants to please Daddy. Even if Daddy is a philistine, even if the daughter is intractably rebellious.

"Pamela is dead. That hurts me more than I can say, Mr. Drake. I'm sure it hurts you, too, and people tend to lash out when they're in pain."

Again she spotted what might have been a ghostly wisp of human feeling, trapped in the darkness of his eyes, quickly engulfed. "Yes," he said, lifting his drink, then replacing it unsipped as though thinking better of the action. His stiff silence, just now, was a license for her to continue.

"If the contracts are bona fide, then my whole life history came out of Pamela's head. It's a great system—with one flaw. There is no provision for the contractor's death. She didn't factor it in; how many people under thirty bother with wills? But now that she's gone, the obligations of the contractees are discharged. Jason is dead. Mickey is gone . . . or changed, I don't know. Either way he's not Mickey anymore. I was on the scene before either of them. Maybe that's how I lasted long enough to talk to you now."

Drake looked the page in his hand up and down one more time. It did not seem to surprise him.

"That's a new contract," said Jaime. "It supersedes Pamela's and grants me an existence independent of hers. It's simply worded to assure you I'm trying to gain nothing through trickery. A simple business proposition, Mr. Drake. You sign, and I hand over Pamela's filebox, plus all her letters to me. A whole aspect of her you didn't see and never owned. No strings. All I get out of it is my own life, and I never bother you again."

He shifted his glass on the black tabletop like a chess piece. He could press a legal claim to the contents of the Smythe box, but the only thing in it had been the contracts. He rested the page Jaime had typed on the table. It took up nearly half the dry area. "You realize I'm under no obligation to indulge this sort of . . . behavior."

She leaned forward in entreaty. "Okay, so I'm as crazy as a firefly in a meths bottle. What's wrong with humoring me if you get something you want?"

Drake laughed. It was a harsh sound, like a cough. "I win either way. With a story like you've just told me, if you bother me again I can have you detained. If I endorse this fantasy fiction you've laid before me, you'll leave me alone. And if I don't—according to you—you'll vanish anyway, like the other two." He could taste the blood. "I think you've prepared for everything in this tactless scenario *except* for your bluff being called."

He produced a pen from a breast pocket and held it before her, like a magician preparing to prestidigitate. Jamie's heart went *bang*.

"I'll sign. But you must do something for me in return." He slid a brass-colored metal object across the slate tabletop. "Let's find out just how deeply you believe your own story, Ms. Ralston."

It was a hotel key embossed with a room number.

"Everyone gets what they want," he said.

The room seemed to plunge vertiginously. In one hideously elongated instant, she flashed back to the crude scene at Pamela's birthday party and realized that in some quarters the war never stopped, ever. The urge toward vengeance had swelled in both of them, poisonously heavy, dense as a tumor. That was how Pamela's letters had become her trump card. Let Drake win them and find out what his daughter *really* thought of him.

His angle of attack was clear. Here was a chance to slap her down, hard and humiliatingly, to neutralize her through collusion. His ejaculate could scorch away the tough fiber of her determination, which, in a way, he had been responsible for creating by founding Pamela's tortuous childhood—the upbringing that made her crave her imaginary allies just strongly enough.

Jaime saw the hotel key as a chance to spit in Pavel Drake's face, for Pamela, for herself. Payback time for all the grief and rotten karma. All the gesture would cost her was her existence.

I love you, Pamela, she thought bitterly, as her mind raced toward the hard truth of her situation. The end it reached was not pleasant to acknowledge.

I love you and I want to do right by you. But I'm also terrified. I want to live very much. Would you call this a betrayal? Or common survival sense? If you would forgive me this, why didn't I tell you about Jason that once? And if you won't forgive me . . . is there anything I could ever do that . . .

Her soul was crippled, and odious, and it did what it had to. "Sign," she said, taking the key, already thinking that the true pain would be brief.

"In due time." His smile was like a pleat in his face. "Excuse me for just a moment." He was all the smooth mercenary now. He had a fast colloquy with Charlene, and pointed toward Jaime. Then he disappeared into the neon murk near the restrooms. There was probably a meeting to cancel.

In Jaime's bag was Pamela's contract. She'd read it a thousand times today, and soon she might burn this mortgage on her life. Tucked into a fold of the document was the postcard, from which she hoped to draw strength. She examined both while Drake was gone. When she saw her signature side by side with Pamela's on the contract's final page, a solitary tear leaked from her eye. Just one. It burned coming out, a generous, salty reaffirmation of her own being. It struck the page and skidded through the middle of her name. The faded purple ink blotted and ran.

You could not buy these pens anymore, she remembered. They stopped making them. Pamela had gotten livid.

Charlene checked in at the bar and glided back to Drake's table just as a raucous stripper's hymn began to bump and grind out of the Object's migraine-sized PA system. She smiled at what she saw. Pavel Drake's latest Bambi had fled back to the forest, forgetting her purse and leaving behind a hotel key, an untouched drink, and a scatter of papers. With schooled motions Charlene swept up the bag and stuffed the papers into it. It was time for her to make a discreet trip to the Ladies. The postcard was the last item in. It featured a timed-exposure of Chicago's Lake Shore Drive at night. It would get chucked into the Object's dumpster along with the other junk just as soon as the wallet was vacuumed of cash and plastic.

Charlene cut loose a snort of disgust that caused her bare tits to bob. That girl, that amateur, had been young enough to be Drake's *daughter*, for christsake.

Dear Jamie . . .

Phone not in yet but plenty of time to write as I got here just in time for the blizards. In re our "what do I want from my friends" disc earlier I gave it some thot and here it is, gameshow style: (1) I'd want a person who'd *always* be my friend and *never* forget me and *always* remember the right dates and places, which I'm lousy at. (2) A handsome-ass lover who loved me enough to die for me (oh romantic notion) . . . or at least say so. (3) A buddy whose more organized than me, but who thinks like me—someone I could COUNT ON no matter what to take care of the odds and ends I allways forget & am too sloppy to finish, or something.

Somebody to be there for me, somebody JUST LIKE YOU, doo-dah, doo-dah.

Its freezing here. Windy City, big dealski. Outta space, stay tuned for next card. Miss you terribly and love you lots. STAY WARM, and XOXOXOXOX

Love,
Pamela.

THE FALLING MAN

In the Major Arcana of the Tarot there exists an almost forgotten twenty-third card.

The known cards are called "keys," and are said to correspond with each of the Paths of Life, or to the twenty-two letters of the Hebrew alphabet. The Fool has no number; it is the card that melds the ends of the circle of twenty-one. The Fool is generally depicted as an inexperienced youth about to step off the edge of a precipice, denoting the passage into maturity and the need to choose a philosophy—to gain wisdom or embrace the bliss of ignorance.

The forgotten card is The Falling Man. It stands outside the unending circle formed by the cards of the Major Arcana. It is a wild card, a skeleton "key." Its subject is the victim of irresistible forces of chaos, caprice, or circumstance. Reversed, it denotes concealed manipulation and too much control.

Catching The Falling Man in your Tarot throw is like having your car totaled by an uninsured illegal alien. It is the one card that forces readers to dissemble, and soften their evaluations. Their eyes would avert, because the eyes cannot lie and make things better.

So, as with all unresolvable irritants, The Falling Man has been swept under the rug. But it is as unfailing a force as the gravity it depicts, and its influence persists

*in defiance of historical subterfuge, touching each of
us to this day.*

The Rolodex card was yellow at the borders with
age, and the little man thumbed it up just as the grandfather clock in his office bonged out midnight in sour
brass tones.

He released a tiny *pah* noise of disgust and hoisted
himself from his desk chair, which creaked as his spat-
ted high-button shoes slapped the floor. Standing, he
was no taller than he had been while sitting. He fought
his way over to the clock, battling the sheer clutter of
the claustrophobic eyrie in which he had secreted himself. Old habits of residence were difficult to change.
His progress across the rathole cubicle kicked up a
wake of dust, and made a legion of tiny insects inter-
rupt their literary dining to scatter. Antiques and gee-
gaws packed the room, and the grandfather clock
presided over the darkest corner like an ancient idol.
Both the clock and the railroad watch the little man
wore on a fob read nine-thirty.

He dealt the side of the clock a savage kick that
made the chimes within clatter rudely. Loose gears
rattled and a terrified mouse fled the premises. Then
the mid-range tubular gong sounded once—the half-
hour toll.

The little man wore a gray pinstriped suit with tails,
a silken vest, and an ascot. His brushed top hat hung
on a peg overlooking the desk, and was the sole part
of the ensemble not spattered in white plaster dust.
The Reverend Charles Dodgson might have asked the
little man to pose on the spot.

Along the obstacle course leading back to the desk,
the little man paused to peer out a congested, porthole-
like window. The entire city of Los Angeles stretched
away below, a quilt of light chasing the horizon in
every direction. The view was one of the reasons he

had maintained this office, away from the eyes of the world, for so long.

"M-hm. Yes, indeed." The little man had developed the habit of cataloging things to himself in a mumbled undertone. It was a personal monologue with an audience of one. "Aahh." The urban view replenished him. Perhaps it was the thought of all those electric lights, and all the lives upon which they shone.

Back at the desk, he glanced at the foxed Rolodex card, then let it drop to the blotter. He wrested open a persistently sticking drawer and rummaged. To the light he lifted a delicate masque of blue glass. Attached near the right eye was a slender, wand-like stick, for holding the masque to one's face. Its features were feminine; its eyes, blank holes deftly cut in the glass.

"Very good," the little man said to himself.

As he sat to resume work, he switched on a refrigerator-sized Victrola and hummed along with Bruce Springsteen. Because he was doing what he was best at, he smiled pleasantly as he worked.

At the last possible moment, Peter Deutsch stepped back from the waiting elevator doors and let the car go up empty. He took the stairs. His entire day had been spent in boxes just like the elevator of his apartment building; chrome and glass cells that hummed and conveyed him from one meeting to the next, with black commas of ground-out cigarette butts punctuating the utility tile of their floors. It was seven floors up and he was wrung out, but Peter wanted to walk.

The stairwell was another box, an enclosure of steel and stone, a clean, well-lighted place. *Thank you, Papa Hemingway.* A box just like all the conference rooms in the Studio City bowl, where it was rumored the majors constructed their monoliths with movable walls, so that hapless employees could discover their need for fresh jobs by clocking in to offices that had become blank walls. They did not just change the names on the doors; they dispensed with entire rooms, as easily as twisting a new face onto a Rubik's Cube.

Peter had not lost his job, but his patience was waving good-bye. He had spent—no, *invested*—a shitter of a day batting his skull against the concrete stupidity of TV moguls and their yes-persons. Preproduction arguments over the TV-movie *Sinner* had been raging for eight weeks; the script was in its ninth rewrite. Peter could only compare the erosion of his soul to spending a year in court. His sanity was being swiped a chip at a time. His creativity had retreated, shrieking, behind a massive writer's block. Today *Sinner* had been passed on to the fifth in a series of pinch hitters, not counting the husband-and-wife team who had conceived the original script and would now get a "story by" credit. Peter was still to direct. Wasn't that what everyone in Hollywood supposedly *really* wanted—to direct?

Like everyone else embroiled in *Sinner* from the publicity flacks on up, Peter was trapped, hemmed in by contract boilerplate, committed to work in which he had, today, lost the last vestiges of interest. "A sizzling look at the real power plays in the boardrooms and bedrooms of high finance." *Sinner* was glitz-encrusted bullshit from head to toe. All jiggle and soap and lies, with all the right advertisers to buttress that all-important American consumer ethic. *Sinner* perpetuated the dumb myth that if you weren't wealthy and wasteful and wanton, you were just *nobody*, dahling.

Peter had spent the day being poisoned by that mind-set, and no purgatives offered themselves as he plodded upward. The climb was the only way he could *ascend* on a day like this. He pushed out self-pity and began brewing a full pot of anger. He should have taken the goddamned elevator.

Thirteen steps. Turn. Thirteen more. Tucked into

his armpit was the junk mail he had pried from the gangbox downstairs. On the fourth-floor landing he let his leather brief drop to the waffled metal and paused to squint at what the stack had to offer. The stairwell floods afforded harsh light. The abundance of trash— YOU MAY HAVE ALREADY WON $50,000!!— was balanced by the sinking certainty that another twenty-four hours had just passed without a peep from Damon about the independent-feature backing he was busy scaring up in Vancouver. Another day without the Mailgram or phone call that would permit Peter to chuck *Sinner* with what the good old Romans termed the *digitus obscenus*. On Damon Fletcher's say-so Peter would be packed and northbound to ''do us some art.'' It was a joke. *Objet d'Art* was the title of the project; the screenplay collaboration that had wrapped both men up in the embrace of true love. If the money came through and the picture got made, there was no doubt that a distributor would rail at the fartsy title and change it to *Art Object*, or maybe *Lewd Mating Positions*. The magic word was *saleable*. Just now, the challenge was creating the film, not what to call it when it was whole.

But the wonderful world of directors' hats held no laughter for Peter today. He thumbed desultorily through the balance of the mail stack.

He would have ignored the folded page as a shopping center flyer if he hadn't spied the red wax seal holding the page ends together in an envelope shape. Then he registered the weight, the quality of the thick, linen-grain stationery. There was no Addressograph label, no stamp. It had been inserted into the box apart from the mail delivery. Peter gave it his full attention for another thirteen steps.

The icon embossed into the cold wax was unfamiliar to Peter. At a glance it appeared to be a woodcut outline of a human figure, arms extended, apparently in flight. He used his thumbnail to pry the seal away without breaking it. He shifted the briefcase to his

other hand and halted on the stairs in order to tilt the
page to the light to read the precise black script.

It was a poem, to him.

He recognized the paraph of Alea's signature before
he was a third of the way through the verse, and his
heart began revving. She had come back. Serious
adrenaline began to punch through his system, making
him giddy in a hurry. He smiled, and then bounded
up the remaining tiers of metal stairs, his chance at
fifty thousand dollars fluttering into the narrow, dark
abyss between the flights.

As he opened the door his eyes were stung. So was
his mind. She knew of his fondness for candles. At
least a hundred were very carefully burning in his living room. Still buzzing from the stairway fluorescents,
his eyes took in meager golden light. There was just
enough to see his way by; no more.

He knew better than to call out her name. A trail
had been left.

He dropped his jacket into the darkness where he
knew a table to be; he grimaced as he heard it slide
off and meet the floor. A marble pedestal had been
deprived of its Kleinst nude sculpture and repositioned
in the front door's sightline, halfway across the sunken
circle of the living room. On it were a tall yellow taper, burning in a pewter holder, a crystal flute of what
he took to be Mumms 1979 Rene Lalou from past experience, and a note, on the same linen paper, folded
into a pup-tent shape. Peter became aware from the
pain in his cheeks that he was grinning like a fool.

Finish Glass before leaving Table.
Remove coat, shoes, socks. Tie
optional. Proceed to Kitchen.

On the butcher block table in the kitchen were an
identical candle, glass, and note. He felt less nervous

about all the burning candles when he saw, close up, the care that had been taken to cup them and provide for wax drainage. All his tinfoil had been used up. While the first glassful of bubbly fizzed coldly away in his stomach, he lifted and sipped the second. By the time the second was down, the first was speeding to his head. No dinner. Too late now, and who cared? He unfolded the next note.

> Bring uncracked Bottles from Fridge.
> Proceed to Hall.

By now Peter's fear of hidden fire inspectors had mysteriously evaporated. His coatrack had been moved to the hallway, and on it hung his chocolate-colored bathrobe. His fingers tingled when he tipped the third glass to his mouth. A very pointed trail of evenly spaced candles lit the path to his bedroom.

> If you are still wearing Clothes,
> please discard them on the Rack
> provided. Finish Glass and proceed
> at once to the Final Room.

The door lay ajar by three tantalizing inches. His glass in one hand and the two champagne bottles in the other, he nudged the door open with his knee. The bed was a gigantic four-poster job in waxed ebony. Dark sheets. No silk or satin crap; that was strictly for the oilier passion-pit mentality. The corners of the room were unfathomably dark. Several strategic candles threw almost imperceptible highlights.

The big bed was empty.

He was two paces into the room when she pounced from behind, whirling him around into a kiss so thorough that both the bottles and the empty flute hit the carpet. She gathered him into her arms, working at him, wanting him so hard that she had to hold him in place to keep him from falling. They stayed that way for a long time. Then she broke away and pulled back just far enough to let him see her hold a finger to her lips before she retrieved the wine and drew him closer to the bed. Talk, its questions and details and problems, was for later.

Tired? He could feel electricity crackling from the tips of his fingers, his toes. . . .

They did not hurry, like eager but inept children. They had time, and their hunger did the rest. Elsewhere, beyond their hearing, was the studied chuckle of a little old man.

"I think I'm falling in love with you."

That was the last thing she had said to him, the last time they had made love, five months ago, the night before she had vanished with no preamble and no heartrending but oh-so-predictable note. Once he had tried to nail her down on who she really was, what she really did for her living, she evanesced out of his life. The days had elapsed one slow century of hurt at a time, long enough for Peter to conclude that the dormant emotions she had kicked back to life in him were just the usual Peter Deutsch overreaction. Hollywood hyperbole. That decided, he had to then deny the *rightness* of the things she had told him, the unspoken validity of the small, telling things she did for him. He had to abort the changes and resonances begun within himself. Opening up—to anybody—was contrary to his will, and when he noticed his own willing vulnerability, he resisted.

His ex-wife Kathryn had cared not at all for such subtleties of temperament; to him, it was a costly emotional effort; to her, it was too little too goddamned late. She did not wish to entertain Peter's feeble tries at dropping his shields. Alea honestly wanted to help. She nurtured, never coaxing. It was proof that

she was different, and this scared him. To Peter it was
a natural fear, and she had anticipated this, and come
prepared to defang it. Peter would have dismissed such
reassurances from anyone else, including Kathryn, as
saccharine. In the real world no one bothered to help
the way Alea did. That final night, Peter had told her
he loved her; the words were a giant step for him.
Hours later she was gone, and he reminded himself of
another of his old personal rules: You only sabotage
the relationships that are the most important to you.
Then came the day sunk in poisonous meditation, the
mental scourging. The bitterness returned and settled
in for a long stay. His insectile plates of emotional
armor began their inevitable recrystallization. Then
came *Sinner*.

At her note, he had come running. There was still
that much left.

She moved above him in a slow and sinuous way
that nibbled his control down to nothing. Her hair, in
a brisk chop, made bangs, framed her face, and hid
her eyes. He hauled in a deep breath as tremors bucked
him, and grasped her rolling hips. The last thing he
saw before he shut his own eyes was her smile, the
lower lip nibbed between her teeth. Maddening sounds
started somewhere deep inside her; furry little noises
of pleasure issuing from the core of the diaphragm and
flowing up and out like dark wine. They were as unique
as her scent, her taste, her movements. She knew what
she was doing. And she knew just how to do Peter
Deutsch.

They had only argued once. It had been a disagree-
ment manufactured by Peter (who had been known to
defend the faulty side of a question merely to gratify
his debate Imp—more fallout from the competitive
mind-set). The topic was long lost; what Peter would
always remember was the way it had concluded. When
it had become hopeless and repetitive, she had said,
''Peter, you're wrong, you know it, and I am going to

crown you with an ashtray . . . if you don't start making love to me in the next sixty seconds.''

That had knocked his pins out, all right. If he could train a film crew to perform with the unerring sense of timing Alea exploited so casually in her speech, he would be in the cockpit of the smoothest-running, most envied machine in the industry.

Alea had manifested shortly after the shipwreck of Peter's marriage. Mrs. Kathryn Deutsch had moved on to become a power broker in Malibu real estate. Dissolution was the mere breaking of a contract; SOP in Hollywood. You broke one pact to ink another, better one. Peter walled himself up behind twenty-hour workdays, not sleeping so much as lapsing into an exhausted coma close to predawn. One day he jolted awake, sheened in panic sweat, as though surfacing from an unsavory nightmare. His eyes opened and he found himself surrounded by *acquaintances* instead of friends, manipulators in the chairs of allies, and vampires leering from behind the lies that had admitted them into his bed, his Day Timer, his life.

The albatrosses pecked at his eyes. There was no one to cling to and no place to flee.

Then, Alea. *Timing.* Clichés had never applied to his life before.

Being with her now brought a lunatic sensation of effervescent optimism. The moguls in their steel boxes became a straw threat, insubstantial, unreal. Fatigue ran away and was supplanted by vigor. Being inside of her solved his problems, made him feel . . .

Safe.

He gasped when he felt her muscles lock him up down there, almost as an expression of his very thoughts. He was staying.

It was against logic, of course, but he had penetrated her in a way that surpassed the physical juxtapositions of mere fucking. Sunk into her, impossibly secure, his limbs and brain charged themselves with psychic strength from the lode she offered. Until it was his turn.

He pushed himself up and kept hold of her hips, pulling her aboard his lap. She grabbed his shoulders to lift herself, and began to drive herself onto him, the gradual increase in sensitivity to friction making her cry out, as though fighting against the new climax. He felt every contraction along with the lush pulse of her blood. She fell back without resistance, one of her throaty, quiet laughs expelling from her lips, and he stayed with her. One more thrust into that loving grip was all it took to completely divorce him from rational thought.

The shorter candle stubs began to wink out in the way dead suns, far away, extinguish themselves and become nonexistent in a second.

The dwarf selected a spatulate blade and carefully planed blood-colored clay from the monster's right shoulder.

Strewn about the litter of the studio were current issues of *Cosmopolitan*, *Self*, *Working Woman*, *Mademoiselle* and more, all open to advertisements featuring male models. Here were the lions that women-conscious sponsors chose to sell their products to the feminine half of the population. Studly-yet-sensitive. Wild-but-secure. Artistic-yet-upwardly mobile. To the monster, the dwarf gave the nose of one, the cruel-but-kissable lips of another, the brush cut of a third. He paged from one glossy spread to another until he located perfect toes. He needed muscular-but-not-steroidal pecs and triceps. The easiest item to scare up was a great butt.

On no page could the dwarf find worthwhile eyes. All were metallic, dead, detached. Billboard entrepreneurs favored that uncaring look. The dwarf's artistic sensibilities were abraded; he gazed into the robot eyes

of these thoroughbred fashion plates and felt all men
objectified.

As he carved, he hummed, taking his time, spacing
out his snifters of Napoleon brandy to make the last
bottle stretch to the conclusion of this current com-
mission. His specially mixed medium was cool and
pliable, receptive to the even strokes of the blade. He
smoothed rough patches with spit and a gentle finger.
Each caress nudged the monster closer to his visuali-
zation; each touch of those cigar-stub fingers brimmed
not only with schooled sculpting talent, but with genuine love. Soft curlicues of clay rimmed the worktable
and stuck to the leather soles of the dwarf's shoes.
More than once he leapt onto the table to loom over
his creation, rubbing flaws to sleekness, his touch
leaving heat trails. The living molding the inanimate,
delighting in the friction of contouring the common
into something extraordinary. He gave the mouth a
succulent downward turn. He made both nostrils exactly the same size and shape—that was a detail you
never found in real people, one even the most percep-
tive would fail to notice.

M. Rogoff would notice, and applaud his audacity.

The dwarf scooped a handful of fresh clay from the
pail and added it to the monster's penis, kneading it
to the proper proportion. On a whim he spit some
brandy into it. He decided against omitting the fore-
skin.

When the brandy flask was down to the depth of a
finger, there remained the riddle of what to do about
the monster's eyes. All options seemed cold and predictable. The diminutive sculptor laid down his tools
before he attempted too much, and messed up what
perfection he had already wrought.

He blew his nose loudly on his denim apron and
rinsed his hands in a tub sink installed low to the floor.
The arrangement of the studio, with its body on the
slab, held the ghostly overtones of an autopsy theatre.

He used a potter's cut-off needle to pry clay from beneath his nails, and felt a perverse urge to snap a few Polaroids of his new work. The terms of his verbal contract forbade a visual record. M. Rogoff's instructions were as precise as ever, and from experience the dwarf knew them to be well-founded. Contracts such as these were best honored.

Perhaps more brandy might lubricate the artistic faculties, he thought with a sly grin. But when he fished into one capacious trouser pocket, all he brought up was a noisy bunch of small change.

At first his eyes dismissed the pair of bright, newly minted copper pennies. Then his attention shot back to target them. They were pristine, lacking scratches or tarnish; they released a musical jingle when he tossed them about in his small palm, contemplating. His heartbeat sped up, and he wondered if the great genius M. Toulouse-Lautrec had ever felt similarly flushed with joy at such a lightning stroke of inspiration!

Humming once more, he dashed the last of the brandy into his glass, and returned to the worktable. He would be able to finish tonight. Then he could contact M. Rogoff.

This was shaping into grand sport indeed.

Peter wanted to hold her hair in his teeth. He embraced her with his arms, his legs, tactile evidence of how long he had starved, how badly he needed someone. He clung. Alea slept.

It had not been an endurance run or point-scoring session. Peter was well-versed in the dance steps of the sexual-politic superstructure of this town, and if need be he could play that in-and-out game with the best. This wasn't that. The points emphasized by their lovemaking struck him as healthy ones.

He remembered what he had labeled her when he first saw her.

The theme of the classic Hollywood party is Business Is Pleasure. The talented and monied are shoved into elbow-rubbing distance; the mechanism is greased with expensive eats, lots of free alcohol, controlled substances, and the usual catalog of incentives. Peter thought of a chess match with all the players in seedy rented tuxes; the pawns in the game were the hookers, the coke, the prurient come-on to sign one's name. Self-important introductions were made between future bedfellows . . . amid future bedmates.

Peter had reported for duty at Damon Fletcher's insistence. *Slap on your happy mask,* Damon repeated all the time. *It never hurts to meet the execs.* He relished thrusting, parrying, coercing. The lies he ran past producer-types slid right off his carapace. Peter had felt conscripted; his visibility would buttress Damon's huckstering. Tonight Peter did not feel like a player. He knew he would suffer this soiree and probably not even get to hang out with Damon all that much. Damon never let his own moves dirty his psyche—to him, it was lying to liars, stealing from thieves. Peter always wanted to bathe afterward. But he let himself be badgered into attending. That was how badly he wanted to make *Objet D'Art* with his fast friend.

All they needed was . . . well, it was obvious, or Peter never would have rung the doorbell.

The clockwork ground into motion and by one a.m. was clanking purposefully along like a wind-up Godzilla toy. Peter smiled at strangers and powered down straight bourbon, instantly gaining an axe-murder of a headache. At Damon's bidding he bared his teeth and shook the proper hands. When Damon was swallowed by the hurly-burly of happy-hour negotiations, Peter stayed behind, a marionette with clipped strings. It was for the best. His bullshit allergy was raging tonight, and he knew he would only muddy whatever pond he stepped into.

He retreated to the far end of a vast flagstone patio, where he could be alone with the rainbow brilliance of Los Angeles spread out below him. He felt pleased with himself in that fatalistic, brink-hovering way that comes from overwork, plus seeing the kitchen help pour dishwater scotch into Chivas jugs. He sat down. Tonight, he just did not have the energy to do it . . .

Alea shifted in his grasp with a groan, twisting half-way around in the bed. He held the palm of her hand to his lips. Kissed. The hand caressed his face, dropped to his chest, and snaked the rest of the way down. He stiffened instantly at her touch.

. . . And so he stared sourly into his glass. No answers there. He abandoned it on the low brick wall without sipping further. Letting the faraway light defocus before him was more comforting.

Nobody introduced her. She was just *there.*

"Drink this."

He looked up at her voice but did not really see her. He passively accepted a delicate glass of what looked like sauterne, because it was extended toward him.

Oh christ, I've been made. He could not keep the hostile resignation from his voice. "Start anytime, honey." He tossed a mocking toast in her direction with the wineglass.

"No. You're wrong." She let silence hang for a few moments. Peter was surprised that she did not launch immediately into a spiel. She sat near him on the brick wall, and watched him, until *he* spoke.

"You'll forgive my vast repertoire of social *gaffes,*" he said gruffly, not caring if she did. He still had not seen her. He kept his eyes on the tree line below the patio. "I am engaged in the only pastimes that give me any pleasure right now. That is to say, getting squiffed and pissing on total strangers."

Another pause of what could have been a minute. Then: "Self-pity is a deadly kind of luxury. You're slopping it all over the place. It's coming off you in waves, you know.''

''Mm. I'm overdoing it. It's like all the dope in town—not what it's cracked up to be.'' The yellow wine was crisp, and very cold, and not a sauterne at all. Peter's palate was at a loss for identification.

''You can talk,'' she encouraged.

He thought he also heard *you've been wanting to talk for a long time*, but it did not come out of her mouth. The comeback that shot up from his mental shuck file ran: *Oh, a hooker psychiatrist; that's a new twist, you should pardon the pun.* His gut cancelled it. The back of his throat suddenly ached with the need to put the payload of acid in his mind somewhere else. She was a stranger. She had asked for it. If puke got on her when it erupted it was her own damned fault. That's what it came down to: emotional vomit.

The wineglass was in his hands. He gazed at some infinity point beyond, in the darkness. He spoke not to the woman but to her voice. He was stark sober now, and his own voice was a deadly monotone. The forces etching his life emerged with a succinct kind of violence, like the confession of an utterly relaxed serial killer: *You see I thought the solution to all my problems was to use myself up faster and when that failed I decided a slow lingering death was better than a short, sharp shock, and so commenced the erosion that kills everyone here, when your sanity dribbles away a dram at a time until you're empty, babe, you can't get a hard-on at thirty-five, or groceries without three pieces of ID, and the traffic cops aren't kidding when they pull you over, and the stench of petrochemicals and madness permeates your clothes, and you have to keep you fingernails manicure-clean because otherwise you'll see the dead tissue hiding there, the residue of all the faceless people you fucked over to get ahead, and you think of all the claws that have* YOUR *blood dried beneath them, and you dwell on this*

*psychotic paranoid craziness until everything even the
ragpickers and shopping-cart ladies haunting the Boulevard, reminds you of how berserk this lunatic hostel
is, they call this living, and your brain builds its own
padded cell, hurling up high walls to trap you inside
and keep you apart from the predators who suck at
your life, your needs, until you become a brain-dead
paycheck junkie, until you can't care anymore, until
you spend an entire year in court because your soon-
to-be ex-wife wants to impress her new sex toy, the
attorney, until you gladly grind out bilge designed to
anesthetize hausfraus and their blue-collar hubbies out
there in Television Land, until you walk like a robot
to stupid social jousts like this one, slapping on a
death-mask grin for the neo-bohos and airheads and
thrill addicts and people who've become walking
ghosts, dead without realizing it, because . . .*

Because.

She finished for him once he was tapped out. "Because you can't run anywhere else. Because with all
the options available to someone like you, there is still
no place to run. Except in circles."

"Social circles," he said with a bitter little smile.

She brought him another glass of yellow wine. A
very peculiar sort of buzz was coming on; he felt weak,
drained, yet purged and somehow more clearheaded
than before. He was suddenly in debt to this woman
he had not acknowledged with his eyes. He was em-
barrassed. With Kathryn, he could never find words
like these, or get past his chagrin at actually voicing
them. It wasn't part of the deal, the contract. If you
ever talked of such things, the razors came out. People
rolled their eyes and pointed and never caught wind;
before you knew it you were shunned, ostracized,
worse than dead.

When he accepted the second glass, he looked up
and began, a trifle too offhandedly, "Look, uh . . . I
usually don't. . . ."

He saw her, for the first time truly *saw* her, and his heart and stomach seemed to swap positions with a *thud*.

"Don't apologize," she said. "Don't back off. You've just been as honest with yourself as you have with me. How does it feel? Better than pity?"

His head swam. Had all the booze slid home at once? With a silly kind of awe he asked, "Are you a—what do they call it—an empath?"

"No." Even her voice was hypnotic.

Peter's arm still hung in midair, holding the glass. She was *so* . . .

"My name is Alea. Now you relax and I'll talk awhile."

Peter always remembered that, too.

Both bottles of champagne lay dead on the floor, the two fingerprinty glasses shot down alongside them. Alea did not awaken so much as trade some of her sleepiness for some of Peter's consciousness. This time it was she who imprisoned him in her arms and legs, grinding with an almost desperate fervor. A wholly unanticipated orgasm picked him up and shook him. She could bring him back as many times as she wanted. And as they fell exhaustedly horizontal, she spoke to him in that low and musical whisper his mind knew so well.

"Welcome home."

In a sense Peter was the one who had gone away. It did not need to be said.

That was how it all began, or rather, resumed. Over the next two weeks Peter Deutsch gradually realized that the alien landscape he explored with Alea was a place he had heard so much propaganda about in his lifetime. He'd thought it a myth and never taken it seriously. Myths were inapplicable to his life. Like clichés.

"Love? I haven't the dimmest notion of what love is," he told her. "Everybody talks about it but nobody *does* anything. . . ."

"You're wrong. You know a lot about it."

"Yes?"

"You know what it's *not*, from experience." Her eyes were a tawny fulvous color, with black-ringed irises shot through with mellow flecks of amber, much like the aptly-named tigereye. They always met his directly. "From what I've seen, you've got a good grasp of the theory."

"What are you talking about?" He shook his head with a little-boy grin. Twice he had tried to defuse the subject by being funny; twice she had deflected him.

"You love rather than *saying* you love. Beware of people who need to hear the words all the time. You love me with your speech, with the things you do, with the way your eyes love me, all the time. You make love to me even when you're not making love to me."

"Gee, thanks. Subtlety was always my strong suit." He felt a faint irritation at being so obviously exposed. But it was true—he thought about her while working, while driving, upon waking, constantly, pleasantly . . . perhaps a bit obsessively?

Certainly some possessiveness might be permitted in his case, if he kept it to himself. She was fascinatingly enigmatic. She told him things about himself that were unnerving because they were so dead-on and cut around so much sweet, meaningless badinage. A misty-eyed portrait she was *not*. Yet she could exude vulnerability while remaining aloof; she could be direct and artfully ethereal at the same time. Sometimes her sheer control made him feel like an unruly adolescent. It was not so much his ineptitude as her mystique—as though she was capable of instructing her pheromones specifically where to go, and what to do.

Alea, simply, seemed more comfortable with the idea of love. Peter had always considered it beyond his reach, *de facto* . . . which was how their conversation had drifted around to it in the first place.

Kathryn had dismissed Peter as a man whose need for a psychological aspirin could always be solved by a bed-slamming, blindingly good fuck. Damon, on the other hand, had always suspected there might be room in Peter's life for another human being. But after Damon had met Kathryn, he decided that capacity for friendship would never get a chance to emerge. Or escape.

Friends never actually understood, thought Peter. If they did, they could not help. If they did help, they could only go so far—never far enough. Before, he would have felt stupid attempting to explain to Damon how someone like Alea could draw the will to love back out of its dungeon. Now he thought that he should at least try to explain it to his friend, because he felt sure it *had* happened. The old Peter, the one pouting at the party, would not have even tried.

He had done her feet and shoulders; now she was doing his. "So—is caring so inadmissable in your life?"

His knotted muscles loosened up under her strong, steady fingers. "No. Just infrequent, that's all. You can't be good at something you've only tried once."

"Sometimes, Peter, you act as though you're waiting for me to get to the part where I finally reveal just what it is I want from you. The hidden agenda that will permit you to revert to your old walled-in self and justify fire-bombing another relationship . . . because nobody will ever truly be good enough for you."

He shifted, suddenly uncomfortable, revealed again. "Wow, I'm sorry if I gave you that—"

"I know, I know," she overrode. "Let me finish. I want you to know something. You are good, Mister Deutsch—very good. At everything you apply yourself to. You stimulate me intellectually, excite me physically, please me generally, and—" she picked at her words, trying for meaning and hitting a difficult patch ''—and sometimes I worry that there will come a time when I fail to keep up with you. You're what I want. You're what I think I need in my life. I have freedom and I can count on you if I need stability. Don't sell yourself short. You've fooled yourself into believing that I have no problems or worries and that I'm the rock you can hang onto. You need a great deal of attention and devotion . . . but that's okay, you deserve it. You deserve everything good in the world, and I want to be everything I can for you. But don't ever think that what you and I have makes one of us superior, especially not me. If you're leaning on me, understand that it's mutual. As long as we both lean against each other, neither one of us will fall down and go boom.''

She tilted his head back, and he saw the imploring expression on her face, a shade of their future together, and it squeezed his heart. She was not invulnerable either. She had been hurt too, sometime far back. It showed in the way her hands stopped stroking him, in the shininess of her eyes as she spoke.

All his previous desire for her was outshone by the way he wanted her now. And thought he needed her.

''Oh yeah. One more thing. I love you, too.''

It was a word he still tripped over. If he had run across the word *joyous* in a screenplay, he would have sneered at it. Now it described precisely how he felt. He was hooked. Joyously hooked. You could never anticipate the snare that would get you. That was *how* it got you.

''You can't know how long this has taken me,'' he said in a diminished voice, thinking perhaps she *had* known all along. The moment was gem-perfect between them. It radiated. Another night lay ahead, and another beyond that. . . .

He felt content at last. Another silly word to pin down the warmth inside him, too long absent.

The next time Peter saw Alea, she was enthusiastically fucking someone else—or some *thing* else, since it probably was not even human.

"I love you! Why do you treat me in this abusive way?"

The little man's bulb nose was red. After slamming the door to his office he slapped his thick-coated arms vigorously, doing a dance in place.

"God! *Pueblo de Nuestra Senora Reina de Los Angeles de Porciuncula!* My darling City of the Angels, my goddess, tell me why you are so unseasonably *cold* this time of year!" He doffed a gray stovepipe hat whose crown was canted forward with age and abuse and unwound himself from a thick crocheted muffler. "Humph! No answers, as usual. Only subzero torment!"

A response issued from the darkness behind the big desk. "Indian winter. Who can say?"

The voice was not warm, either. It was a reedy buzz from a crooked-lipped mouth that hated to squander, in speech, time better spent drinking. It pronounced words off-center, with an accent. A stranger might be left with the impression that a huge French cockroach had journeyed far just to scare the little man by addressing him from behind his own desk. But the little man's startlement was momentary.

"Very funny, Maurice." He tossed his hat toward the tarnished rack. He never missed. The visitor flinched, anticipating something heavy and deadly.

"Wah!" The dwarf's feet flashed in the air as the top-heavy desk chair upended and dumped him on his butt. Moths fled toward the ceiling and jostled paper floated like big cartoon snowflakes.

The little man would never let the dwarf see the hint of a leprechaun smile on his face. He had to keep a tone of disdain in his voice. "You know, Maurice, it annoys me beyond mere words when you burgle your way into my office. My office is my sanctuary, my cathedral . . . and here you are, using the font for your *toilette.*" He tugged off thin gloves a finger at a time.

The dwarf, in the light now, shook his head and walked around the desk with his peculiar rolling gait. His head barely cleared the desktop. He lifted a stack of ancient manila file folders from the seat of a bar stool that rose from the chaos, placed it on the floor, clapped his hands of dust, and scampered aboard. "Sorry," was all he said.

The little man sniffed. "I did ask you not to, you know."

"But . . . Monsieur Rogoff . . . I . . ."

"Yes, yes." The little man waved a dismissive hand and used his muffler to rub his nose back to warmth. "You wish to impress me with your stealth and expertise in all things. Fine, good. I am suitably dazzled. I would not summon you at all if I lacked for faith in your multifarious talents, yes?" No need to stroke the dwarf's ego more than necessary, he thought. His brow wrinkled. "And should you do it one more time, I shall find myself forced to engage equivalent talents elsewhere, yes?" It hung in the air. The dwarf was silent. The little man took this as an acceptance of terms, and terminated the topic by saying, "Ah. Good."

The dwarf sanded his stubby sculptor's hands against each other. "To the task at hand, then?"

"Mm. Yes. Once more into the breach, and all that, yes? But on the way over here, Maurice, I was thinking . . . a few changes, a few variations on the normal theme. This time I want something for myself. On this case, we get a little extra, I think."

It was clear to the dwarf that his employer was still doping out what his intended deviations from the norm might be. This was stimulating; almost as good as a full flask of cognac. "There is danger, perhaps?" he said, eyes aglint.

"No. As a matter of fact, I want spice, not salt."

"But . . . improvements on your classic procedure, Monsieur?" The dwarf checked the grandfather clock. A lot of theoretical time had been lost. The clock was always wrong. So they had never possessed the time to lose in the first place. To Maurice, if it was ten past anything, he deemed himself late for his metronomically recurrent cocktail hour.

"Improvements? No." The little man picked out a careful pathway toward his desk and draped the muffler beside the hat. "As I said—seasoning. A good cut of meat is delicious without seasoning. Sometimes, with the right spices, it can become even better, yes? Not that I wish to equate my work with meat, especially dead meat. Did you bring the death mask?"

"At your feet. You nearly made me crush it."

"Mm." The little man reached into the carpetbag he found next to the desk chair and lifted out a hemispherical plaster bust. He turned it in the light, admiring the strong, archetypally masculine peak of the nose, the brainy forehead, the almost ruthless cut of the mouth. The eyes were blank white convex surfaces. They always were, on a death mask casting. The featureless chalk-toned eyes seemed sealed, locked, mortared up from the inside. On the masque of flawless cyan glass the little man had utilized earlier, the eyes had been holes—equally devoid of detail, yet ingresses, permitting passage in either direction. The glass had been polished, glossy, seductively cool to the touch. By comparison, the plaster half-face was a riot of rough texture; from it still ebbed the heat of its injection and hardening.

That, thought the little man, was a small but apt illustration of the difference between his own work, and that of Maurice—the littler man.

M. Rogoff laid the death mask next to his Rolodex. "And the body?"

The dwarf palpitated excitedly. "Oh, Monsieur! A

true work of art. I have outdone myself. Only the most exotic raw materials, coupled with my secret formulae! By my watch, three entire days of curing the medium. I nursed it, yes, I baby-sat it. I think this one may last five, even six entire hours!''

That brought the little man's eyes up. Six! Unprecedented, even for Maurice. The dwarf sitting high across from him had a face like a baked apple, bad teeth, and darting black seeds for eyes. He wore threadbare rags, coat upon sweater upon shirts. Sometimes he smelled unpleasant. Nothing exterior hinted at the ability within that compact and eccentric package. His newest monster was good for six hours. Someday Maurice would reach the little man's own level of craft and skill. Someday he might become capable of making them the way M. Rogoff himself made them. But that would be all—Maurice, sadly, would never cultivate the other talents that the little man wielded with the same measures of care and adroitness.

That was exactly why the little man needed, on this job, to vary his technique somewhat. Thus, spice.

Now that the monster was ready, and he approved—even of the too-perfect nostrils—it was time to click on the switch and watch the whole vast machine go up and down.

Today's cockfight over *Sinner* had been postponed due to the line producer's dental appointment. Stupid.

Peter strolled down two offices, nodding and smiling at the receptionists and scurrying workers. The xerox machine was down, and a panic was simmering. In places like this, the xerox machines were always down.

Finding a vacant office was easy. Someone had gotten promoted or cashiered. He put his feet up on the desktop, empty except for a blotter, an in-out box with a broken strut and no papers, and a digital clock. The telephone was a given. If there had been no desk in the vacated cubicle, there would still have been a phone.

Peter punched in Damon's number in Vancouver.

Damon laughed out loud for a full thirty seconds before catching his wind. The revenge was tasty. Make those studio munchkins pay, pay, pay.

"Still with me, Damon?"

"Jesus, yeah. You're a beautiful man, Peter. Let's talk for a couple of hours."

Peter couldn't damp down the huge, loony grin on his face. Even if nothing had happened, it made him feel good to talk to Damon. "Five-to-ten odds that that club of lawyers and doctors you corralled together are still sitting around trying to equate you with the movin' pitcher biz."

"*Au contraire,* ace," Damon said. "A bank account was born yesterday, and you and I are the proud daddies. Five hundred large. You see, it's that time of year again, and those lawyers and doctors discovered a sudden burning urge to invest. The point-five gets us the loan for the rest we'll need. Is the name *Flying A-Hole Productions* okay by you?"

Peter was glad for a hearty laugh, because the news had otherwise struck him speechless.

"You and I are set, captain. You have but to plonk your ass on a red-eye and make an X on some contracts. Of course, I've gotten pretty good at forging your signature, so you don't really have to—"

"This is going to knock her out," Peter whispered.

"Oh—by the way, guess who's interested in the part of the smuggler? Lawrence Banks."

"I have to tie off this mess here, first, and—"

"Banks got interested as soon as I told him *you* were involved, and that you were the guy who wrote and directed *The Big Casino—*"

"I haven't even told her about *Objet d'Art* yet. I wonder if—"

Neither was receiving the other, and their conversation sounded like the madly overlapping dialogue in a Howard Hawks or Robert Altman movie. They both clammed up as if by telepathic agreement. Then each said, *"Hold it!"* in chorus. They wasted the next few seconds of prime phone time giggling madly.

Peter would have to re-read the *Objet d'Art* script for the hundredth time. Maybe on the plane. More crucially, he would have to review his contract for *Sinner* to find whether it would be easier to dump it or do it fast. Nothing in a contract was non-negotiable. You could even change the date on top if you used the right kind of *baksheesh*. Like brandy into coffee, his thoughts gradually sank into priority order and were assimilated.

Alea floated to the top.

"Peter? This is gonna knock *who* out?"

"Oh, christ. That's right. You don't know yet."

"Who her? I mean, which her is 'who'? You know what I mean."

Peter chuckled, then sighed. "That's some question, really." His brain filled up with her. "Her name is Alea. I don't really know how to begin this . . . listen, Damon, you've got to meet her; she's . . . I mean, let me tell you about her!"

"Aha—my friend, your overpowering verbal ineptitude clues me that this is no couch-versus-starlet routine. Unlike the cheap, sleazy affairs littering your past, as perverted, disgusting, and downright illegal as they were. So how're you doing?"

"You don't know how good I feel, buddy. With Kathryn I was never such a wonderful person."

Damon's ready sarcasm was blotted out by the silence of growing awe. "Peter. Dear Peter. All of a sudden this sounds like something that is very real for you."

All the things he wanted to say funnelled down to a telling smile. "Yeah. God help me, Damon, she's important to me. She pulled me up out of the quicksand. A friend *and* a lover.''

"Whew." Long-distance static crackled. Damon knew what this meant without having it spelled out. "I thought you were in an emotional nosedive you'd never pull out of, ace. I gave you about two more months, max, before you tied one of those GI Joe plastic parachutes around your wang and leaped off the top of the Black Tower. *Nude Director With Uzi Hoses MCA Execs During Death Plunge.* But you sound one hundred percent. You actually sound happy. I don't think I've ever *seen* you *do* happy before . . .''

"I'm a fucking rocket. With you and her both, I'm on the verge of the highest high you've ever seen in your chemically enhanced life. I've got to tell her the news!''

"Hang back. First tell me where you met this angel.''

"It was—'' He felt the jump-start jolt of memory. "It was at that party you roped me into attending. The one at Shepard Bonnard's little hedonist villa in the Hills.''

"There were dozens of women there; if I saw her I probably forgot her immediately.''

"No, Damon, you'd remember Alea if you saw her even for a second, and she was with me nearly the whole time. You knew everybody on the guest list. Are you positive you didn't see her?''

"Whoa, boy. I know where you're headed. Listen. I was in hustle mode. I probably saw her, didn't track, and moved on. Next case. That party was like a subway car at rush hour, and a lot of pretty kiddies were on the carousel, and nothing personal. Okay?''

"Yeah, right. Sorry.''

"Trot her along if you can. Scenic Vancouver. Use a gun if she needs convincing.''

They both laughed. For a while they repeated themselves, more to run up the phone tab than to insure memory of particulars they already knew inside out.

Peter sped down Cahuenga West, leaving the sunroof on his Mazda open in defiance of the cold snap. The bracing rush of air made him cocky, exuberant. These were sensations that were too long in coming home. For someone like Alea, Damon's news flash could not be contained by another phone call. Peter marveled. What had not been real an hour ago he was now going to deliver in person.

Out of the garage, up the elevator, double-timing down the corridor, he rehearsed, whispering to himself as he dredged up keys and unlocked his apartment deadbolt.

He shut up as soon as he was in. It was as if the very timbre of the air inside his home had tripped sensory alarms planted in his flesh. The door swung quietly back and the very ambience of the room hit him as sour, skewed. Something was wrong here.

His face crinkled the way it normally did when he smelled something offensive. It was not unlikely that he was walking in on a burglary in progress; an innate and nonspecific caution deep in the pit of his stomach warned him that if he was going to proceed, he should do so without a sound. He walked heel-and-toe, circumventing the sunken living room, sticking to the carpeted areas, breathing with jailbreak shallowness and not feeling a bit ridiculous.

In an insane fit of humor his persona vacated his body in order to observe the action through the eye of a director: Here is the ominous establishing shot of the hallway, shrouded in darkness; here, the Arriflex shot, jerky and hand-held, traversing the hall with that oddly cocked point of view that tips what we're seeing as being through the eyes of the butcher-knife wacko as he creeps up on the bedroom door. It is ajar by inches. Of course. More cinematic that way.

Alea made a noise.

It was like a gasp for breath, hard, distinct, perhaps cutting pain loose. A flashbulb image of Alea in jeopardy welled up but Peter suppressed it. The thudding of his heart was making his throat and temples pulsate. It became difficult for him to inhale.

She had made that sort of sound with him in bed. That was what kept him from bursting through the door in the role of white knight. Now a new image played across the screen of his mind, one that could not be shoved down. By the time his hand touched the bedroom door it was almost as if he had willed that dreadful picture into reality by the sheer force of his concentration.

Again, as on the night of the thousand candles, Peter saw his own empty bed. The room was lit in faint gold tones by the track lighting on the ceiling; the rheostat was turned up about halfway. The sheets, blankets and pillows were strewn across the floor like the trail of clothing he had left on a night not so long ago. His view tracked along from the bed until he saw them on the floor.

They were enthusiastically missionary.

Peter watched a round, almost girlish ass thwack up-out, down-in, with the frenzy of a machine. Alea was beneath, feet in the air, legs bent at the knees, hands hooked so she could rock backward with each thrust. The man on top was sunk into her like a baby into a cradle. Broad shoulders, muscle-knotted back, short, badly styled dark hair. He pushed off into a quicker, rabbity pace as she enwrapped him, legs and groin rocking faster. Her feet, angled down in a dancer's point, flattened back as orgasm rollicked through her. Peter had never noticed that before. She clutched at him, pulled him down to meld with her, gasps tearing out of her throat. With a suicidal detachment, Peter marked the ascension and declination of each cry—up, up, peak, plateau, down, down, downdown.

Then laughter. It rose, as familiar to Peter as pain.

A steel web, strands thread-thin and ice cold, constricted around his heart.

Her partner uttered not a sound.

Instead, he pushed up from her just enough to turn his head and glare directly at Peter through the two-inch crack in the door. His pupils were solid disks of bronze; they caught the overhead light and glinted as though chatoyant. Peter knew he was not visible, yet the eyes transfixed him, shimmering copper from lid to lid, no irises. They locked with his own eyes and held. Slowly, the man, the thing atop Alea, smiled at him. It was vampiric, hideous; the face seemed to rupture and shift thickly like molten wax.

Peter reeled from that malignant gaze, sucking in a startled breath and groping blindly for support. His knee bumped the door and it swung freely open. Alea's incubus was still staring at him with its death's-head grin.

The plans of attack that had capered through Peter's brain—of kicking in the door, of doing violence, of using stealth and surprise-freaking them, of doing the manly thing, the macho thing, the mad reactionary thing—all shrivelled to nothingness under the targeted power behind those inhuman eyes. Peter froze.

Alea's voice unfroze him.

"Peter. Get out of here."

Her tone suggested that his intrusion had been expected. The resonant and calm modulation of her speech was even more frightening than the soulless gaze of her demon lover.

Peter began to tremble. No stopping it.

The lover with the sculpted torso devoid of moles or blemishes resumed fucking her, penetrating to the hilt, his buttocks clenching with each push. Alea's hands scampered over his body, grabbing the protruding shoulder blades, touching the smooth small of his back, cupping his ass, her fingernails leaving white and bloodless indentations in the perfect skin.

Amputated from those eyes, that smile, Peter swallowed hard and stumbled back. His body forced him to flee on a purely autonomic level; his mind was stunned and shut down. Numbly, stupidly, he slammed his own apartment door behind him as he fled into the corridor.

In five minutes he came back.

He had run like a gazelle down the stairs. He took the elevator back up. It had not taken him long to wrest control, to come back into himself. In the grip of his right hand the claw hammer swung pendulously. He had gotten it from the Mazda's trunk; a carpenter's hammer, a foot-long haft of wood terminating in several pounds of drop-forged steel. Two metal wedges cinched the head solid.

Peter smiled pleasantly at the elderly woman in the car with him as the numerals blinked upward. The two poodles at her feet yapped and danced. Peter smiled. The woman watched the numbers and pretended not to notice the crazy roadmaps of dry tears that formed a shiny latticework on his face. He was disgorged on the seventh floor. His smile remained cemented in place.

He was thinking of what he could do to his visitor's face with the hammer, what the claw-end would do to his unearthly eyes, how the vee of the claw would become clotted with hair and blood and skull and brains, oh yeah.

He unlocked his door normally, shifting the hammer to his left hand. Everything was unchanged inside. He shifted the tool back because the biceps were better in his right arm—more swinging momentum, more impact. He moved back down the hall, strolling now, skin tingling, ears pricking for sounds, but otherwise totally composed.

The smile hung improbably on his face, like a mortician's final joke on a corpse.

He used the head of the hammer to push the re-

closed bedroom door open again. The hammer
thunked heavily against the hollow-core door, which
rasped back along the carpeting. The knob bumped
against the back wall.

The trailers were over and it was time for the main
feature.

The bed was still empty. But this time, so was the
room. Five minutes, and they had cleared out.

He glanced around, double checking, the metabolic
backwash requesting permission to throw up now,
please. He fancied he felt his soul emit a soft hiss of
relief. In a second, he knew his fall had been aborted.
What might have happened was not going to happen.
The thought of what he had intended did not sicken
him; it became a dull ache that settled in alongside the
others already imprisoned inside him. He could deal
with it. The apartment was empty. Alea was gone.

Again.

His big mirror, five feet on a side, was canted
against the bedroom's west wall. He caught sight of
himself. He looked haggard and old. He thought of
the body bills he had run up on his compulsive all-
night shoots, using caffeine as collateral for one more
hour, dexedrine caps for one more night. He thought
of where his life had been *invested,* of karmic loans,
and considered the hammer in his hand, his gaze moving from it back to his own face, as if requesting not
absolution, but just a simple explanation.

This was the crash point. Crash, as in bankruptcy,
as in the Great Depression, as in what happens when
you slit a computer's throat, as in that's all there is and
there ain't no more.

He planted the hammer into the center of the mirror,
into his own burned-out image. *Crash.*

Crouching behind the seventh-floor door, Maurice
monitored the corridor through the rectangle of wire-
gridded window until Peter Deutsch emerged from his

apartment. The man was disheveled, off-kilter; there were slivers of glass in his hair. His eyes hung in purplish sockets. They saw little, recorded nothing. Maurice thought of feeble bulbs flaring their last, then smiled.

They almost always looked this way when the fun began.

The elevator doors met, terminating his view of the lost man with the hammer still depending from one fist. Maurice eased the fire door open. He had blocked the latch with a slip of cardboard. Since there was never much traffic within these high-rent filing cabinets, he quickly padded down the corridor, his nudity of no concern. His comically exaggerated phallus bobbed from thigh to thigh like a bell clapper.

From behind his ear he plucked the key, fabricated several days back from a wax impression, and unlocked Peter's door. He vanished inside, water slipping past oil.

The smashed mirror was strewn about the bedroom floor in ten thousand pieces. Maurice did not even slow his pace, and wicked silver barbs punched deeply into the soft soles of his feet. A jagged, five-inch wedge caught and pierced, erupting through the top of his right foot just behind the big toe. The point jutting from the split flesh was dulled with gobs of red clay.

In Peter's bathroom Maurice gave the counter mirror a jolly salute, then gouged out his eyes with the white points of his tapered, perfect fingernails. Two clay-smeared Lincoln pennies rang merrily as they spun in the bowl of the sink. He pushed the stopper down to keep from losing them. Then he unfolded the ivory-handled Gay Nineties straight razor that had been presented to Peter as a birthday gift, used once, then left on display . . . where it could do no further damage.

Maurice jabbed the point of the stropped blade into his throat below the Adam's apple. A drop of oil oozed forth. He held firm and sliced shallowly floorward, stopping at the root of the penis.

The monster, gutted, eyeless, was still standing before the mirror. Still smiling.

Maurice's stubby hands eased out of the monster's chest and grasped the lips of the slit. He shucked the entire carcass like a scuba suit, and once he was out it piled up bonelessly on the floor. He herded the rubbery mass together, scooped it into the bathtub, and cranked the shower tap to full hot. While steam clouded out from behind the pebbled glass door, the dwarf grabbed one of Peter's bath towels and mopped sweat.

In moments the shell of Alea's non-human fuckmate had dissolved and escaped into the pipework. Now it was just several gallons of liquid clay headed for the city sewer network.

Jingling his pennies, Maurice fetched his carpetbag from the bedroom closet. He pulled out wads of his own clothing and replaced them with the jeans and tee shirt worn earlier by the monster. Maurice had known Peter Deutsch would be too preoccupied to ever notice the extra, alien bag amid his own closet clutter.

When he raided Peter's bar for a congratulatory nip, he discovered some excellent VSOP and decided to liberate the bottle. It had gone very well tonight. Now it was time for M. Rogoff to work the magic, as only he could. Time now to fire the clay lovingly initiated by his master's hands. The next item on Peter Deutsch's agenda was the blissful hell of M. Rogoff's kiln.

One more thing, I love you, too.

Peter paid pathological attention to packing. This, too, was an autonomic thing, this ability to pack for a trip in a great rush and not forget a toothbrush or a checkbook or a needed file folder. A skill his shell retained when the rest of the relevancies of his life had dropped away. Stuffing balled socks into a sling bag, he let this skill run full auto, trusting that nothing critical was overlooked. He sensed, if only subdermally, that once he closed the door of this place and boarded the jet for Canada that he would never return to his home.

''Home'' had lost all meaning for Peter in the past few hours he had spent preparing to abandon it. Until Alea, home was never what he'd called these rooms where he bathed and slept and never quite found the time to put in the oak shelves, or order the deskwork, or hang pictures, or invite peers for diversion. It was an enclosure that kept at bay certain inconvenient elements—heat, smog, rain—and imposed a sameness that was simplicity to ignore. It was a numbered door in a corridor of like doors, mazed into a floorplan that mirrored itself above and below and beyond. The building was a vast filing cabinet for people, an upscale address stocked with all the amenities. It was a mail slot individuated by initials and a phone number with a taped message.

Never a home, not truly.

It was the place where he had made love to Alea. That made it a home. They had never had sex anyplace else but on his carpeting, his mattresses, his iron-gray pillowback sofa group. Few areas in the apartment had not had their virginity violated, but it struck him that they'd never gotten naked at Alea's place, or a hotel, or anywhere but here. Home was the place where he and Alea had made love.

But this was also the place where Alea had fucked and been fucked . . . where she had enjoyed spreading her legs for something that did not look totally human. Where she'd told Peter to get out.

Betrayal seemed to seep from the wallwork. This was no longer Peter's place.

Slow rage steamed in his gut, subsided, marshaled again, until his mouth tasted foul. The wraparound

picture windows showed him the Hollywood light-
scape. Damon Fletcher had told Peter about Hollywood in all its bilious glory; here was a place where
nothing was guaranteed to be lasting or sincere or real.
No causes, no motives, no blame to be placed—this
was Hollywood. It was where they worked because
they could hack it and millions could not. Schwab's
was boarded up and the Brown Derby shut down.
Grauman's Chinese had been Mann's for more than a
decade and the famous Tiny Naylor's drive-in coffee
shop was history.

Hollywood.

Peter was supposed to be progressive, tolerant. Simple sexual infidelity had nothing to do with his anger.
And the Pacific Ocean was not really wet.

Jealousy was a dragon with emerald eyes, one he
had to engage in battle to deny what he felt. All the
tender and private moments, and telling interludes between two human beings in sync, had been cleared
away by a fierce possessiveness as frank as a jamming
signal. The soft confidences he had shared with her
were now drowned beneath thick, oily waves of self-
ishness and anxiety with a suddenness that sent the
bowels plummeting and struck the brain comatose. He
had heard her make those sweet sounds he thought
reserved only for him, heard her laugh in a crushingly
familiar way.

*Sir, you got took, sir, and fell hard, sir, and offered
the knife your shieldless back, stupid, and . . .*

Truth buffeted through the windows of his mind and
knocked asunder the card house he had been tilting
together. Alea's feelings had been not only reciprocal,
but had radiated from her and come home to him two
hundred percent. She had never been seduced. Despite
the fact that Peter was wounded and hurt, he could not
honestly round-file the one truth that defied the prime
rule of Tinseltown: She had not *used* him for anything.

The bedroom scene played countless encores in his

head. He was well into triple-digit reruns—the flash of
Alea's cinnamon skin, the flush of intraorgasm heat;
shock-cuts of moisture and motion and love-grunts and
the too-perfect monster filling her over and over . . .
and two inhuman eyes full of molten copper. The
memories stung and flew away and zipped home to
sting again, like subliminals tucked away between the
frames of film. Unfair. Subliminals were supposed to
be outlawed.

At first he'd been destructive, throwing things like a
petulant child, punching the refrigerator so its contents rattled and broke. He hit hard and opened up his
hand. The blood calmed him, cycled anger out and
exhaustion in, let him trade seething rage for false de-
spair. He cried. Time elapsed. He did not drink.

He stared toward, but paid no attention to, Nicholas
Roeg's *Bad Timing* unspooling in the predawn on cable. Art Garfunkel, who had sung of sounds of silence, was fucking a dead woman because he was
obsessed with her. The TV became an insect tonal
noise, snowing Peter's inputs and insulating him from
the sounds of the city. He fell asleep in the wing chair,
packed but not departed. Dreaming permitted him to
hear Alea's voice almost at will.

Peter. Get out of here.

It was the same dark, soft voice that had once ordered him to leave his sperm nowhere but inside her.
Doors opened by playful sensuality slammed with amplified violence because Alea's words held the unique
venom of being unforgettable. They seemed designed
to brand themselves into his memory. Peter had been
neutered; his manhood wiped out by a single soft sen-
tence in the dark. How could anyone fight artillery like
that? How in hell to scour away the shame of turning
and running? Nothing could win him back that lost
dignity.

It hurt to think of Alea, but he was unwilling to
forget any facet of her. He would not blank her out

even if it meant his own survival. She had melted into the palpable Los Angeles darkness as easily as a wraith. Peter would not have thought it so simple to merely erase a person who had so much sheer presence that he thought of her anew every thirty seconds or so. Too many unfinished conversations hung between them, too many moments yet undecanted.

The bright chrome feelings he had embraced were oxidizing now. Alea had been a wish-fulfillment practically from the beginning. To get her back, what could he do, what might he give up? Damon's voice welled up inside him, laid behind a sardonic echo track: *You actually sound happy.*

"Happy," Peter mumbled, and woke up.

A key was ratcheting in the front door lock. All Peter's sensory knobs cranked to full tap. His vision targeted the door and his heartbeat hit runaway.

Light sheared in from the corridor and a small, hunched shape darted inside, hurriedly slamming the door. Peter heard furtive breathing in the renewed darkness, followed by a muffled slapping, as though the intruder was hastily brushing himself off. Then came the shuffle of short, waddling steps across the carpet, then a voice.

"Merde! Flaneur, indeed! Pah! Is not even a loafer entitled to a small, eh, restorative—*urp!*—nip now and again?" The voice was brackish, and seemed to emanate from somewhere near the floor, as though the speaker were muttering from the bottom of a well.

Peter bolted out of the chair, still woozy, trying for a good Clint Eastwood tone and missing: "Who the fuck are you!"

"Ma foi!" The dwarf's volume matched Peter's. He jumped, clutched at his chest, got tangled in his own feet and tumbled into the two-tiered section of sunken living room. Peter, unmoving and not quite buying all this, watched the dwarf scramble back toward the front door. It was like blundering into the third reel of a

silent movie comedy; he had no idea of what was going on, but it sure looked funny.

"Hey." His voice came out conversational, comic. He sprang for the door and easily intercepted the tiny interloper, spinning him about and shoving him back. He blocked the door with what he hoped was an aggressive stance. "What do you think you're doing here?" It was hopeless and trite. He would have cut it from a script.

The dwarf smiled with forced ease. The dirt on his face cracked. "Heh, heh . . . I clearly have stumbled, ah, literally, into the wrong apartment, Monsieur . . . I, em, I . . . am down the hall . . ." His eyes were rheumy and flammulated, and the special aroma of bargain port wafted up from his soiled and threadbare coat. Disturbed fleas settled.

"You are *not* down the hall," Peter said. "You *will* be out the window very shortly if I don't get a straight answer from you, you sawed-off little pisswah." Yeah, that was manly, he thought. It was taking all he had left at full power to toss a scare into a dwarf.

"Well, er, Monsieur, I . . ." The voice trailed off. The cheesy grin remained. The dwarf shrugged.

"Let's have a drink, you and I," Peter said. Changing tack was a good way to keep the upper hand. "Sounds like you could make good use of a spot or two. Shall we?" He waved the dwarf toward the kitchen, but the tiny man did not budge, unsure, nervous. "Come on, come on. A drink is what you want, right?"

The dwarf looked around to make sure Peter was addressing him. As he approached, Peter thought of Poe's character groping around the rim of the Pit. Once the dwarf was settled onto a stool at the breakfast bar, Peter pulled down the Chivas.

"Ah, good!" said the dwarf. "I was going to request something more potent than wine."

"Ice?"

"Do I look like a barbarian?"

"No offense." Peter handed across a thick-bottomed highball glass. The dwarf gulped the full whack and handed it back for more, smacking his lips.

"Sounds like you're in trouble for goldbricking, mate," Peter said as he poured.

"Eh?" His eyes never left the glass.

"You called yourself a *flaneur,* a goof-off. You always so charitable to yourself?"

"Of course not!" He banged the glass on the countertop for emphasis. "It was *him.* My employer. He watches. He checks. God help you if you fuck up." More scotch was within range and his truncated reach was sufficient to win it. When he made the grab he eased his hold on the bundle of keys he'd kept fisted tight and they hit the polished bartop with the jangle of small change.

Peter recognized Alea's keys as much by their unique sound as by the snapshot glimpse of them he caught before his guest executed a noisy recovery and swept them into a dark, dirty pocket.

The keys were grouped, Peter knew, by a circlet of ball-and-socket gold chain, not plated, but apparently solid gold. Where a conventional person would have attached an oval Gucci plate with embossed initials, or one of those stamped metal ticket facsimiles for *Cats* or *Les Misérables,* there was a tarnished brass knickknack the size of Peter's thumbnail. It was rectangular, with a raised border like a miniature playing card, and enclosed a deep-cut contour of a human figure, arms extended—the same outline that had previously appeared in bas-relief on Alea's waxen seal. The figure no longer looked to Peter like it was flying. It looked like it was plummeting toward some uncertain and ugly end, helpless to arrest its fall.

The dwarf downed two more burly swallows of scotch and muttered on about his philistine boss. Peter canceled the lunatic urge to laugh in favor of strategic timing.

He watched the dwarf's glass ascend, then caught him with a mouthful of liquor. "You made some kind of mistake?" he said. "Involving Alea."

"Oh, no, she was *perfect*. But I'm not supposed—" His gaze bounced up to Peter's triumphant face as the firebolt of Chivas burned its way down the wrong tube. It was a perfect double-take. He spluttered and turned an alarming shade of scarlet, veins bulging at the temples as he spluttered and gagged. *"Zut!* You!"

"You thought I was just a fellow burglar, right?"

The dwarf mopped at himself.

"See, pal, I'm an absolute security nut. Only Alea had the key combination that would open the front door. I changed the upper deadbolt myself; not even the building manager has a key to that one. But you did."

Swallowed air resolved into a broad panic fart. "I— I only saw your—back before."

"Tell me about your employer." In a taut suspense script, the next line would be: *His name, for starters.* Peter leaned across the counter and pointed. "His name, for starters. Window's right over there."

"Monsieur Rogoff." The dwarf's tone was exasperated.

Peter thought that alcohol and self-interest were melding to get admirable results so far. "And does this Mister Rogoff know where Alea is?"

The dwarf shrugged again, sighed. "Ah, Monsieur. She is gone for always. Of her you will never see again." Said with the species of bogus regret the French believe is terribly sympathetic. "She was very beautiful . . ."

"Does Monsieur Rogoff know where she is?" Peter's face crimsoned, his eyes growing starkly white.

Maurice recoiled. "Monsieur Rogoff knows—everything!'' He hiccuped and silence lagged between the two men.

Peter poured himself a belt—over ice—and tipped it back.

''You will take me to meet Mister Rogoff tonight.''

''Oh, no, Monsieur, I cannot! He would terminate me! Not for any price!''

''I didn't name a price.'' The dwarf's protest sounded a bit too rehearsed, so Peter kept on his deadly smile and lunatic-calm demeanor. ''I'm offering you a once-in-a-lifetime opportunity—a chance to get back to the ground floor via the elevator instead of the fast way. Cheers.''

Maurice lent the window a queasy glance. ''It is useless for me to argue, I suppose.''

''Bingo,'' Peter toasted. ''Or *splatooey.*''

Maurice winced at the indelicacy. He regarded his empty glass as a gallows-bound convict might his final taste on this world, with regret that he had not made it last longer. *''Zut.* So be it, then.''

''I'll need my keys back to seal our little pact.'' Peter held out his hand.

The dwarf's phoney expression of camaraderie under fire dissolved into an acid look of daggers and poison. He rifled within his several coats, kicking up dust and gnats, every contortion punctuated by a grumbled checklist of curses in French, just in case Peter did not sense what an inconvenience he was causing.

But he relinquished the prize.

Peter's grasp closed on the keys, affirming their reality, his heart surging almost as if he had physically recaptured Alea herself. On its tiny ingot of gold, the man-like figure fell, and fell. . . .

Kind of like the pose Maurice would strike on the way down, as he picked up speed. If.

''Don't fret, Shorty.'' Peter felt gruffly hale now. ''I'll put in a word with your boss, after he and I take a meeting.'' He hesitated just shy of the sunken portion of the living room. ''Unless, of course, *you* really do know where Alea is right now.'' He raised his eyebrows and considered the window again. ''Hm?''

''That is something I wish with all my heart, *mon ami*,'' Maurice said in his saw-toothed voice. He spread his open palms in a theatrical gesture of impotence. ''But, truly, I cannot say because I do not know. If Monsieur Rogoff wishes to divulge more to you, he shall.''

Maurice's exaggerated courtliness was as grotesque as his expressions of sympathy were patently false. Peter found himself wishing for a pistol, something big and phallic and lethal, loaded with lead wadcutters. A mushrooming slug to the head; instant checkout. He was still thinking of death, and that was inappropriate, and he glimpsed in a flash just how absurd he was.

Play tough, he thought. *Let's see if you can maintain a degree of physical intimidation for* this *little errand, at least. Can you keep it up?*

''I think I might just be able to charm Monsieur Rogoff,'' he said. ''Just look what I've done for *our* relationship in such a short time. Move. Now.'' It was essential tough-guy dialogue.

Maurice belched, picked snot, moved as ordered.

The grandfather clock stubbornly bonged four times. It was two-fifteen in the morning.

''Useless!'' the little man snorted from his vantage at one of three high, narrow windows that took up most of the north wall of his cramped quarters. He was far up enough from street level that security bars would have been paranoid in the extreme. His exasperated comment formed a corona of mist on the chilly glass; from across his customary anarchic disarray, the cantankerous clock endured another of his mordant glances. "Old World craftsmanship . . . don't make 'em like they used to . . . *pah!*"

He fantasized sweet-talking the senile timepiece closer to one of the vaulted windows, then defenestrating it. It was fully twice the little man's height and might offer a heroic struggle, if it could anticipate anything other than a splendid view of nighttime Los Angeles all the way to the Hollywood sign. He could watch it somersault end-over-end as it achieved terminal velocity, the building's floors blurring past ever faster, and then the sweet harsh kiss of impact, the sundering of oiled mahogany, the splintering of joists, the glittering spray of cogs and gears and an end to years of temporal suffering.

He remained at the window, imagining himself a thane in a high keep, and watched as car headlights curbed on Highland Avenue and extinguished. The railroad watch in his fob pocket declared the arrival of two-fifteen a.m. Maurice, as expected, was spot on.

The Victorian clutter of the workroom resembled the overstock of an antique shoppe and a thrift store, ignominiously mingled by one of California's overhyped quakes. There was no obvious regard lent to cataloging, and none for display—the little man knew how to locate whatever he might require. He gently shifted a dust-laden afghan, so as not to precipitate a barrage of sneezing. He thought: *I am healthy but I am old, and would spare my pipes the violence.* Beneath the afghan was a maplewood chest, rough-hewn like a rural coffin. It might adequately accommodate Maurice, should the dwarf ever decide to decease. From the chest the little man lifted out a cloudy bottle of very old, venerable brandy. Maurice's well-earned reward, for Peter Deutsch was a prize of rare worth. The little man resisted the temptation to puff the dust from the bottle, remembering to spare his pipes.

"Our Mister Deutsch has no idea of just how valuable he is," the little man said to the bottle. "Eh?"

He hummed and laughed, in the manner of a child at play alone. "Right about now, our dear Peter is waxing tragic, pillorying himself in the most classical terms imaginable!

He settled back in his creaking office chair and steepled his fingers expectantly. "Hm. Some people just don't appreciate good *melodrama.*"

Peter Deutsch vacillated between waning anger and bewilderment, both dwindling to irrelevance in the face of his ever-amplifying exhaustion. He lifted and dropped each foot, climbing stairs again, thinking that the only reason people like great altitude is that it provides such a wonderful view when you fall.

Hysterical laughter seemed the most viable of all his options.

The dwarf, Maurice, no last name offered, had directed him over the hill of Hollywood proper, then to the ancient Bekins warehouse that loomed against the southern skyline as a decaying smog-tarnished colossus, way the hell down Highland Avenue. It looked like a decrepit Deco-era dirigible hangar.

Then came the chain-link barricades, the locks and fences. Maurice, like a rat, seemed able to squeeze through any opening the size of his head. Peter was forced to scramble over. The rusty coil of razor security wire sharply depreciated the value of his tailored shirt. A deviously crooked nailhead did likewise for his trousers, once Maurice had lifted open a rotten plank hatch much like an old root-cellar door. Down in the darkness, Peter deftly sank ankle-deep into a cold engulfment that wasted both his shoes. Then Maurice led the way up flight after flight of groaning metal stairs barely a yard in width and sandwiched between mildew and verdigris-encrusted walls, like some forgotten fire escape. Peter's hand came away orange whenever he gripped the rail, which came and went like a cruel practical joke. He yawned. He was sweating. His socks were soaked through with something vile. *Keep climbing.*

He was crazy, all right, to be following a dwarf who had burgled into his life with maddeningly vague tidbits about the fate of the creature he'd once thought of as a human being named Alea. Alea, who right now symbolized his entire capacity for love, sealed up in a bottle and thrown overboard. He felt as if his entire life had blown a tire.

He thought of freeway wrecks, of the shucked husks of destroyed tire treads, of disintegrated safety glass, of tardy paramedics and lives permanently off-course thanks to an errant second of high-speed traffic. Some people who worked in Hollywood commuted from San Diego. Three hours plus, coming and going, nearly a fifth of each waking day consumed by travel and drive-time radio and maybe, just maybe, a collision that could unmake your existence. It could all change in an instant. *Crash.*

Peter kept climbing.

He began to hear the wind cooing through the structure; thought he could feel the mammoth building swaying. It was an illusion, of course. His body told him that he was nearing the very top. In Maurice's wake he completed the final flight of risers, then wrestled past an acre or so of junk in an attic the size of half a football field—the discards and obsolete detritus of hundreds of past lives. Then came a narrow stretch of planks laid across fat girders, sloping slightly downward, then more junk, now enclosed by close walls reaching not quite to the dim recesses of the ceiling.

Then, incongruously, came an office door with a tarnished brass knob. The pebbled glass was cataracted to ivory at the borders and held despite a heroic, curving fracture through the lower left quadrant. Flaking

gilt proclaimed the MORRIS BUTTS DETECTIVE
AGENCY. Detective Butts had gone wherever failed private eyes go, decades previously. The door was still in
the world, and its glass was lit from within.

Maurice beckoned. "Enter." The door creaked. Peter thought: *This is not real life. This is an episode of*
THRILLER *and I'm about to meet Boris Karloff.*

"Is it Deutsch as in *Sprechen sie Deutsche?*"

Peter nodded. A small man behind the desk was
squinting at a crumbling Rolodex card.

"Maurice, show Mister Deutsch to a seat. The barstool will do."

Peter's eyes tried to deny the input—the little man's
vest, the faded dignity of old silk, the swallowtail coat
in gray pinstripe, the musky ascot and vintage pearl
stickpin. He noticed a watch fob, and, in a fall of light
beneath the desk . . . spats? The costume was natty,
but had suffered rigors of wear. It made Peter think of
that odd mixture of senility and majesty which char-
acterized elders whose minds could lock with crystal-
fine resolution into the minutiae of the Depression, yet
got only fringe reception on the here-and-now. He
watched the little man pay meticulous attention to the
flicking of dust—real and imagined—from his outfit.

"My young friend," the little man began while
Maurice was still peering about for the location of the
barstool. "Permit an introduction. The name is Rogoff."

"*Monsieur* Rogoff," Peter said vacantly.

A courtly nod, modest. "Thank you. Is something
amiss, Mr. Deutsch? You're staring at me as if I had
a third eye. Oh, Maurice, it's over by the clock, for
heaven's sake!"

Maurice grumbled and heaved. Butlering was beneath his station.

"You look like one of those Hollywood Boulevard
loons," said Peter. "The ones in the castoffs and the-

atre costumes you see picking in the litter baskets at three in the morning.''

"And just now, you, Mr. Deutsch, look like a news composite of a crazed killer." He waved Peter's notice toward a foggy bureau mirror leaning atop a dresser missing all of its carved knobs. "Or perhaps more relevantly, a *hammer* murderer, eh?''

Maurice gave up trying to hoist the barstool and instead cleared it off and scrambled aboard. Let the new guy get his own goddamned seat.

Peter saw, staring back at him, an overused face, barely organized around manic eyes, darkened, hollowed. His hair was lank and dirty and sticking forth in windblown licks. The corners of his mouth were pulled back in a smile he could not feel. His face was numb; but here was that face, grinning. Several days of stubble coarsened the view. He could have been a denizen of the alleys himself.

"So let's forgo snap judgment by appearance, hm? Let's go for the meat, the substance, the inner man, the details—and not the 'high concept,' as you might say. If I may presume." He seemed enormously pleased with his own banter, his face aglow, ruddy and elfin.

Peter abstracted past his own image in the mirror and took in the little man's bulb nose, the eyes like glittering chips of black quartzite. In defiance of cliché they, in fact, twinkled. His facial topography seemed to indicate the little man spent a great deal of time smiling. His hair was white as duck down, healthy but clipped very short, like that of an old Navy man. Peter rose, considered all the junk again, and sank his hands into his pockets. "I'll stand." He thought of poker.

"There is a question that brought you here," the little man began. It had the quality of a rehearsed speech; dialogue, a script—perhaps that was why the tone seemed weirdly jolly to Peter. "It caused you to follow Maurice into this strange place. Why bother?

You're a fellow who knows how to cut his losses. Why indeed? I've devoted a goodly amount of meditation to my response to the question—"

Peter fixated as though seeing Rogoff for the first time ever. "Where is she?" His voice was a whisper.

"Ah, precisely! That question!" A look of vindication fleeted across the leprechaun countenance. His hands fiddled with air. He was excited. "I shan't tell you she does not exist, as Maurice might have awhile ago. That sort of answer was designed more for . . . um, titillation, don't you think? Wouldn't serve my purpose, now that you're here. And I surmise that your patience is probably as worn down as your demeanor. I notice everything, you'll notice. . . ."

M. Rogoff's voice was drubbing and hypnotic; Peter had to remind himself to ask again: "Where is she now?"

"Ah. I put it to you, sir: Would you like to see her again, now, tonight?" M. Rogoff tossed Peter's card onto the desktop, and reclined to relish the effect. Good scenes were Peter's business. Here was a man who could appreciate pains taken. "Academic, really. Of course you do."

Peter fought the surging anger inside himself. He wanted to face this *monsieur* evenly matched, emotionless. It almost worked.

"Of course I do." The rage, swirling crimson and cobalt, seethed just shy of boiling, and Peter's voice was low in the oppressive room.

"And the car you have brought with you, I presume it is a two-seater?"

"Oh, Monsieur!" exclaimed Maurice. "Such an automobile! Flashing green lights, little bells that ding when you leave your door ajar. Fairie voices that tell you to fasten your lap belt. Like something from that space movie!" Maurice had liked *Star Wars* a great deal.

"Don't hasten to invite yourself," M. Rogoff told

the dwarf. ''Mr. Deutsch and I have several private business matters to discuss. In the meantime, Maurice, as a reward for your sterling service, you'll find a bottle of extremely old brandy on the bookshelf right behind you, next to the clock. Also an envelope.''

M. Rogoff rose from the desk, his height not changing all that noticeably. He flexed his hands into a pair of white linen evening gloves and fetched down the brushed top hat from its wicker roost. He directed Peter to pick up a large Gladstone bag in brown leather.

Peter's toes were almost touching the bag. He had rehearsed a lot of angry things to say—good, raw, punchy stuff—but could bring none of it to the surface. He remained speechless, as though dubbed into silence. It all seemed to follow some predetermined course no matter what he did.

M. Rogoff indicated the room's only door. ''Come along, Mr. Deutsch. We are going to attend a party. Don't worry—we shan't stay long.''

Maurice had screwed around on the barstool to locate the brandy that had been shelved right behind him the whole time. As Peter and M. Rogoff picked their way to the door that once belonged to Morris Butts, P.I., Maurice said, ''Just behind me! You are too crafty, Monsieur! To change the scent of the bottle so that my seasoned nose could not inform me of its presence, that is wickedly clever, Monsieur, bordering almost on cruelty.'' At the threshold of the door Peter heard a cork pop. The dwarf's final words to him stopped him short. ''Be wary of the Monsieur,'' he told Peter. ''He is a sly one. He could sell the Devil's own lost soul back to him, with interest!''

Night colors flowed across the streets like liquid neon; the air smelled vaguely of impending rain, giving the cold a sharper edge. Alea had blended into the blue-on-blue juncture of LA sea and sky, embraced the velvet black of the city's night, and tilted herself seamlessly into invisibility. Peter's flesh tingled with her presence, as if she had become a chameleon, and all he had to do was look hard enough to see her again, there against the vapor lamps and slick tarmac and the heavy, wet air.

By this time of night, everything was closed, and that impression summed up Peter's state of mind. He felt locked out. Her loss was like a scalpel sewn up inside of him, and he craved her the way a battlefield craves silence and sanity. He knew defeat. *This is how it ends, always.* Alone, wearied, never quite brave enough to finish it all.

M. Rogoff pointed; Peter drove, keeping his eyes on the road until he could think of something to say.

"Maurice," he said after a few more northbound miles.

"Hm?" M. Rogoff was bestirred from some private reverie. He was doing just fine watching the sights and sounds from Peter's big, fancy motor car.

"He was terrified you were going to cashier him for leading me to you."

"Oh. Mr. Deutsch, Maurice's instructions were explicit. Specifically, he was to be caught by you, and he was to reel you in by whatever avenue best suited your mental state. Maurice is a talented chap . . . though to tell him so goes straight to his head. Unlike spirits. If he used his intoxicated-dwarf ploy on you, be sure it was a sham. He drinks constantly, but I've never seen him drunk. I *have* seen him drink five longshoremen-types under the proverbial table with virtually no deleterious effect."

"You mean he's like that all the time?"

"Mm, yes, give or take."

They caught the Hollywood Freeway. All of Peter's roads in life seemed to lead inexorably back to Studio City. He was about to ask again where Alea had gone when the little man interrupted.

"You seem on the brink of giving up. Please don't.

Not sportsmanlike. Tonight shall be quite an educational night for you, Mr. Deutsch. All you shall experience, even my seeming inattention, has vast relevance to *your* problem, which centers on the woman you have named Alea.'' He sounded like a low-budget swami.

"*I* have named—?"

"No explanation I could offer, here, in traffic, would make any sense to you right now. It is better to just show you. Dwell on this, in the interim: You never would have met her, if not for me. Nor lost her. She is no longer a part of your life because her core purpose has been served."

An angry stab of feeling in Peter's gut, perhaps the scalpel, slicing away, told him a desecration was being enacted. His eyes steeled and would not admit the image of the little man in the next seat. "So this is all your fault, is that what you're telling me?"

"No, no, no, Mr. Deutsch. It's my *job.*"

He wanted to scream, to slow the Mazda to a tire-rending halt and pummel the little man in fury, to jump the curb and paste a pedestrian, to somehow vent all the frustration and defeat, to cut to the chase. To terminate this two-bit melodrama and end Rogoff's bloody endless narrative. But his passenger cut in ahead of him again.

"Oh. Look. Look!"

They flashed past a three-dimensional billboard the size of a parking lot turned on-end. It presented to the world—noisily—the latest live-action spectacular attraction of the Universal Studios Tour. *See it now.* It was not a request.

Monsieur Rogoff is a master of misdirection, Peter's brain advised, oddly, in Maurice's raspy voice.

See it. *Now.*

The freeway sloped down, lane upon lane of racing red taillights and bright speedbump reflectors and green signs offering choice exits. You couldn't see the

Black Tower from the freeway as easily as a few years before; it had been dwarfed by more imposing monoliths. Peter's eyes sought it from habit—a monarch now deposed, yet still more intimidating than the bigger boys. It was a ruler-straight dark rectangle cropped into the postcard shimmer of the electric skyline, a box of black metal windowed by black glass, which absorbed all surrounding light. To question the Tower with your eyes was to peer into the plunging uncertainty of a mine shaft or abandoned well, and wonder what testy things hungered there, night vision ready to fox you if you were reckless enough to go groping in the dark.

Peter's Mazda had a sticker; it was waved through the main gate by the night guard. One of the studio's vintage jokes was that a corporate presidency automatically opened for the person who could provide more parking. Peter now saw the trick—simply clock in at three in the morning.

M. Rogoff was probably waiting for him to ask what in Satan's butt-hot Hell they were doing *here*. Peter decided to deny the little man the satisfaction of being so goddamned *right*. Familiar aches began to roost in his shoulders and spine; crossing the studio lot's threshold brought all the fatigue and frustration of *Sinner* home to his bones. He shrugged, felt them slide away. It was amazingly easy to shuck any sense of obligation to *Sinner;* it had become trivial, disposable.

Above, the Tower reached to blot out the stars. M. Rogoff was looking reverently up one broad black flank. Lights nicotined the tinted panes at the very top. Elsewhere in the building, and throughout the backlot, workers were braced against the predawn cold and getting eyestrain in cubicles, attending to what the moguls, in their exquisite simplemindedness, called *product*.

As they approached, another man in security livery unlocked the big lobby doors from within.

"Wasting time," said Peter. He was so tired he was leaving words out of his sentences. "Can't get in without a pass."

"You mean an invitation," said M. Rogoff. By means of elementary prestidigitation he produced a stiff white card. The guard grinned at the trick, nodded toward the card, and admitted them.

M. Rogoff stopped, made room for himself, and bowed formally. Then he led Peter. "I believe the lifts are this way."

Peter knew bloody well where the fornicating elevators were, thank you very goddamn. . . .

"You're about to ask one of those questions again," M. Rogoff said, punching the UP panel. "Just wait. Wait and see."

Anodized doors parted with a *ding*. Peter thought of big, nasty single-edge razor blades sliding wide. He held fast, worrying his lower lip.

M. Rogoff browsed him, bottom to top. Then he smiled and went first.

The door gofer looked at Peter quizzically. Suspiciously. "Excuse me, sir," he said, "but that is hardly the proper attire for this—"

"It's fine, Dolph," M. Rogoff interposed. "He's with me." The gofer retreated. "This evening's soiree is a masque, Mr. Deutsch," said Rogoff.

Peter stared as though consulted about particle theory or recombinant DNA.

"A masque. As in *Bal Masque*. Yes? Or the grand masque of the Red Death, as recounted by Poe?"

Peter closed his eyes as slowly as a turtle, to try to keep more headache from leaking in. It did not work.

"A masque. A masquerade. Where people wear masks."

For some goofball reason all Peter could think of was music. Mahler's lush Symphony #10; the Adagio. The "Bus Station" theme from Tangerine Dream's score for *Near Dark*. Gabriel croaking about red rain; Exene Cervenka crooning on hungry wolves. Thirty seconds elapsed and his double-crossing memory reminded him to think of Alea once more. The abrupt, scary ending of "She's So Heavy," as unpredictable as the slamming cell door at the finish of Eurythmics' "Room 101." If you donned your mask—your masque—backwards, did the devil get you with his subliminals?

No mask. No costume. Peter mumbled "Hammer murderer," to the gofer as he entered.

Three interconnecting suites commanded a westward panorama of the Valley, the middle room—the one with the bar—opening onto an Astro-Turfed rooftop patio. Peter could smell dance sweat and Turkish cigarette smoke. Ice clinked. Strangers laughed; the sound was piercing and harsh. A spider-like disc jock deftly puppeteered a five-turntable spread, spotlobbing random tape spikes into the gutters between tunes, a different flavor for each room. Butthole Surfers howled through "Sweat Loaf" in the chamber containing the bar. Further back, E. Power Biggs did his Bach thing on Harvard's Flentrop pipe organ. 'Gasm rollicked to the end of "Cock Knock" and was supplanted by the Ramones bellowing "Beat on the Brat." M. Rogoff and Peter were standing in the Big Chill chamber. Etta James wrapped up "The Blues Don't Care About You" and the jock set the Temptations to spinning. A CD unit waited its turn while the rotating vinyl discs broadcast soft petroleum rainbows.

"Wondrous!" said M. Rogoff as the intro to "Psychedelic Shack" hit speed.

Grotesques and arabesques whirled; the dancers spilling through the door and engulfing part of the patio. Easier breathing there, amidst the frenzy. Typically Hollywood. They were all trying to out-Herod one another. Tonight the predominant peer-clique brag of choice manifested in the preponderance of masks crafted by an ex-Las Vegas fashion designer named Russell Zanoza. Killer momentum, gathered around midnight, was still peaking.

"So colorful and alive!" M. Rogoff, again.

A worthy in a jewelled frog mask and leather tuxedo blundered into Peter, drenching his shirtfront with fresh piña colada. He did not ribbet. He said, "Sorry, love," and bobbed off, leaving Peter to swab himself with cocktail linens. His garments were three days stale. He found himself queerly grateful that their odor had just been neatly masked by a socially permissible accident.

When he saw M. Rogoff again, the little man was holding a straight double scotch toward him. He expected a *bon mot* about quenching the inner man now that the outer man was drenched. Mick Jagger began to sing of chainsaws on the Bois de Boulogne a room away.

Peter killed the scotch with a grimace, fortifying himself against what promised to be a long charade. Ahh. M. Rogoff took his free hand and led him, like Fred before Ginger, cutting through the throng to home-in on the bar. Long tables supported the savaged remnants of chips, dips, cheeses, rumaki, jumbo shrimps, chicken in Chinese mustard, assorted fondues (now cold) and crumb-strewn hors d'oeuvre trays. An Iranian with a mole near his mouth drew endless espressos and cappucinos from a steaming brass faiyima. Milk hissed into froth.

M. Rogoff located a high stool. "We shall—how should I say?—hang out here, until we fade from notice. Until new faces obtrude. Finished with your drink? Hm, perhaps you *could* give Maurice a manly contest. No matter. Do have another. It might render you less hostile toward what I shall reveal to you."

The noise quotient was jarring, yet despite all the aural competition, Peter could capture every syllable.

M. Rogoff paused a lot when he talked, enunciating like a scholar who knows the camera is on.

"Wasn't she beautiful?" he said clearly.

Peter began to smell the slant. This was like dialogue. He was supposed to say, *wasn't* WHO *beautiful?* He sipped his scotch. It was good, aged, the real stuff, not like the bogus Chivas at Shepard Bonnard's party, where he had met the *who* woman. It seemed centuries distant, but it was easy for him to replay that party now. Here were music and dancers and an available patio.

"I thought she was a party whore. In fact, I think I called her one."

"Yes. Your hostility was returned with understanding and love. Beautiful. I really cannot conjure a superlative for her, Peter; she was so . . . superior. And there was the benefit of excellent timing. Timing is everything, is it not? You could not have met her at a more opportune time. You were thrillingly ripe; as vulnerable as a safe-cracker's sanded fingertip."

"Misdirected. I fell for a con. Sue me."

"Peter." M. Rogoff had become familiar, easily shifting from the formal *Mr. Deutsch.* Peter lent it no notice. "I do not take my work lightly. It was not merely a charade, as you think."

"No, it was your *job,*" Peter mocked.

"Am I correct in saying that when you met Alea, you were—I believe the common parlance is: 'Going down for the third time'? You were being thoroughly abused by shallow and predatory people, yes? And you were lucky enough to receive exactly the reinforcement you required at just that precise moment. You were not deceived."

"Just fucked." Sour.

M. Rogoff considered his own small, fine hands in their white gloves. "Sexual compatibility *is* my forte."

"Not what I meant," Peter said. He was annoyed enough to speak while not looking at the little man.

"I demonstrated one last jog of faith and got shucked and hung out to dry. I wanted not just anyone, but *her*. I wanted—"

"Mr. Deutsch." Mannered, again. It had the desired effect—it got Peter's attention. Time for serious goods. "Do you *always* get what you want?"

The caperers beyond, the dancers and laughers, had melted into an abstract living artwork of flashing colors and crude motion. The noise seemed to fade back further still, to die a small death. Peter watched for a very long minute.

"No," he said. "Never. When I did get what I wanted, for once, I could hardly believe it. I doubted."

"Ah. Ahum! Now we're back on track. Nobody can recognize perfection right off the beam. You can't. *I* can, rarely, but only because I do the planning. It took time for you to *learn* that she was perfect for you. Just what you wanted. That matured into just what you *needed*. Correct me if I err."

"Great timing. Perfect." Peter's voice was losing inflection, lifeblood leaking from an uncoagulated wound.

M. Rogoff was excited now, prodding the thought chain ever-forward. "And when she began to seem just a tiny bit *too* perfect to you—?"

"She displayed weakness. She admitted self-doubt to me. Showed me a crack in her armor of perfection." He ran playback in his head, then shook his head ruefully. "I didn't fall for it. I swan dove. And hit like an anvil into a duckpond."

"But all because of me, Peter. It was all my doing. I love art a great deal."

Peter had fought hard to loathe the image of her face, to summon aversion-therapy at its most brutal. Alea was evil; she had been the destroyer; hers was the fault. Despise her that you might cleanse her from your mind.

It didn't work. It was a patchwork membrane of ra-

tionalization too fragile, too transparent for his anger
to sustain. Even if Melvin Belli and Perry Mason
slapped him with irrefutable documentation that she
was a berserker, right here right now, Peter knew that
he would never be able to talk himself into hating her.

"Peter." The repetition of his name had a succoring
effect. Peter might have used the same technique to
hold the attention of a happy dog. "Peter, it simply
could not be permitted to last. There was the *work* to
consider, after all. You had *Objet d'Art* and your friend
awaiting you in Canada—a definite first step down the
path you've craved for so long. The path that leads to
the artistic recognition you need as fundamentally as
love. But for you to venture there an easy cynic, em-
bittered, walled away from honest feeling, glib and
shallow. . . ." M. Rogoff sighed. "At the point I in-
jected Alea into your life, you had been working too
long, too hard. You had been through too much. Your
divorce. The courts. The psychic decay. Unfulfilling
labor. No end in sight. You had inured yourself to pain
so heavily that no honest emotion could ever shine
through your work. Not even the pain itself. Can you
see it now, comprehend it?"

"Bullshit." He hated perceiving only edges. Out-
lines. And he hated the idea of being outgunned by a
little old lunatic who lived in a Bekins warehouse. He
drew scant solace from the fact that it wasn't the *most*
humiliating thing that had happened to him recently.

"You're trying to get me to believe that if I'd taken
Alea with me to Vancouver, I would've turned into a
romantic klutz on *Objet d'Art?*"

"If you had gone without meeting her, the film
would have been too dark. Too unforgiving of humanity. If you had taken her there, it would have become
worthless hackwork. It would have been a very—ah—
cute film."

The scalpel stirred, slicing Peter's stomach into strip
steak. *Cute* was a word that had been mated with his

directorial output twenty times too many. The Curse of "Cute" was on his head. VARIETY—*Cute concept; pedestrian execution. Cute characters. Cute enough to matinee for one week.* HOLLYWOOD REPORTER—*No depth; fails dismally. But cute idea nevertheless.*

Peter to Damon Fletcher, a week before the party at Bonnard's: "Cute! Fucking *cute!* I would put my left nut in a garlic press and give it a mighty squash for the *paparazzi* if I could just evade that goddamn four-letter word just *once!"*

Damon to Peter: "Nahh. You'd be down one *huevo* and they'd just look up a synonym." They'd both laughed.

M. Rogoff's voice had assumed a lectorial hue. "If you protect yourself from feeling intense pain, you also erect an equally impenetrable shield against being intoxicated by pleasure. Tipping the balance became . . . ah . . . paramount. How could you be expected to produce anything of honest artistic significance?"

The little man had in his mind a sepia-toned picture of Maurice, at work sculpting his monsters. Talking to himself, but also vocally coaxing the blood-colored clay into behaving. Investing tears, first the spicy salt ones of anger, then the honeysuckle tears of joy. Sacrificing a mouthful of his precious brandy to knead into his creation. M. Rogoff knew these emotions, and his speech to Peter was born of rough experience.

"Alea served her purpose for you. Are you not now packed for Canada? You're telling yourself that distance is the answer, that escape will win you perspective. What you are not prepared to acknowledge is that now, as a result of your travails, you are girded for the challenge that *Objet d'Art* will be for you. Alea's work was accomplished." His eyes sought the dancers. "She could not be permitted to last for you, any more than she can be allowed to last for that gentleman over there."

Peter followed M. Rogoff's gesture past the dancers.

"Willard Pell?" He recognized the writer instantly, even from behind. They had been introduced in the ebb tide of business. With the debut of his second novel, *Come the Wind, Fear the Storm,* Pell had been hailed as "the new Salinger" by *Publisher's Weekly.* He took seriously the advice to relocate to Hollywood. A dumb movie was produced from the groundup remains of his premiere book, *Jackals,* and the offers that sprang from his second novel all died in development hell. Pell could thrash out scripts as well as any word-processor chimp doing TV, but had ignored the movie-biz truism that the execs don't pay you for pretty writing—they pay you for the bullshit you are expected to endure, selling your talent to people who have none of their own. Pell made money. Book Number Three somehow never materialized. He tried not to let the great big cogs of the machine munch him too much. Now he stood at another elite party, being seen, a touch overweight, a touch egg-eyed, one more Hollywood victim in a roomful, disinterestedly watching a teller of party tales struggle his way ineptly through some humorless anecdote.

In a crowd where blithely bared tits, mooning, and ostentatious gropery formed the behavioral norm, Willard Pell was holding hands with a blonde woman whose back was also turned toward Peter.

M. Rogoff pretended to hunt for pineapple juice at the bar. "You wanted to see her. There she is."

"Sexcrime" fired up. From the room beyond, "Addicted to Love."

Peter pushed off his stool and instantly felt the scotch slugging him. He executed a sort of dreamy beeline for Willard Pell—the only other attendee not in costume. Like Peter, he did not require one. They were both clowns. Fools, but in the medieval sense.

As he reached to tap the blonde woman's shoulder she spun as though they were waltzing. She held to her face a masque of immaculate blue glass which complimented perfectly the azure of her gown, a floor-length job in drifting gossamer. Cuts of it lagged in the air like Indian veils with each of her motions; they wafted to rest as Peter stood unmoving, trying to see through the masque.

He saw that the blonde hair was not a wig. Details piled into his toil-worn and prostrate brain: Same height. Same general build. The planes of her face, even concealed by the masque, were different. He knew the lips would be fuller—the upper with more pronounced peaks; the lower more rounded and plumply sensual. The cheekbones would be more Scandinavian. Her hair, her massy handfuls of natural wheat-blonde hair, left her scalp in a different pattern, framed her face in a new way.

Gone was the tiger-eye; through the cut cyan glass he could not see the amber flecks he'd expected. Peter thought of Tragedy and Comedy with their eyeballs gouged out. Glass could be sharp and sneaky. The eyes, the only humanity the glass masque would permit him, were the amplified blue of the Arctic sky, a color you saw if you held a flawless blue-white diamond to the sun. Peter fancied he saw a borealis in each.

She removed her masque—it was on a wand—and smiled at him. "Have we met, sir?" It was neutrally pleasant; an open, civil smile for an as-yet-unintroduced friend.

He tried to say her name and his voice drowned. His hand tried to reach for one of hers but didn't quite make it.

Willard Pell cast a nervous glance—he had to—toward his clique before cutting in and snatching the hand Peter had missed. He was almost petulant. "Uh—Peter?" He stammered. "Why, Peter Deutsch! I'd . . . um . . . like you to meet my fiancée, Michelle—"

Her smile harpooned Peter, and emptied him of hope. It was more notice than he'd given her upon their first meeting, at another party, so far away now, and her smile had not changed in any way. Peter knew its form indelibly. And now, in its depths, he saw nothing of himself, nothing for him, nothing whatsoever.

"I'm sure you've seen Peter's work, love, he's the one who—ah, directed, right?—*Mad Horizon,* and—"

Her teeth are identical, Peter thought through rocking waves of disorientation. The veins in her neck trace exactly the same way. Her smile, her eyes. . . .

"Geez, what *was* the name of that miniseries you did for Daystar last year?"

It was bullshit, pungent, Hollywood's finest kind, and Peter was expected to spoon it up like everybody else. It was why the pay scale was so high. *"Dead Steady,"* he said, empty of inflection.

The woman smiled at him diplomatically, from a vast distance, as Pell leaned forward. "Peter," he whispered, "What in hell is the matter, man? You look like a sack full of curb scoopings." The writer's face was a runny amalgam of mild shock, slight embarrassment, fair-weather brotherhood, light revulsion.

You deserve everything good in the world.

From the stool, M. Rogoff nodded, a buoy in a typhoon. Already Pell's group sought some detour from Peter. *It's okay—he's been drinking.* Peter backed off with a choked-off utterance he hoped sounded apologetic. *I heard he actually signed to do that garbage script for* SINNER. He had to get back to M. Rogoff. *He hasn't been the same since his second wife dumped him, I heard.*

His mouth was amazingly dry. M. Rogoff handed him a delicate stem goblet of amber wine.

"You see?"

Peter gulped the wine, then pinched the bridge of his nose hard enough to whiten flesh against bone. He renewed his long-distance overview of the woman in the blue gown. "It *is.* Christ. It's her." His face was

contorted by a soft wonder. It was nearly awe. Beneath
it, the anger remained, on hold. "What have you done
to her? I don't understand how this can happen.
Who—?"

He was cut off by M. Rogoff. "Ask me just *who* I
think I am; that's next." He patted Peter's shoulder.
Good puppy. "Now we can go talk a bit in a more
salubrious atmosphere. And eat. I'm famished, young
man. These cocktail calories just won't suffice."

Peter tried to stop the little man as he gave up the
barstool. "No. We . . . can't. Can't go. I can't just
leave her. Here. Like this."

M. Rogoff took his hand again. Frankenstein leading his feckless creation. "Dear Peter. My friend. She
is not yours to leave, or take. Can't you understand?"

Peter did not understand.

Peter. Get out of here.

The party sloshed noisily into the hole left by their
departure. Five minutes later, it was as if the director
and his eccentric little companion had never been there
at all.

In the elevator, M. Rogoff tapped the panel for the
sub-basement and the doors knifed back to frame the
chintzless underpinnings of the Tower—concrete cor-
ridors, stacked cardboard boxes, cold fluorescent
tubes; workers' restrooms, dead inventory.

Peter remembered the tunnels. Universities had
them, government buildings had them, Disneyland had
them, and the Tower, that maze of shape-shifting mod-
ular offices and incredible shrinking tenures, had them
in spider-web profusion. They were the secret panels
that the veepees and attorneys used to shuttle script
revisions, executive edicts, and angst from one sound-
stage to another. They accommodated electric golf
carts. M. Rogoff and Peter hoofed it.

The tunnel into which M. Rogoff led him was damp
and poorly lit; Stage 13 was gloomy and oppressive.

"Where are we now?"

"Safest place in the world," said M. Rogoff, his voice booming in the stage's cathedral acoustics. Light bled into the vast and empty blankness, then gushed, and Peter's pupils shied from the brightness as he saw a bank of lighting rheostats with M. Rogoff's white-gloved hands on the levers.

They were standing in a graveyard. The little man's eyes sparkled with their own interior current.

It was a movie sham-Necropolis, larger than death, an exaggeration. Studding a carpet of gray moss were chipped and canted monuments, custom-eroded to highlight their uniform age and decay. They were boxy and massive; the names emblazoned upon them ostentatious. Lost memories that had never existed. Tombstones of this ilk were illegal now in sunny Southern Cal. Ordinances demanded that grave markers lie flush with the turf to facilitate groundskeeping.

This was not real. Peter's eye shifted to director mode. The set was huge and visually contiguous; shots could be effected from almost any angle. Tinder-dead prop trees leaned upward without off-camera support. No visible wires. A forced-perspective crypt stood in arrogant shadow against what he assumed to be a large sky cyclorama, shaded for twilight. It would dissolve to an impressionistic limbo once the smoke hoses were turned on. The whole gag was a monster movie; vintage 1940s.

They were beyond backstage, two paces deeper than behind the scenes, alone in the dark heart of the cinema beast.

This evening Peter had been shown what he'd asked to see . . . and the sight had ruptured a valve in him, greedily suctioning out the dregs of his emotional pain. He'd been left giddy and reeling. He felt just like Wile E. Coyote on the downside, snoot bashed crooked and eyes crossed, just as the cliff ledge shears away an inch past his clutching toes. The plunge into the bottom-

less blue of Alea's new eyes had rendered him vacant
even of pain, and everything might somehow come out
all right—if only he did not look down.

"Peter?"

Chemical mist seemed to follow M. Rogoff down
into the middle of the cemetery. "Don't gawk back at
the reality we just left. Do come forward, into this
one." He resumed his window shopping amongst the
tombstones. "That Forest Lawn. Pah! A disaster area.
Immortality of a most repugnant sort. Ah. Right here,
I should think."

Peter waded in and caught up with the little man at
a stone oblong like a tipped-over refrigerator. The
name etched into each face in florid Gothic characters
was DEUTSCH.

M. Rogoff cracked his Gladstone bag. With a magician's flourish he shook out a checked tablecloth,
spreading out the creases atop the gravestone, which
rose to waist height. "Voila!" Next came neat plastic
cases containing summer sausage, a wedge of white
cheddar, a cluster of green seedless grapes. A skinny
loaf of sourdough bread followed. No preservatives.
A pair of matching goblets in hand-blown green glass.
A knife. A flagon of wine with a crooked cork.

"Good heavens!" Peter said. "You forgot the candles."

"Tut, tut." M. Rogoff withdrew a pair of thin tapers. They were wilted into bow shapes. "Light these,
please, while I eat. I'll try to be satiated by the time
you arrive at the next of the questions burning into
your soul." He set about slicing precisely into his vi-
ands. "Isn't it intriguing?"

Peter balanced the first lit taper into a puddle of
melted wax. It froze and held. The candles smelled of
jasmine. This time he spoke his line on cue: "Isn't
what intriguing?"

"Two hours ago, all you could think of was seeing
her again." M. Rogoff chewed and swallowed a

mouthful of bread and sausage. "You'll notice she wasn't on your mind again until I mentioned it. Have some more wine."

The bottle unstoppered musically, and Rogoff poured more of the mystic yellow wine Peter had already sampled at the party. They watched as amber liquid met green glass and produced a mellow blue light. Its taste made Peter hungry. He filched a disk of sausage and reluctantly let it bring his appetite back. He had tried to run too far powered by alcohol and stubbornness alone.

"What is the next question burning in my . . . you know."

"You wish to know—*why you?* Why all this pain for you."

Almost everything M. Rogoff said hurt. This did not. Instead of feeling exhausted, Peter was beginning to feel tired, yet capable. "Isn't there enough pain for everyone? Did I get a double share or something?"

"Yes to the first question, no to the second. You were specially chosen. I never choose frivolously. Ah. See? You *can* hold the steamroller impulses of youth in check. That's refreshing. It allows an old man like me to indulge his sense of the dramatic. Some of us can't help viewing life from the proscenium arch, don't you know." He popped grapes into his mouth as conversational punctuation.

"I noticed," Peter said. "Presto change-o." The scalpel jabbed his soul; took a biopsy.

"Pah! Even our dear Mr. Pell shall derive ultimate benefit from *his* private pain. But only for his art, and thus, for himself. There is another great novel in his future."

"He loses a blonde and gains a magnum opus by suffering? Terrific formula for success you've worked up, there. Maybe you could bottle it. How are you at suicides?"

"No need to get caustic, Mr. Deutsch. Hear me out.

You have much more to accomplish than does Mr. Pell. That woman will serve the purpose for him the way her Alea incarnation did for you. But you are not merely going to make an artful film. I would not have selected and cultivated your emotions and brought you here if that were all. I need you to do still more. For me. Permit me a touch of uncertainty as I search for the correct words . . . you *are* very special and I've never tried to present a case like this before.''

"Hm. I owe you so much.''

"You shall. What do you think of what you saw upstairs tonight?'' M. Rogoff's voice notched down into dead seriousness.

Peter had devoted some meditation to that one. "It implies processes I don't even want to consider.''

"Ah. But regardless, you still love her boundlessly, and would do nearly anything to win her back, correct? You see the path as insane. The destination to which it leads is quite rational. That's not linear thinking.'' He speared a shard of cheese with the knife, using it to point at Peter. "You, sir, are a true romantic.''

The draughts of amber wine were buffering Peter's adrenaline and calming his raging stomach. His head stopped hurting. He felt extraordinarily lucid. "And you—sir, have never been in love. Of course. Have never made such an ass of yourself.''

"*Au contraire,* dear Peter—how do you think I got this job?''

That was good for one more near-overload of Peter's circuits. His eyes flashed up to meet the little man's. Trauma lurked in there, laying ambush.

"Oh, I *know* what you're going through about now,'' M. Rogoff proceeded. "And I'm very good at what I do. You are proof.''

"Great. I feel like shit. Which, according to Willard Pell, I also look like. Doggy doo, to be specific.''

"Normally, I would have been finished with you the

other night,'' M. Rogoff elucidated. ''And now you would be in Vancouver, morbidly filming a depressing box office failure. Naturally, you'd continue to work. But you'd never get better than average. Better than 'cute.' ''

Again the scalpel, poking minute holes, starting leaks. ''But I had to go and get *chosen* by you,'' said Peter. He toasted the little man with a smirk and found his glass empty. ''Wonderful. But what for? The pallid cemetery fog stank of CO_2 and dry ice. Now what?''

''Now your career will regain lost ground and sail into the black.'' M. Rogoff was still eating.

''I tell you now that this shall be a project that shall dwarf all your previous achievements—ahem!—drawing its inspiration from the most unusual of biographies.'' One gloved finger jutted skyward as he struck a declamatory pose. ''My own!''

Incredibly pleased with himself, he held the pose and watched Peter's awareness dawn by degrees.

Peter's glass drifted down. He shook his head, then spoke, to the gravestones. ''Son of a bitch. It really is true. Every single person in this goddamn town WANTS TO GET INTO THE FUCKING MOVIES—!''

The little man recoiled a half step, hat tottering, his chin pulled in at Peter's outburst. ''I was hoping you would accept your good fortune with a bit more, ah, *decorum*. Peter, I was expecting a tot more gratitude.''

''*Gratitude—!*'' Peter had quickly learned he could discomfit his opponent by screaming. He enjoyed watching the little man flinch. In fact, this felt pretty goddamned good.

''What has happened to manners, respect?'' M. Rogoff was running on, like a dribbling faucet, back in monologue-land. ''*That* is what one reaps from tilling a solitary field, I venture. Hm! No sense of peers, of community! One loses touch, I suppose, eh? Well! I am not accustomed to such . . . *extreme* and—''

"Stop prattling or I'll yell again," Peter overrode flatly. He sensed leverage. Maybe now was the time to haggle.

"Young man, as of this moment you know more about me and my work than any mortal. I've outlived generations of my . . . well, my subjects."

"Your victims."

"Mine is a story that needs to be told, and by someone of your fine sensibilities," he continued, suddenly seeming no more confident than the hungry independents and self-conscious on-spec writers Peter routinely fielded as a necessary evil.

"You're not kidding?" He felt groggy. "You actually believe I'd do something like that for you?"

"I'm not a *child*, Peter." M. Rogoff turned his tone cold and pragmatic. He was quite adept at speed-shifting. "You would do anything for even the slimmest chance at getting Alea back, if only for a moment, so you could tell her the lines you so *need* to tell her."

A shudder squeezed a chilly egress up Peter's backbone. He had dismissed Alea from this weird equation, concentrating on how best to blot out the dull ache of loss. Now the boneyard made hideously logical sense. This was the ultimate Hollywood pitch: the dealmaking over comestibles, complete with clandestine bribery and the ceremonial proffering of perks. *Have your girl's machine call mine; we'll do lunch.* Sometimes such words were the invitation to one's own execution. Now Peter perceived the proposition, and it provoked a shiver in him despite the warm glow of the booze.

M. Rogoff gave the nail one more good whack before Peter could react. "Now—given that you must learn literally everything about me in order to faithfully represent me in a script, why not then take the next step and do it? Take my actual place in the world. My inheritance is yours."

"Wow. Such a deal." Peter was hanging tough.

"I am a durable old wretch but I shan't last forever. Maurice, as you've seen, would make a lamentable replacement. This artform demands so much more—excellent taste, finesse, a stringent sense of proportion, stylish choice-making, and, most critically, *timing*. That last, I think, is a specialty of yours."

Stylish choice-making, thought Peter. Some choice! It reminded him of those dumb comparisons you make as a child: *If you could pick the way you hadda die, what would you pick?*

Peter assessed the man who had engineered his emotional destruction, a man now tossing him a pitch so unhinged that all he could do was hang on and fight to pay attention. How weird could it get, and when would it quit?

Don't sell yourself short, she had told him.

"Mind you, I am not going to shuffle off the coil anytime soon. Past the chore of my biography—I don't wish to die undocumented, you see—how would we resolve the wrinkle of having two men qualified for the same unique and esoteric job?"

"Why don't you be so bold as to tell me?" Peter rolled his eyes, impatient as a tourist at a border-crossing. Was there or was there not a hope of seeing Alea again?

"Delighted to." He paused for effect—he did everything for effect—and dabbed wine from his lips with a corner of the picnic tablecloth. "We give you, as your first assignment, a case I am emotionally incapable of processing objectively. I have been holding in the backlog file a case in which I have a personal interest. That prohibits my involvement. I'll need you to handle it. Eh—finish your cheese. Peter. Don't tell me you've come this far, reached this high juncture and are still capable of disbelief? Yes? Would you prefer some slight of hand as reinforcement? Elementary magic? The cup-and-balls trick, or the magic slates?"

Peter shook his head *no,* and finished his cheese.

"It is my misfortune, and perhaps the world's, that neither I nor my position are genuinely unique, as I've said. You'd think *one* of me would be enough, as *you've* said. But, in fact, there's someone else." He tapped off into an almost moonstruck sigh.

The relays in Peter's brain clicked positive even as he gulped to swallow surging hilarity. This was all getting a tad too nineteenth-century. "A woman. A woman who does what you do. Your opposite number. . . ." He let it hang.

"With whom," submitted M. Rogoff, still munching, "do you think I was in love, Peter?"

At first, Peter's laugh was only a strangled noise of hilarity. "I don't believe it." He murmured this knowing what rotten dialogue it was. *It's crazy, but it just might work!* Or: *We can't stop now for a lot of silly native superstitions!* He believed it, all right.

"Would you care to consider the processes *that* implies?"

M. Rogoff returned the smile, made it encouraging. He urged Peter, with a nod, to continue. "There's a woman . . ." said Peter, *"the* woman . . . and *you* want *me* to . . . to . . ."

"Exactly," said the little man, proud that Peter had read his basic plotlines accurately

That was all it took to burst the crumbling dam.

Peter laughed out loud. The laughter, freed, ripped from him. He hooted and capered and slapped the bogus tombstone with his name on it. He sucked wind and giggled and choked and blew forth vast salvos of laughter, possessed and scruff-shaken by mirth. Fake fog hightailed it away from his lips. His sounds made monstrous echoes.

"You want—" By now he was gasping. "You want me to bring you two back *together?"*

"Who knows?" M. Rogoff overdid his shrug. "The woman is bloody near impossible. Intractable! Contentious! But look at your own crystalline reasoning! Look at what you've just told me and deny you are exactly the person I require. Deny that I have chosen correctly!" He recharged his goblet with triumph, smiling too.

"You were in *love* with her." It was honest incredulity.

M. Rogoff waved his hand. "You were in love with Alea. She began as you are now; her first step was also the fine vintage you are enjoying at this moment. I amplified her astonishing capacity for giving a lover exactly what is needed. By consenting to allow me to amplify you similarly, you shall not only function at the apex of your talent, but you shall become like her . . . therefore closer to the essence of what she is. No two works of art are alike."

He raised his full glass in a tentative handshake toast. "So, sir, why don't you and I both get started?"

Consummation time. Time to ink the pact, to get on with it . . . or go sniffing for a new deal.

Peter's gaze was magnetized to the little man's free hand. The spotless white glove now held aloft the masque of cyan glass he'd last seen in the possession of the woman now called Michelle. It absorbed the light. M. Rogoff placed it gently, almost reverently, between them in the center of the monument.

Abruptly, Peter knew the graveyard as pure facade— saw the baby spots and lighting rigs bolted to the overhead ironwork. Saw the wall padding and seams. To the peripheral left he saw refrigeration vents and the squat, oily smoke generators. They had a hydraulic stink about them. Real dust swam in beams of ersatz twilight. He saw the machines and gears that made it all so atmospheric on film, and hesitated.

Not real. This graveyard was a bastille of illusion. He lifted the blue glass masque and saw the ghost of his old face flowing over its smooth contour. The image hit one of the eyeholes and dropped in; cloudy water down a drain, one swirl and gone.

Then came the ticklish feeling that the teleplay for *Sinner*, probably in its eleventh revision by now, was going to stay tented on his dining room table, destined for coaster service. The hair on his forearms raised as though charged.

In Peter's head, the voice of the little man, always two steps ahead, always so goddamned sure. *Now your eyes are supposed to flare, and in a spasm of rage you smash the glass masque. Ready? Action.*

"We should get started." It was not a question; not really a repetition. "Since I already know this story by heart, we should get started, huh?"

Almost casually, he spun the masque back toward the middle of the checkered tablecloth. They were playing chess, for godsake. It clattered—the sound of real glass being threatened—but did not break.

With an irritated puff of breath, M. Rogoff bent forward—the height of the monument stone was a nuisance—and slapped the masque with the flat of his hand. It made a death sound like fracturing a mirror tile with an elbow inside the rolled-up sleeve of a flannel shirt. When the little man lifted his hand, Peter saw the masque had gone to sand the color of Bimini diving water and a thousand sharp tongues and slivers. The eyes were gone.

M. Rogoff picked points of blue glass out of the palm of his hand. Some were seated deeply. There was no blood. It looked to Peter like film of the fragments being meticulously inserted, like pins, into the cushion of M. Rogoff's hand, projected in reverse. Little punctures. No blood.

"Are we *happy* now?" said the little man.

What in hell did he have left? Peter reached for his own goblet and stopped short. The sound of the masque breaking had startled him; this sound of glass disintegrating against the stone bearing his name. It was hewn of actual mineral; it had to weigh a ton, minimum, no bullshit. Why wasn't this a foam rubber fake? Papier-mâché?

"Mr. Deutsch?"

Staring at the broken, eyeless face of the ideal lover, Peter swallowed his goblet's last sip of yellow wine and broke it, experimentally, against the stone. *Crash.* Rock beats glass.

"Oh, good," said M. Rogoff. His tone did not mock. It was appreciative.

He thought of all the deals that had been near enough to soil him. The lies, the ass-covering, the grabs and misses and fervent wish that nothing stinks *too* much beneath the teak paneling when the first weekend box office grosses roll in. Everybody gets what they want . . . except the ones for behind the scenes, where someone always got trodden, where one more ethic wound up dead and rotting. The way they sucked you in was with the felicity, the seductiveness of their offers. The way you kept control was by calling the setups. The essence of survival in such an arena was to insure that the fall guy was never you, and as a director, Peter had only understood that power one way. Until now.

Inside him, the scalpel excavated, uncaring.

The little man needed an apprentice. A biographer. A matchmaker. And beyond. Peter knew what he needed, or rather, knew with sky-blue clarity *who* he needed. A perfect deal, and a perfect excuse to break all those old pacts, with escalators and incentives.

Even for the perfect deal, Peter did not think he could sign his name in that sort of blood.

The little man cocked his head, as though reading his thoughts. "Peter? I don't personally believe in gods or devils or deities vain enough to capitalize their own pronouns. I believe in people. I certainly believe in myself, and I love doing what I'm good at—arrangements. I had felt sure I'd come to the right place and chosen the correct candidate for my very special offer. This matter is no trifle to me. But now it occurs to me that even I, with my spotless record, might have erred. If so, I heartily apologize. You are, naturally, under absolutely no obligation to accept my offer."

The phrase was so clichéd it reminded Peter of the junk mail come-ons his eye automatically dismissed. YOU MAY HAVE ALREADY WON $50,000! He experienced brief phosphene flashpops of being able to engineer love, processes; to multiply a millionfold the pain he had been convinced he'd felt.

"Peter, if you did not know the story by heart, you would not be standing across from me now. Don't you think that I know my job?"

The scalpel ceased prodding and gave Peter a gallows tickle. He found himself helpless to resist one more yank of the chain.

"You mean you wouldn't be just a tiny bit disappointed if I told you to get stuffed?"

Blood evacuated from the little man's face in a rush. His own goblet slipped between slack fingers to break apart on the monument stone. Wine flowed into the checkerboard weave, darkening it as a good, robust Red might have. Lees spattered the fragments of cyan glass on which her special smell still faintly lingered.

"Thought so," said Peter, realizing that the little man would know the breaking of glasses to be a very traditional way of sealing a bargain. He did not need to be told. Peter was getting the hang of this sort of thought. "Never mind. Just kidding. So when do we start?"

As artificial twilight yielded them to genuine night, the two men walked together from the graveyard, discussing, with much expressive waving of hands, how—precisely—they might begin.

A buck impelled into death by a speeding car has no concept of why its concert of musculature feebles into painful unreliability, or for what reason it finally crumples to earth, husking autumn air. While the planet whirls in its orbit, the buck dies with no sense of event, not even feeling chosen, just as the automobile lacks a sense of having been selected by the creature into which it is destined to crash. On freeways with no mouth and no terminus, it rushes headlong until it stops or flies free of the path. Animal and machine, primitive to modern, hurtling together in shared ignorance, cognizant only of motion and impact and pain.

And so in the lost card of the Tarot, The Falling Man falls forever—unaware of how he was precipitated, or whether his plummet will end in a soft, corporeal cloudbank or in the fatally unyielding flatness of a round Earth. His role is to guide superstitious mortals in their affairs by continuing his fall for eternity. The card cues a Path of Life not trodden in symbolic soil, but inscribed upon the wind itself, as transient as skywriting, as fundamental as oxygen, as mutagenic as love.

MONSTER MOVIES

The green ones were Martians. The orange ones were Indians by deferral, since they'd stopped making the red ones. Light brown ones were Mexicans; darker brown, Negroes. Yellow—Chinese. That left green. Martians.

Jason popped the M&Ms before they could smear a rainbow across the warm palm of his hand. Commercials were so full of owlshit.

Oblivious to the classroom natter he sat, letting the excitement build, as it always did on Fridays. The first thrilling temblor struck early in the week, whenever the new *TV Guide* hit the racks. It oscillated until Friday night at 11:30, when his pent-up anticipation went *bang*.

Plain M&Ms were the prime taste (Peanut M&Ms were for perverts), followed by Lipton's iced tea and Lay's potato chips. Texture was embodied in a fortress of musty cushions and Jason's ammo stack of magazines, the elder issues furry or lop-eared with handling. The unforgettable aroma was that of the tubes inside the Motorola console firing, scorching off dust.

Nothing good seemed to last; good stuff was forever being stolen, and to Jason the red ones classified. He had always liked them best. Their candy shells seemed hardest, therefore the most fun to chip artfully away with your teeth. They stayed crunchy the longest. And now they were supposed to be bad for you and had been outlawed. Nobody had warned him, so that he might hoard up a stockpile. His father had mentioned something vague about red meaning Russian and Russian meaning Communist, and thus the *true* reason for doing dumb things like meddling with the colors of candy and disrupting the universe of children.

Jason was not a child. He was nearly twelve, and he owned his own bike and radio. And his personally cultivated Friday-night ritual was about to commence.

Fairchild tossed back his second Tanqueray martini of happy hour and scoped the catch of the day.

Diffused to soft focus by the neon haze and cigarette smoke of the lounge, all of the women in attendance looked tasty and desirable. He knew from experience that up close, the ratio of physically attractive eligibles would nosedive fifty percent: About half were actually as good as they looked.

Once they opened their mouths, the odds crashed another thirty percent.

Benjy, faithful bar ramrod that he was, had stocked the snack dishes with smokehouse almonds today. Fairchild's fingers dallied in a silver clamshell. Best just to nurture a comfy buzz and cab home. Cable was all titties and gore; the late show, all TV reruns, and most assuredly not what it used to be. Fairchild felt betrayed. Home, then, to an early bed and perhaps a fat, sleep-inducing novel. After one more jolt from Benjy. Weekends sucked.

Lacquered nails tapped the shoulder of his Verri Uomo suit. "Psst, hey meester. Buy a drink for a real lady?"

"Why, Ms. Masterson. Thank whatever gods are left."

She moved in close so he could hear; the din was amping up. "I think it's safe for you to call me Kris; we've been off the company clock since five. Come on, I've secured a booth. You can sit and tell me what in hell you're doing, cruising this meat rack. Unless you've got to go?''

From Fairchild's barstool vantage his own apartment was no longer succoring, a shield against the world. It had become a dank trap.

She hailed Benjy, then slid in opposite Fairchild, the swish of her smoky hose lost in the cocktail din. He imagined the sound—silky, sinuous, calculated. What was up?

"Well," she said. "This is the biggest victory of my business day so far."

He raised his eyebrows. Let her call it. Automatically his hands sought the martini glass, the almond dish.

"You didn't say no."

His smile was genuine, and he was pleased. "Are you kidding?" He opened his hands toward her, shrugging, as if her virtues were obvious to any fool. Not beauty, his brain amended. More like magnetism. Her hair looked fulsome, tactile. The lines framing her mouth were pleasantly human; the mouth itself tempting, beneath frosty gloss. Her nose made her face impress too aggressively. She was aware of this and turned it to her advantage when she chose. Her eyes were the best—the irises clear as Zeiss lenses, bordered with green-flecked black rings, so stark and powerful that she kept them damped behind wide executive glasses with spidery white frames. Turn her down, was she kidding? Her posture was charm-school perfect, her legs distracting, her voice commandingly husky. She looked about two inches shorter than him. He imagined the way a serious kiss would tilt her.

"I was just scrutinizing the male element in this joint. Half of them are tuned to Age-Wave, half to metal rape music . . . and most, to dead air." She was drinking Long Island iced teas.

"Not much room left for anything with a melody."

She saluted his observation with her glass, ruefully.

"So clearly, the fields are fallow. I have decided to take bull in hand—or something—and declare that the time has come for you, Mr. Fairchild, and I to have a talk about us."

"Us?" Thus far he was being a moron in the banter department.

"Mm-hm. You heard right. You. Me. Us. And the first misconception we need to chuck off the sill is the excuse about how you don't dare approach me because of how it might *look*, me being above you, corporately speaking. I have been dying for you to say more than *hello* ever since the Fullerton conference. Do you remember when that was?"

He could not. In his mind it reran, overexposed, her image searing hot-white as she strode into the boardroom: attache case, flunky in tow, power suit, girded shoulders, legs to die for; god, every man in the room must want her. That had been . . . a couple of weeks ago?

"Four months." She pointed, for emphasis. Simple high-gloss nail polish, no silk-wrapped bullshit. She'd done it herself. "You sure know how to hurt a lady. Four months, during which I haven't invited you anywhere, either. I could plead prior commitments. Truth be told, I think we might be equally chicken. Care to grab a stab at Excuse #2?"

"Sure. It's too soon after the divorce." He mimed a tiny violin.

"Yours? Or mine?"

"Yes." That brought on their first shared laughter of the evening. A foundation, in case they cared to build something.

"I guess that makes it time to impose a testing criterion. Always good company procedure. You have to list your faults. I'll go first." She sipped her drink and worked up a mischievous expression. "I don't just wear these glasses to read. I wear flats when I'm not trying to thrill strangers. I don't sleep in the nude. I despise cats. If I drink too much I think I'm too gorgeous and that my jokes are all hysterical. They aren't. I'm a workaholic. I don't plan on being anybody's mommy. I listen to my answerphone to see who's calling before I pick up. That's not everything, but now you can start.''

He duplicated her ritual with the glass. "I wear tinted contacts. I eat too much Italian. I punch elevator and crosswalk buttons more than once. I'm drinking more and enjoying it less. I talk about getting 'back in shape' someday. Except for coffee I always skip breakfast. I think clothes *do* make the man. I terminally adore old monster movies.''

"Those things from the Fifties? Giant bugs and UFOs?''

"Yes. Especially the Shock Theatre package.'' He could see she did not know what that meant. No one did, these days. He shrugged dismissively.

She raised a hand, as if in grade school. "For me it was beach movies, Elvis. In neighborhood theatres. Oh, by the by, congratulations on your promotion.''

"Thank you, ma'am.'' He flipped open a leather wallet and did a bit of prestidigitation. "Check out my new card.''

Her eyes narrowed. They were potent at any volume. "You're not thinking of trading that for mine, are you?''

He looked up and fumbled for a response, thinking now that pulling out his card had been artificial, gun-jumping, stupid . . .

"Because every man I've ever met has insisted on giving me his business card. A casebook of shitty and shallow relationships, summed up in a stack of paper rectangles. It's too goddamned easy to collect them.'' Some past hurt turned her gaze bemused, maybe wistful. She averted her eyes and extracted a cigarette case from a calfskin clutch bag.

He decided to wax Germanic about it, to cover his

noise with a louder noise. Rather than stowing the card, he held it over the pebbled orange globe of the table candle. His name, J. ADRIAN FAIRCHILD, browned, smoldered, and then crisped left to right. The card stock was quality and took its time burning. He offered it to her.

Her eyes approved. "Apology accepted," she said as she held his hand to steady the flame, then leaned in with her filter-tip. They both watched the card eat itself, until it was a curl of black in the ashtray, its stored energy gone forever. The ashtray was identical to the silver nut dish.

"Fire mesmerizes," he said. "Like boiling water or snow on a TV screen. Or a cursor on a computer."

"Pyromania as recreation; now there's a blast from the past. Remember when you were a kid and set fires to see them burn? Fire was forbidden. Uncontrollable. That's why I liked to watch it."

"Not me. It was oppressive, undiscriminatingly destructive. It turned into a childhood fear I had to get over."

They traded enigmatic looks, instead of cards.

"You did, I see," she said, indicating his own pack of Winstons.

"A subtle acknowledgment of mastery over that old fear. How'd *you* come to smoke?"

"My parents told me not to, the way they told me not to play with fire." Smoke puffed out with her mild laugh. "I always did the opposite of what my parents ordered. They ordered me to pray before bedtime and I retaliated by proclaiming myself an agnostic at the ripe old age of ten . . . just as soon as I found the word in Dad's *O.E.D.*"

"I invented my own private religion," he said. "A congregation of one. Let me tell you about it."

Dusk was bringing on a landmark night.

At the Hilltop Liquors magazine rack, Jason discov-

ered that his long-ago fan letter to *Famous Monsters*
had proven worthy of print. His legs shook and turned
unreliable; this was literally the first time in his short
life that anything this enormous had coalesced into
printed history around *him*. He was ultimately forced
to walk his bike partway home, pausing at every in-
tersection to page back to where his name was writ
large in bold black and savor his own words, inscribed
with monkish patience months before, over and over,
until what he had to say on his college-ruled paper was
purged of the tiniest error. He had signed his name
with a modest flourish, then written it again underneath in the same careful block lettering used for the
body of the letter, just in case his fancy signature
proved illegible.

He reread it a hundred times between the store and
his driveway, throat dry, heart thundering, triumphant.

At dinner, his father misunderstood, overpraising
Jason for "getting published," as though cracking Un-
cle Forry's letter column was level with the achievements of Mary Shelley, or Bram Stoker, or Gaston
Leroux. *They* had created brand-new monsters with
their pens, monsters with names, monsters that had
not existed before the writers thought them up. Jason
found himself unexpectedly belittling his own accom-
plishment, just to press past his father's well-meaning
lack of comprehension. His stepmother, who had
bought him a copy of *Freckles*, which had collected
dust for months on his bedroom bookshelf, thought
the letter was "nice, dear," after wrinkling her nose
at the photos of the Creature from the Black Lagoon
throttling an oceanarium worker, and Lon Chaney Jr.,
as Mary Shelley's monster, carting off Evelyn Ankers.
Jason's stepmother looked at the letter but did not see
what Jason saw. To contravene her would be as self-
defeating as brushing his teeth with cherry Coke. Parents could be so frustrating; between the two he could
neither brag nor be humble.

Still, sundown came and his pulse quickened. Sometimes the best stuff in the world was not for sharing.

In monster movies, sundown usually signaled the start of the good stuff.

One critical factor of Jason's Friday-night logistics was adequate provisioning. He picked at dinner, leaving room for the goodies to be raided later. A cursory run-through of homework permitted him to dismiss school from his world for the next forty-eight glorious hours. The triad of upstairs rooms was already empty of his older brother, Marcus, who had trotted off to dinner with Monica McMillan and would be spending most of the evening attempting to plumb the mysteries inside Monica's skirt and blouse. She was one of Buddy McMillan's girls . . . and if Marcus and Jason's parents didn't cool it with the embarrassing jokes, Jason might not ever have a future with Laurie, currently the youngest of Buddy's brood.

Two years back, girls would have been unthinkable.

Jason's parents liked to call the third upstairs room the "TV room," which was akin to calling *Revenge of the Creature* just another movie. To Jason its purpose was more sanctified. The *TV Guide* for this week had promised potent mojo indeed: *The Mummy's Tomb, The Mummy's Ghost,* and *The Mummy's Curse,* all kicking off half an hour before midnight, with a *Twilight Zone* repeat.

Bulling through the haul from nine to twelve was the toughest; he knew that a triple feature that late at night would knock his body out too soon and he'd sleep through the crypt cave-in at the climax of the final Mummy film. But he was too agitated to nap. Napping was for little kids. The ability to stay up late was proof of incipient adulthood. Snooze now? No way. He passed the time boning up on Mummy minutiae.

Famous Monsters contained most of what he sought,

augmented by *Castle of Frankenstein* (which he was growing to like better and better; here was a magazine unafraid to say a movie was a stinker from time to time or to print photos of naked women getting fanged by British bloodsuckers). For a balanced newsview there were the second-string publications—*Mad Monsters, Fantastic Monsters of the Films, Horror Monsters*—and the *Mad* magazine approach of *For Monsters Only.* Jason tended his pile of monster mags with the reverence of Egyptian supplicants for the dreaded Scroll of Thoth. He read again what an idiocy it would be to dare to break the Seal of the Seven Jackals, and the aroma and texture of the brittle pages of the older issues made it easy to imagine the smell and feel of Tana Leaves.

The *first* Mummy of note was Im-Ho-Tep, Karloff, Thirties. While Jason maintained what he thought to be the accordant degree of respect for what Forry J. had dubbed the classics, he favored the more dynamic monsters of the subsequent epoch. Universal Pictures, Forties, *after* they dropped the growling, propellored plane from their logo, when *any* monster in the gang could be depended upon to come lurching back for more. *Kharis* was who Jason preferred to think of when you said *Mummy.* He favored the idea of a monster who could kick butt despite obvious structural disadvantages. Kharis dragged one lame foot; his right arm had curled into a crippled claw and frozen against his chest; the conflagrant finale of *The Mummy's Hand* had welded his right eye shut forever. Kharis was a handicapped monster, for christsake. You could outrun him, sure, but he'd catch up while you were sleeping, the tortoise beating the hare, and Kharis never gave up or stopped, ever. Jason visualized a business card, gold, bordered in diamond-shaped Cleopatra eyeballs and bird-headed guys wearing skirts. *Vengeance Our Specialty. Slow But Inexorable.*

Kharis was implacable, determined, and mean. He

even strangled a German shepherd that barked at him once. The sound of a dog barking in the night could still suggest to Jason that perhaps Kharis had found some excuse to serve him with a personal termination notice, and perhaps he was shuffling silently up the front walk right now. Jason's stepmother would discover his wide-eyed, almost-twelve-year-old corpse at breakfast time. His father would exclaim that, why, those grayish marks on his neck look . . . almost . . . well, like *mold*.

That had been the original justification for the fortress.

An important component of Jason's Friday night setup was raiding the TV-room sofa for cushions with which he constructed a sort of open-ended pillbox, facing the screen. It was superior to a mere monster blanket (not to mention more snug and certainly more grown up), and the fortress helped enclose Jason and his supplies within the influence of the picture tube and its monochromatic shadow plays. His tradition was to kill the lights and entrench with the sound turned down until the *Twilight Zone* faded in, just him, deliciously alone in the dead of night with his monster movies. Beyond the rearward limits of the fortress there was nothing to see, save darkness, a buffer between Jason and a world of retribution.

''Put that way, it really does sound like a classical religion,'' Kris said.

The bar traffic had gridlocked, and two uncollected empty rounds loitered on the table between them. His butted smokes were mingled with hers in the clamshell ashtray. Their tab kept their booth locked down during the lounge's prime trolling time, and they stood secure against assault from all comers. They held, oblivious to the flesh-shoppe/slave-bazaar ambience and in spite of the clamor level. An inversion layer of smoke hung stubbornly and rendered all sights beyond three feet of the booth ghostly and nimbused, as though viewed across a moor clogged with swamp gas and St Elmo's Fire. He had begun ordering water chasers to keep from dehydrating.

"Your basic coursework in classic monsters always reminded me of the hierarchies of Greek and Roman gods," he said. "More like the Egyptians, actually, where the roles were separate but equal. No real pecking order; no monster was especially more powerful than another. The focus is on the mythology of genesis and transformation; how they all got to *be* card-carrying monsters in the first place."

Her existence in the corporate megastructure had been defined by ladders, and the idea of equal power equally portioned held a special appeal for her, whether it was among monsters or vice-presidents. "I heard the movie companies just invented a lot of that stuff—about how the Wolf Man only wolfs out during the full moon, or how Dracula can't hack sunlight."

"I thought you weren't allowed to watch those things when you were a kid."

She laughed at something personal. Her smile involved her eyes every time, with an effect more soothing than any cocktail. "I don't know what sort of youngster *you* were, sir, but as I mentioned awhile ago, I generally considered any parental ukase to be a gauntlet cast down. I invented the most elaborate hookup imaginable for reading after curfew. My bed was tucked into a nook below a semicircle of cupola windows on the second floor of our house—a big old rambling coastal thing in Florida. By hanging my comforter between the edge of the bed and clamping it to the wall molding with clothespins, I made a lean-to. I sneaked a 25-watter into my bedside lamp; normally all my parents had to do was look out their window and see if the cupola windows cast any light on the lawn. My weak lightbulb outfoxed 'em. If I heard them coming up the stairs, I could kill the whole outpost in ten seconds flat.''

He nodded, mouth full, anxious to reveal his own version of the subterfuge she had just outlined.

''I had one of those rough-hewn wooden treasure chests, the kind you buy in Mexico? It was hasped with a cheesy brass padlock. Guess what I kept in it?''

''Doubloons?'' Her lips encompassed a sliver of bar ice. It slid into her mouth. He could feel his own tongue cooling. ''Human skulls? Some nasty-ass boy shit I'd rather not know about?''

''Lipton's Instant Iced Tea.'' He said it with newscaster gravity, as though copping to the sale of bomber specs to the Russkies.

Her glass hesitated midway. ''You're not serious. You mean I'm sitting here chatting up a man who *actually* . . .'' She pressed back from the table edge. It was like opera, in its way. ''Omigod.''

''Yeah, I know. Child molesting pales. Necrophilia is more forgivable. But I feel compelled to bare the true ugliness of my soul to you.'' He clasped hands over heart and sought divine sanction in the direction of the ceiling.

He reminded her of a bargain martyr. ''You're starting to drip.''

''No doubt. Anyway, I drank tons of Lipton's, more than any soft drink, and my measures in composing a glassful would shame NASA with their precision. If I didn't get my tea, I'd die. I powered it down by the gallon but mixed it one glass at a time. Some procedures you just don't rush.''

''Or compromise—like the rules in monster movies.''

''Exactly.'' He pulled the green olive off its pic, thinking of stakes and vampires. ''My stepmother—Wicked Stepmom—took a dim view of my guzzling what she called 'caffeine product' on school nights. And water didn't make it—it wasn't a *flavor*. I couldn't sneak tea up to bed, but I could take a glass of water from that cold jug in the fridge. I made sure she saw me pouring that water and taking it with me upstairs at bedtime.''

Child's mischief glinted in her steady return gaze. ''You conned her. Because up in your room you had your pirate chest with the instant tea inside.''

''That, and sugar, in carefully purloined margarine tubs, plus long-handled spoons I had to keep from the Dairy Queen. Napkins. I couldn't manage your light setup, but I did have candles and matches.''

''You little turd. So you were probably up way past the witching hour, grinding your teeth to sleep.''

He swatted this serve back. ''While you were skulking around with your nose in . . . what? Nancy Drew? *National Velvet? Dick and Jane Hit Puberty?*''

''Sherlock Holmes. When I found out the Speckled Band was a snake I nearly wet my bed. No sleep *that* night.''

''What, no boogeyman alarms? No tucked-in sheets?''

She shook her head vehemently. ''I hate that. Still do. I have to poke my feet out or I feel trapped. Another fault for the list: Hospital corners are too confining.''

''Gee, I thought I was the only one. We ought to keep this to ourselves. The mob might lynch us by torchlight.''

She surveyed the singles on the hoof. ''My. Yes. Definite bounce-a-quarter-on-the-blanket types. All the men in here have the same haircut.''

It was easy to laugh with her. ''It's actually a vinyl skullcap they swap on a timesharing basis. Even some of the women are wearing it. See?''

They mocked the players around them. Kris had a way of holding in cigarette smoke that was terrifically contemplative. When her thoughts were organized and ready for articulation, the smoke would then stream out in gray plumes. "Well, despite all this peer pressure I think I still turned out fairly unimpaired." She executed a stiff little bow. "Thanks for not contradicting me. I really have to visit the Ladies'."

He had always used cigarettes primarily for gesticulation—elucidating some point with an unlit smoke, then pausing to ignite it, almost as punctuation. With no audience, he felt no need to enkindle a fresh Winston. He tapped it back into its hard pack. When she returned, he watched her cut through the lounge's bustle—great legs, to be sure. Traffic jammers. Her eyes favored him with another smile, as though they had shared a secret.

They talked rationales, and another Long Island iced tea was conquered. "My family moved all over the country," she said. "New classmates virtually every year. Families aren't tied to towns or states or even other family members anymore. People get divorced so routinely."

He saluted that. "Parents die."

"And there are no constants. Except the bad stuff—the disruptions, the adjustments, the constant restructuring of your life. Tough on a kid. Ultimately there's no one to really depend on, except yourself."

"And the Creature, and the Mummy, and Frankenstein's friendless Monster. They're weird looking, they're alienated, they're picked on, and they're so dependable that when you're a kid it's almost blasphemy to think that *Midnight Frights* won't still be dutifully on the air when you're *aged.*" He said the word with a comic downward twist of mouth. "You know, it's funny. All those monsters in all those movies frightened me. Yet I kept their pictures, cutouts, taped to the wall where I could even see some of them in the dark. They scared me, sure . . . but once the sun was up I couldn't wait to make sure they were still there."

"You didn't really fear them," she pointed out. "You respected them."

He lifted his Winston pack, drew, and fired up. "Is that intuitive, or are you just preternaturally astute?"

"It's both. Plus intellect, style, and great legs. Made me the success-hungry power bitch you see before you today. Your *superior,* I'd say, if it didn't make me want to start giggling." She did anyway, helplessly.

"I think you're right. Them, I respected. Loved, even." He could see the coal of his cigarette bouncing back from the lenses of her glasses, combining with the candleflame already living there, and the sparks of her inspirations, nebulae dancing in her eyes.

Whoa, back off on the gin for awhile! he thought.

"Family and friends might fall apart or move on or betray you, but those monsters were always there for you."

"Not always," he said. "But I agree. I was unusually forgiving where they were concerned. Those movies frequently lost track of their own rules. I compensated. Instead of being offended when the Wolf Man got offed with something other than silver, I made elaborate justifications. Sort of the way TV evangelists can twist a Bible verse to mean anything they want. Creative reinterpretation."

"*Were* you especially religious as a kid? Conventionally, I mean?" When she saw the sour expression cross his face, she said, "Oh, I see. Dumb question."

The *Twilight Zone* was the one with the thing on the wing. Good warmup. Jason sank back and let the cushions of his fortress embrace him.

The Mummy's Tomb was two Mummy movies in one; its first half consisted almost entirely of flashbacks from Kharis' debut feature, *The Mummy's Hand.* His entire cinematic chronology, therefore, waited for Jason within the palm of a single night, and for once Channel 13 and *Midnight Frights* got the order right.

To all those who violate the tomb of Ananka, a cruel and violent death shall be their fate!

Princess Ananka had been Kharis' girlfriend, back when he wasn't the Mummy yet. They weren't supposed to be fooling around. Then Ananka croaked from some lady disease, so Kharis swiped a tea chest full of Tana leaves that would bring her back to life. Which was . . . sacrilege! So the Egyptian guys caught him and *cut out his tongue* before wrapping him up and burying him alive to guard Ananka's resting place for eternity. They fed him soup made out of Tana leaves to make him into an immortal sort of night watchman, and everything was cool until a bunch of guys from museums started digging everything up. Ananka began this habit of getting reincarnated as gorgeous women living in small rural towns in the USA, so after Kharis bumped off everybody related to anybody who had bothered her tomb in the first movie, he had to keep chasing her around. Usually the High Priests of Arkhon (swarthy guys wearing medallions and fezzes who knew how strong to make the Tana-leaf soup) fell in love with whatever version of Ananka was currently wandering around the woods in a nightgown. And that usually pissed Kharis off to the point where he'd smear the priest by the end of the movie. Getting shot or set on fire didn't bother Kharis much; that he could go three thousand years without going to the bathroom puzzled Jason more. And the world supply of Tana leaves had to run out eventually, even though that carved coffer always seemed full up. Various High Priests of Arkhon gravely maintained that if one fed Kharis too much Tana-leaf soup, he would become— ominous musical sting—"a monster such as the world has never seen." Kind of a Turbo-Kharis.

For that, Jason could hardly wait. He just hoped he was not distantly related to anyone who had ever seen a pyramid.

The World War Two vintage of these films permitted Jason invaluable access to the social and courting rituals that had, no doubt, influenced how his parents had turned out. All the women were frail, shrieking things. They fainted a lot, in order to get carried around by either the Mummy or the good guys. Said good guys had pencil mustaches and black hair that gleamed like casket polish. Everybody smoked a lot; it was adult and sophisticated. Jason took mental notes, mimicking the cigarette gesticulations with a toothpick. Secure in his cordon of night, his fortress awash in silver light, he could study the behavior of adults in black and white without getting interrogated or yelled at. Or worse.

Sometimes the heroes were foolhardy enough to try taking on the Mummy fistwise. It was the only time their oily skullcaps of hair ever got mussed. But exhibiting bravery by slugging Kharis usually won you the fainting girl . . . unless you got your voicebox imploded in that bandaged vise-grip. Kharis just sort of pinched your neck shut, and you ate pavement faster than a snipped marionette. He had no reservations about choking girls, either. Or dogs. Just *glurk!* And dead.

After prying potato-chip shrapnel from between his teeth, Jason theorized, holding his toothpick, mannered, between his index and middle fingers and jabbing it toward the TV's iridescent eye as though debating a crucial point with the screen. He had read about the transmutation of fossilized dinosaur bones. Maybe beneath Kharis' rags, after thirty centuries, was a skeleton of solid iron. That might account for his invulnerability, and why he did not crumble to ash whenever one of the Basil Rathbone lookalikes clouted him with a club.

During *The Mummy's Ghost,* Jason gobbled up the scene in which Kharis makes the museum security guard go bye-bye forever. As the victim thrashed, he busted a huge plate-glass window. *Famous Monsters* had tipped Jason to the fact that Lon Chaney Jr. had accidentally gotten wounded during the filming of the scene. Jason fought not to blink, and there it was, by god: two big dots of blood on the Mummy's chin. Real blood. Real *actor's* blood. Unplanned bloodshed, captured on film for all time.

Wow . . .

Against tradition, Kharis, even though he was a monster, usually got the girl by the final reel. In this particular installment, Princess Ananka's reincarnation began to age into the real thing as she was being lugged away, having fainted. She grew this broad streak of white in her hair, then got all wrinkly just in time for her and Kharis to waltz into a bog and leave hardly any bubbles. The End.

Until *The Mummy's Curse,* when the bog gets drained, and guess what happens.

Jason must have drunk several quarts of tea, if what he peed out was any clue. In defiance of his stepmother's admonitions about caffeine product, he dozed off ten minutes into *The Mummy's Curse* but awakened in time for the crypt cave-in at the end. Once a monster got mashed, good old Universal Pictures would wrap things up so fast it made your eyeballs throb. He liked the idea of falling asleep during a Mummy marathon, then waking up to find himself still safely within the fortress and the world of Kharis, where the hard and fast operational rules handed down by the High Priests of Arkhon were constant. If you fell for this week's Ananka reincarnation and Kharis found out . . . so much for your fez-wearing status, bub.

Only on Friday nights like this did rules make any sense to Jason. These rules he could pace and comprehend. Unlike those of his parents.

"I'd say *atheist,* if I didn't find the *theist* part so . . . prejudicial. God-ish."

"You're talking to a wobbling agnostic, remember?" She tapped ash. "The conventional stuff was already superfluous for you, even redundant. That's clear. You didn't need a prefab holy writ because you already had one inside those monster magazines. You had your own communion wine and ceremonies. You had your pantheon of deities—Frankenstein, the Wolf Man, Dracula, and especially the Mummy.''

"Kharis. Who sprang fullblown from the box-office receipts of Im-Ho-Tep.''

"See? You even joke about it mythologically. Don't underestimate magnetism like that. Jesus, you even had a fixed weekly time for worship.''

Oh, Kris was very good.

"It's tough to convey how *important* that was, once,'' he said, sucking the water from a template-formed square of cocktail ice. "My generation fell into the interstice between theatricals and videotape. It was a brief span of years in the Sixties during which a kid *had* to depend on *Midnight Frights* or risk never seeing *I Married a Monster from Outer Space*. It's easy to get homesick for the ritual aspect of camping out Friday nights, waiting for the monster movies to commence. Faithfully.''

"One thing you never realize is how fleeting a period like that can be in your life.'' She tried to head him off. "But a time machine would be useless, you know. Because it would be impossible for you to warn your younger self how fragile some moments in time can be. You couldn't do anything . . . except maybe spoil the fun.''

"Like trying to explain to a kid the difference between an agnostic and an atheist, I suspect.''

"The nomenclature isn't really cardinal,'' she said. "The underlying emotions are. I think my parents sensed that. They were fairly noncommittal—or open-minded, to be fair—about their daughter's interface with belief systems. Common sense and thrift and, later, wit were more valuable. I think they were more apprehensive about what species of boy-monster I'd eventually drag into their parlor to soil the throw rugs.

Turns out they were right. . . ." She made a face in remembrance of the day she had decided white knights were extinct. "You could arguably call it a learning experience. Vietnam was a learning experience, right?" When the flash-replay of her love life finished behind her eyes, she caught up with the question she'd asked earlier. "So, let me rephrase: Were your parents religious? Was it a problem?"

"My brush with 'conventional' religion," he said, making quotation marks in the air with his fingertips, "was akin to a car getting sideswiped by a bus—the kind of accident where the car gets totaled and the bus drives on with a ding in the bumper. Soon after my dad married Wicked Stepmom, she decided it would be 'spiritually' prudent to inflict me on a Christian Sunday-school class." Again the quotes, stirring trails in the smoky air. "Or vice versa. My brother, Marcus, was exempt. Why? He was older. And he, for whatever reason, attended grownup church with Wicked Stepmom, without a fight. Maybe he was doping out religions for future use. Anyway, like Mojo doin' rock 'n' roll, I found myself compelled to *do* the Sunday school *thang.*"

"Trapped like a rodent in a holy Catch-22. Looks like God really wanted your ass."

His laugh came out crooked; more a snort. "Not for long he didn't. He'd already rounded up a kid in the class named Eric Lowrey. I sat in his vacant folding chair. He'd died of leukemia, just like my real mom. *His* mother was teaching the Sunday-school class, and she nailed me, mine being the new face and all. I got sniggered at for never having read the Bible. So I bit her back; I knew about Eric's death and remembered what my mom had looked like the last time I'd seen her in the hospital. I was six or seven; they had brought her out in a wheelchair and she was all blotchy. I'd had no concept of death then. By the time I was pushed into the Sunday-school class, I'd formulated some pretty definite ideas. Rules for death. And I concluded that if Mrs. Lowrey's 'god' had killed my mom, then he or she or it deserved to get run over by a bus. He or She or It spells *horsh'it*. And I said to her, 'You don't *really believe* that Eric is in some place called 'heaven' you can't really *see* . . . do you?' "

"Omigod."

"Yeah. It hit the fan, no lie. Poor woman burst into tears. Bet your ass she filed a full report."

"Oh. Oh, no." She covered her face with one hand, then peeked out between the fingers. "What happened to you?" She spoke softly. Harsh words might leave dents.

"I didn't have to worry about attending Sunday school much after that. I got grounded for three months, two of which were June and July. I got a thorough yelling at." His words came out in a huge exhalation of smoke. "While Wicked Stepmom was bellowing and asking me *just what did you think you were doing,* she finally lost it and backhanded me. She wore this massive emerald ring that split my lip in three places. I stood rooted, unmoving, scared, crying my head off. I thought, goddamnit, I'm almost twelve, I'm nearly a teenager at last . . . and here I am, crying. Baby. I sure didn't cry when my real mom died."

He took a drink, aware it was melodramatic. Kris let it ride—in fact, she sipped her own, to balance, to encourage.

"She hit you."

"Mm. *Pow.* " He swatted air to demonstrate. "Having perpetrated sacrilege, I found myself playing Town Heretic. I had tampered with her religion . . . so she destroyed mine. Burned it down. Funny—just like the lab going up in flames at the end of a Frankenstein movie. Conflagration bashed down monsters better than Raid on roaches. She tornadoed upstairs to my room, and tore all the pictures off the wall, dumped all my magazines into a trashcan, and set fire to it in the back yard. I'll never forget the sound of that trashcan being dragged down the stairs. Clunk, clunk, clunk; worse than blows in any beating. I watched out the window. A line had been drawn, you see; a new rule set up without warning. Now I couldn't leave my room, couldn't even go downstairs for a glass of water. Everything in the can went up in smoke while I stood there watching and doing nothing, and after it was clearly hopeless, I turned away and went into the bathroom. There was blood all over my chin. My lip was swollen and felt novocained.'' His fingers, remembering, sought scars where there were none.

Kris watched him snub the half-smoked Winston. The twisted wreckage bled tendrils of gray, then gave up for good.

''Next weekend, no monster movies,'' he said. ''I missed *The Thing* and *Frankenstein Meets the Wolf Man.* I tried waiting until my parents hit the sack, then sneaking into the TV room and watching with the sound and brightness knobs turned way down. Until Marcus ratted on me. *Pow,* again.''

''It's almost Shakespearian,'' she said. ''Brother betrays brother. I used to try to read in the dark. When the moon was full and bright, you could. Hell on the eyes but exciting in its way, when you found out it was possible. Your mom, did she—''

''Stepmom.''

''She didn't burn the magazine with your letter in it, did she?''

''She only missed that one because it was in my school pack with my books. I carried it with me everywhere, feeding off it. Eventually I read it until it fell to pieces. Whenever I opened it up I was afraid she'd pounce and take it away. It never took her long to make the stairs when she suspected I was up to no good.''

"The barking dog," Kris said, with a hint of a smile.

"What? Oh." He had passed the memory, and now it receded the way a sleeping town dwindles behind a train in the night. His mouth had become quite dry. "You know, contrary to this blather, I'm really not a nostalgia nut. It's too rosy. If I was inside the skin of that twelve year old, this moment, I wouldn't relive how great those movies seemed to me. What I'd feel again would be the terror, the impotence of what it is to be that age."

"And Wicked Stepmom? Did you ever reach detente? That sort of thing seems to take forever when you're a kid."

"She eventually forgot it or found new things to be angry about. But that didn't bring back my magazines or erase what happened. In fact, *she* erased it; she never mentioned the incident again. She died not long after I left home. Pharyngial tumors. Her throat closed up and she died. Ironic, huh? But you're right—I did respect the Mummy. Kharis was my pal. It was Wicked Stepmom I was afraid of, Freud preserve us."

"I knew you were a boy who loved his mummy."

They cracked up. She had seen how this reverie might turn wet, and she wanted to yank him out of it. It worked.

"Hey," she said. "It's nearly eleven. You have to think about leaving soon; *you're* working tomorrow." She held, slyly. Clearly she was not going to dash for an exit herself, just yet. Sip, puff. "I like this. We've been here for hours that have passed like minutes, talking like old buddies, with hardly any social bullshit." She toasted this sentiment with a modest nod.

"Bullshit makes the world go 'round. It's our day-to-day coin. You'll pardon the residue? Sometimes it's difficult to shut down the alarms in your skin—the ones that order you not to try, not to get involved."

They clinked glasses.

Mischief had sneaked across her countenance again. "Oh—just so you'll know: I fully intend to close this evening with a kiss that deserves immortalization in a book of bests."

He could not stop the arch of his eyebrows, nor blank the pictures her words thrust into his head. It was past the time where the *will she/won't she* game retained any flavor, and she knew it. The struggle toward the easy comfort they now felt in each other's space had been long in arriving for both of them, and to cap the event with a quickie would be sordid and inappropriate; it would vindicate the predatory callousness all around them. To rush matters would be like gulping Veuve Clicquot—no savor, and certainly no latitude for appreciation.

She had foreseen this and jumped ahead to the perfect answer. Just enough spice. He no longer wondered at her obvious administrative talents.

Her own thought chain would never become public record, but it turned her smile into a cherished, private thing. In the smog of the lounge, her clarity dazzled. "What I'm talking about is my lips, stalking yours," she said. "Most people are lousy at osculation. You'd better not disappoint me, because I'm taking a huge chance here. And no, I'm not normally so flamboyant."

"Blame the booze."

"Actually, I'm a sucker for that little boy."

"I doubt most of the yupsters here even know what *osculation* means." It was his conversational escape hatch, and he used it to dodge the ripe red blush her bold words had set to creeping up the collar of his Pierre Cardin shirt. "Fish-lip kisses. Yucch."

"How about the car crash of lips, the kind that chips your teeth? I hate those. Or those wormy kisses, where the lips are ashen and cold. French-the-cadaver."

"Hm. And then we have the Neanderthal oral rape kiss."

"Ow. Yes. The onrushing mouthload of meat. Suddenly a tongue has invaded your face, a quarter-pounder boxing your tonsils. And it reminds you of the last time you woke up face down in your pillow and couldn't breathe, except the pillow wasn't soaked in saliva."

They wrung out a bit more fun at the expense of amateur kissers everywhere. Somebody should start a school.

"Not guilty on all counts," he assured her.

"Good. I just wanted you to contemplate this forthcoming kiss for awhile. The kiss with which we shall end this evening. You were beginning to look a touch blue, kiddo." She let her tongue-tip test her lip gloss, just a flicker, a tease that brought his dormant blush flooding to the surface. "Aha. Good sign. I did it again."

"Evil," he said. He rode it out; there's no way to duck a sneak attack by your own metabolism. He parried. "You have to promise not to faint, though."

He thought about the kiss a lot over the next hour or so. If this was torture, he never wanted it to end.

After midnight it began to rain. Droplets tamped brittle leaves of pulp-paper ash into black muck, and the lingering ectoplasm of smoke was beaten down. The trashcan's sides had blued, then scorched and peeled in the hot shimmer of the fire. Its contents grew more insubstantial the wetter they got. The rain made the dross of combustion collapse upon itself. Soon there would be nothing left.

Getting outside took Jason a lifetime. Thousands of heartbeats, pints of paranoid sweat, a triple helping of jumpy stealth, with a veneer of patience he strained against with each tic. Window to shingles to trellis, the ground a blurry dark void somewhere two stories below, the footing on the roof treacherous, yet irresistibly inviting. To *not* venture out, to remain uncertain for the rest of his life, would be the ultimate horror. His friend, the darkness, was with him, rendering him invisible and keeping from his eyes sights that might have kept him off the roof.

It was cold, and he regretted having to creep out barefoot. But his stepmother might notice wet shoes the following morning, and the surface of the roof was slickly waxed. Hairy.

The can in the middle of the back yard still exuded heat; Jason could feel it from three feet away. He groped for the steel lip and tentatively snaked both hands inside until they collided with the topmost mound of cinereous residue. It fell away at his touch.

Tears were sluiced saltless on his face by the rain as he felt the bones of his magazine stack crumble and puff into soot beneath his fingers. This time he was not crying, merely running off at the eyeballs—internal emotional pressure seeking the easiest vent. He was in control now and okay. He was not so successful keeping his teeth from doing a castanet dance in the wet, windy chill.

Logic demanded remains; even cremation left *something*. Dust was enough to recorporate Dracula. Fire could never totally obliterate the good Doktor's namesake monster . . . could it?

The magazine had landed, bent double, on the very bottom of the can. The glossy cover and front and back pages had peeled away a sheet at a time as they had browned and shriveled, heat pounding paper back toward basic carbon. From the edges inward it had tasted flame and succumbed to crawling buglike embers, neon orange, burrowing their feed paths in the darkness. They spat and hissed as the rain killed them. A finger-length of binding glue, still hot enough to sting, clung to a smatter of barbecued pages the size and shape of a round-shouldered paperback. Jason's questing grasp had stumbled across the prize.

One *Famous Monsters* had pulled through. Some of it, at any rate. About a third.

Back inside, he sank his hands into a basin of warm water to shock back feeling. He washed his blackened feet, listening to Marcus snore obliviously in the next bedroom. How could Monica McMillan bear the noise? It sounded like a foghorn with a crawfull of snot. Maybe she hadn't actually *slept* with Marcus yet. Yeesh.

The magazine remnant, Jason decided, was fragile as mummy dust itself, and dead. Best not to attempt life support. He unlocked his tea-stash chest, scared up a candle, and struck a Blue Diamond match. The tang of ignition stung his nostrils and caused the bite of pages in his hand to expel a postmortem smell like dirty ashtrays. It weighed nothing. By candlelight he parted the page fragments.

A single picture of the Mummy had survived the inferno. The entire photo had been magical—Kharis hoisting Elyse Knox's (fainted) form onto a crypt slab while an oilslicked Turhan Bey watched, from *The Mummy's Tomb*. The center had pulled through: half of Kharis' profile, truncated by a binder gutter where the magazine had been stapled.

The corona of char made it resemble phonied parchment. Jason flaked it away and used scissors to trim it to a tight shot. He taped it safely inside the lid of his treasure chest. Other salvaged portions followed.

The pressure of Kris' lips on his had blessed him with a spontaneous erection.

She tilted her head, cradling the nape of his neck with one slim hand, gracile fingers tickling the fine, rising hairs there. Her eyes were slitted to black and wet with the sight of him. He saw them close. The best stuff happened in the head. He heard her inhale nasally, as he had, neither of them daring to break the seal.

His brain got full up, outdistancing him.

Her teeth caught and caressed his lip with the slightest excruciating pressure, and her own mouth proved as generous as his imagination. So commenced the tango of brushing and sampling, tempo accelerating, that divorces adults from all reason.

The pit of his stomach slid giddily into zero-gee. Alone in the foyer of her building, she had beckoned and he had RSVPed in kind, both of them in a hurry, hearts like cheetahs wildly battering their cages of ribs, the anticipation of tasting her nearly boiling forth and blowing off his scalp. Their mouthwork grew hotter, more fervent, starving strangers taking what they needed, then waned to a gentle softness, friends now, with time, a calm eddy of passion. So much could be said just with lips, without words.

Their embrace slid and wound and wrapped tight. They fit. In that instant he realized how it would feel to be sheathed inside of her, shed of their workaday business armor, caught in the grip of cunning musculature. This time he could hear her stockings whisper past each other, and the sound flinted sparks behind his eyelids.

She offered her throat, and he began in the delicious hollow where jaw and ear and neck cojoin. By the time he had chewed his way to her shoulder and the arch of trapezius, she was berserk and trembling. She returned a nibble of her own and he felt gooseflesh shoot all the way down to his heels.

He had not been kissed this way nearly enough in his life. Nor could anyone ever be. No matter how fast you ran, some things never stopped stalking you.

The following Friday night was historic, damned near a religious experience.

At Kris's behest, via intercom, the foyer sentry permitted Jason to elevator up to five. She awaited him, arms folded, chiding stylish tardiness, leaning against the threshold of her open door, just barely inside of a deep-cut evening number that swiped his first few breaths and made promises that knocked his train of snappy patter right off the rails.

"Hi, stranger," she said, and kissed him again.

He had been a skinny kid who had turned out a thin adult; something metabolic. No swap of hair on top for gut on bottom. He remained symmetrical. His eyes were brown, almost generic, behind long, almost feminine lashes. These eyes caught and held, their gaze frank, frequently challenging, but open and friendly for those who had the backbone. Right before bidding adieu to his 20s forever, he had asked why some people found his facial package a threat and was told "It's the 'stache." He lost the goatee but kept the 'stache as his first line of defense. And now he stood awash in mellow amber light, Kris embracing him full length, and wondered like a fool what had attracted her, thinking that the sum of his outward masque made a difference. Fooled, even in honest romance, by surfaces. His marriage had been a surface thing. Snapshots had boasted the perfection of the union; pictures constituted hard proof of happiness. Photos were important, especially to parents, but he had never cared to prove anything to parents past the age of eleven. Judging from what Kris had mentioned about her first husband, some samaritan ought to introduce their two exes; united they could live the illusions fostered by their mommies and daddies and shoot lots of keen pictures to prove what fun their programmed, dead lives were. Hi, Mom!

"Hi, stranger," he returned, unable to stop the grin. Too boyish.

Dinner was catered, and throughout Kris reserved some secret amusement, extra baggage to her usual smile which she declined to illuminate until dessert and digestifs. Crystal and wine and tapers did unforgettable things to her eyes.

"Okay." She cocked a thumb toward the living room, where a sparkling panorama of cityscape waited beyond floor-to-ceiling glass. "Here goes almost nothin'."

She led him toward the sofa group and he made a joke about heeltap. When you tried to get the last drop out a glass, it coated the glass on the way out and never emerged. Her solution was to refill the glass. Things were at that precise stratum of silliness.

She sat him down and, with very obvious pride, enumerated the items ranked before him on the low coffee table. The arrangement was shrinelike.

"From your left," she said, "Lipton's Instant. Your own personal Tana-leaf high-octane liquid-fuel input." Next to the jar was a carafe of icewater. "For completeness' sake. I'd prefer you didn't actually switch to this stuff right now because this Moet is bloody good."

He nodded gravely.

She lifted a flat, opaque plastic bag by one corner, holding it gingerly, like undusted murder evidence. "Do you have any conception of what this thing costs in real money?"

"Jesus Christ—*Famous Monsters* . . ."

"In what they call *fair-to-good* condition. I call it criminal. Have you ever *been* to one of those grotty little shops? They're full of people who—"

He dropped the foxed magazine open on the table, as though afraid to mangle it. "There's the photo. Almost exactly as I recalled it."

"—Yeeucch. I don't want to guess when they bathed last. Anyway, *attendez-vous*. I presume your lightning intellect has by now divined the intent of that stack of videotapes, there. Now hold out your hand and close your eyes."

"Sure you're not going to put a snake in my hand, Sherlock?" He shut up when he heard the rosary-bead click of his palm filling with candy.

"They've been putting the red ones back in for some time now," she said. "Remember you told me they'd banned them way back when because they thought the red dye was carcinogenic? Turns out it was guilt by association; there was never anything bad about the red dye used in M&Ms. But a different red dye cursed *all* red dyes. It took all this time for the dust to settle."

"God." He deposited most into a dish on the table, then popped a single M&M—bright red—thoughtfully, as if sensitized to the possibility they might vanish again at any moment. "This is truly weird, Kris. Incredible. I think I'm nervous."

The Martians had landed, too. He ate one.

She scooted closer and soon her hand was on his neck again. Soothing. He likes to be petted.

"I thought I oughta check out these here Mummy movies in case I was missing something fundamental in life. Backstory from a lost age. Here, I need your help."

They denuded her corner group of cushions and set up for a triple bill.

"I'm notorious for dozing off midway through. I think I mentioned that."

"I guarantee you will not fall asleep."

"Ever think of putting a white streak in your hair?" She raspberried him.

"Guess not." He toed off his shoes before her big-beam TV screen. Her sofa had offered more building blocks. The fortress was an improvement over the old version. Only the bad stuff had been left behind. Until now the good stuff had not been for sharing.

They had been putting the red ones back for some time now. He had simply failed to notice.

"Peelers," she said. It was what she had called pillows as a child. She settled in, barefoot, legs tucked, achingly attractive there in the semidark, a champagne flute to her lips. She had fathomed him well and knew just how much anticipation was good for him.

On the screen, Kharis lurched again, pinching shut the necks of the Banning descendants one by one, shuffling ever onward, for love, the vigilant caretaker of a hopeless and unconsummatable devotion.

"A toast," Kris said. "Here's to dark rooms, things that go bump in the night, staying up past bedtime, and magic shadow shows."

"And being grownup enough to know what to appreciate."

"Humph. So practical." She frowned.

"Cheers." They clinked. It was good old crystal, thin and musical.

"Cheers."

The concrete canyons surrounding Kris' highrise worked acoustically, like cathedral archways, bringing to them from an unknowable distance the sound of a dog barking, shortly past the witching hour. It stopped abruptly. Somewhere, in some other dark bedroom, a child might remain wide-eyed until the predawn, in fear of barking dogs. But not Jason. Not tonight.

ALWAYS: There are always people who deserve my boundless gratitude (and your appreciation) for helping, in multifarious ways, to get this fiction onto paper and into print. And always, it's a pleasure to list those who gave a damn. If you don't, then skip this page.

SUB-DEDICATION: This book is also for Michelle, Michelle, Michelle, Sara R., and the legendary Madame X. "The Falling Man" was written especially for Janice, with love.

LOST ANGELS also honors new daddy John Silbersack, the editor who responded when nobody else cared to. My pal Richard Christian Matheson somehow found time to wade through copyedited manuscript *and* write an introduction, thereby avenging himself for the stuff I wrote about *him* for the record in SILVER SCREAM.

My thanks to Tappan King and Karl Edward Wagner, who helped "Red Light" into the record books, and to Steven R. Boyett for suggesting the title LOST ANGELS.

AND NOT ONLY THEM, BUT: Marcus "Boho-Man" Nickerson for swell artworks, Bob "Garage Band" Sabat, Lisa Feerick, Ellen Datlow, Terri Windling, R.S. Hadji (hi, Bob!), Jessie "Quit That!" Horsting, the staffs of *Midnight Graffiti*, Outer Limits Bookstore, and the murdered, much-missed *Twilight Zone* Magazine, Anya Martin, Amy Thomson (did I spell it right this time?), Charles de Lint, Alan Rodgers, Dynamo Dave Silva, Beth "Two Hugs" Gwinn, Debra Richardson, Tim Walker, Jim and Elizabeth Trupin, Ed Bryant for the critical support, Bill Warren ("Monster Movies" owes a lot to Bill, for obvious reasons) and . . .

. . . Roselle Campbell and Elly Bloch, my surrogate Moms.

(And hi to the Texas Contingent: Ardath Mayhar, Joe and Karen Lansdale, Jo Foshee, Susan Brown, Melissa Mia Hall, Lew Shiner, Jerry Heilman, Carol's twin sister Cathy, and Dave Webb and his Chainsaw Girls, Glenda, Holli, and Robin. And Avatar, too.)

—DJS